The Diabolus Legacy

S. Kenneth Falconer

Cover illustration and artwork by

Mitchell Nolte

For my father, gentleman and scholar, historian, lover of crime novels, sudoku and cryptic crossword master.

First published 2019

© Paul Bird 2019

National Library of Australia
Catalogue-in-Publication-Data:

Bird, Paul 1965-

ISBN-13: 978-1724935533

ISBN-10: 1724935534

.......the innocent sleep,
Sleep that knits up the ravell'd sleeve of care,
The death of each day's life, sore labour's bath,
Balm of hurt minds, great nature's second course,
Chief nourisher in life's feast

Macbeth, Act 2, scene 2

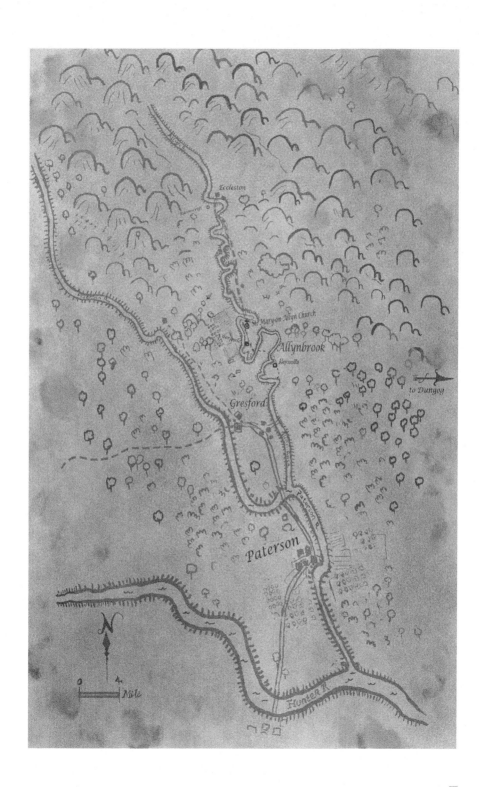

Sydney Cove

March 1875

i

Blood is *slippery*. Released from the body it relishes its first moment of escape, spreading, pooling, ebbing. Then it slows, coagulation factors bridling its onward race, until it becomes sticky, clots, clumps. But in that first minute, before it is hampered from within, it is free to do as it pleases, released from the vessel bonds of the victim, pouring forth unheeding, unknowing.

And he was used to blood. His own blood spattered over his uniform at Balaklava and Lucknow, the blood of his enemies staining his hands, the blood of his fallen comrades on his boots. Spilling blood was part of his existence, part of *him*. But that was another lifetime and in war, one could excuse each other, blood was part of the battle, part of the struggle.

The blood of this girl was different. As she lay on the dimly lit street, her throat cut to the windpipe, he felt the rage intensifying. Eyes half open, mouth slack in mute protest, blood spattering her dress, shoes, hands, spilling out onto the cobblestones and pooling as the rivulets of red coalesced.

Macleod looked along the line of Campbell's Stores. The doors shut tight, closed against the thieves of the night. Peering into the darkness towards Waterman's steps, he could discern no movement. The smell of rotting fish and sewerage wafted toward him on the salt breeze. Masts groaned and creaked as the ships in the harbor rocked gently on the swell. In the distance, music dipped and rose from taverns on George Street and the sailor's home on the harbor foreshore. Turning south towards the Mariner's Church, straining to see in the darkness, the gaslight struggling to disperse the shadows. There was no movement there either. No chance of any witnesses.

He turned back to the girl, her body lying on the corner as if the murderer had thought at the last to conceal his deed. She was sitting upright, against the stores, her head slumped forward.

Bending down on his haunches, he felt his knees pop and a sharp bolt of pain shot through his thighs. He ignored it, taking off his hat so he could examine the girl more closely. Her throat savagely cut; her clothes spattered with her own blood. Picking up her hands he turned them slowly, discerning no signs of any damage to the nails, no indication that there was a struggle. She wore the clothes of a street seller, one of the flower girls who frequent the markets. Her hair hung loose, and as the blood pooled around her, hair framing her face, her lips pale and face ashen.

Macleod tilted his head, side to side, waiting for a clue, knowing it had to be there. And then he saw it. It was peeking out, as if hiding and teasing, beckoning him to find it. He gently pulled it out, a colorful neck scarf, bloodstained. He knew who would have been wearing it.

"Should we get the doctor, sir?"

Macleod nodded. In the distance, he could hear retching as the young constable emptied his stomach into the water.

"Sort that young man out. We can't have him emptying his guts every time he sees a body."

The sergeant turned, "McDermott," he said, "pull yerself together! Get over here, the inspector needs you."

The young boy wiped his brow and turned pale-faced to walk back to the scene.

"You need to go and fetch the doctor," said Macleod, "and ensure you stay with him until this lady goes to the Dead House."

"Yes sir," said the young constable, standing to attention.

He staggered and Macleod was about to admonish him but let it ride.

"What are you waiting for?" asked the sergeant. "Go!"

Needing no further encouragement, Constable McDermott scampered off toward the mariner's church and dead house.

"You stay here with her," said Macleod.

The sergeant took out his police rattle. "I'll call for other officers," he said.

"No. Put it away," said Macleod. "The less attention we draw to this, the better."

"But am I to stay here on my own?" asked the sergeant.

"What else would you do? Do your duty. Stay with her until the doctor arrives and go with her and the constable to make sure she gets to the dead house. We will need to identify her and notify her family."

"Sir..." said the sergeant.

"I don't expect to debate this with you, sergeant. Stand here, keep it quiet and wait for the doctor."

The sergeant nodded, nervously twirling the right side of his moustache.

"Yes, sir."

He stood beside the body.

"Where are you going, sir?"

Macleod strode off, his six foot five frame ambling toward the sailor's home. He held up the bloodstained kerchief.

"I need to find the owner of this," he said.

He strode off to the south, around the corner of Campbell's Stores, towards the mariner's church. As he passed the sailor's home, he could hear raucous singing. He paused for a moment, weighing the options, and decided not to burst inside to see if there were any witnesses or the offender. He knew this would be a waste of his time; he knew who the perpetrator was, and he knew where he would be, and it wasn't in the sailor's home.

As he strode around the corner of Cadman's Cottage and turned onto Argyle Street, he caught his breath. There they were, standing in the darkness of the dockyards. The Russian soldier, his guts split open and his intestines like worms writhing on the pavement. His comrade, half his face missing, and his teeth scattered on the ground. They looked at Macleod imploringly, their blue and yellow uniforms spattered with blood. Macleod took a step back and felt the familiar chest tightening, the knot in his guts, heart racing.

They did not advance toward him but stood witness to him as he stumbled further up Argyle, backing away. As he lurched backward, the half-faced one put his hand toward him imploringly, as if to beseech him for help, even though Macleod knew he was beyond it. He tripped and fell, sprawling backward and hit the pavement, smashing his elbow. The pain jolted him and as he pushed himself to his feet; the apparitions had disappeared. Shaken, breathing hard, he started again up Argyle, then into George Street toward Reynolds Lane.

The streets were full; the gaslights witness to the depraved spectacle. Drunken men vomited in the street, whores plied their trade and excrement and filth coated the buildings along the crowded corridor.

He tightened his grip around the kerchief and cut left pushing past sailors fornicating in the darkness, flittering away their wages on the carnal pleasures of the Rocks. And then to Reynolds Lane where no-one went at night and the rocks Push reigned. The narrow alleyway squeezed between the buildings; as he tried to enter, they met him; two lads, larrikins dressed in the street attire of The Push, short jackets with bright kerchiefs and bell bottoms. In their lairy attire, they waited like spiders, beguiling sailors who were unfortunate enough to come to the lane, seeking pleasure. Too often they were robbed and brutalized.

"What do you want copper?" said the taller one, blocking Macleod's way.

"Well now," said Macleod, "you know me, but I don't know you."

"You don't need to know my name," said the larrikin. He put his finger on Macleod's chest. "You don't need to come up here copper, so I suggest you turn around and walk away."

Over his shoulder, in the darkness, Macleod could see all manner of writhing shapes.

"I don't want to enter, but I want to find the owner of this," he said, holding up the bright kerchief, bloodstained and dripping.

"Don't recognize it," said the larrikin, "so why don't you push off and take that with you. Push off now before something nasty happens to you."

Macleod measured his assailant for a moment and then moved quickly. He brought his right elbow up to the man's jaw, hitting him on the point. He felt the bone break as the jaw fractured and teeth clattered on to the pavement. The man groaned and slumped, and has he dropped, Macleod kneed him in the stomach and brought his elbow around to the top of his head, knocking him to the ground where he lay groaning and rolling, blood spilling from his mouth.

The second man stepped forward, the knife drawn, and lunged. Macleod stepped to the side, grasped the man's hand and brought the knife around so he controlled the weapon, and then pinned the man to the wall. He put the knife to the larrikin's ear and brought his face close. The larrikin's breath was foul with the sour smell of whiskey mixed with rotten meat, but Macleod did not wince and pressed ever harder against him. He took the knife and pinned his arms behind him against the wall, bringing the knife up to the man's ear and sliced... just enough to draw blood.

"I know you know who owns this kerchief," he said, "and I'll take bits off you one by one until you tell me who it is."

The man was frightened, but he had front. He spat in Macleod's face and in reprise Macleod sliced the top of his ear off. Blood poured from the ear, dousing the man's shirt and Macleod's hand.

"We can keep taking bits off you until there is nothing left," said Macleod, "or you can tell me where the man is owns this kerchief."

The familiar give when a man yields became apparent as the larrikin began to slump and urine trickled down his leg, pooling on the ground.

"And now you've lost control of yourself", said Macleod. "What a sorry piece you are."

"No more... outside the Fortune of War," the man stammered with tears in his eyes.

Macleod pulled back and kneed him hard in the stomach, so he doubled over and fell to the ground. While he was down, he kicked him, making sure that the blow landed squarely in his solar plexus, so he could not draw breath. He threw the knife at him as he lay on the ground and turned, walking along George Street to the Fortune of War.

There he was in all his glory, but without his kerchief, looking somehow more ordinary without his usual paraphernalia. He had a poor sailor by the scruff of the neck and was dragging him towards Reynolds Lane but as he saw Macleod he scarpered north along George, toward Argyle and down to the docks.

Macleod pushed through the revellers and pursued him, keeping a close eye on the man's form as he weaved down the street between the revellers, running to Argyle Street, turning right down toward Campbell's stores. He closed in, watching as the larrikin tripped and fell regaining his footing quickly and taking off down to the wharves and then to the right, towards the park, into the darkness.

Macleod realized he would lose him, and he slackened his pace, gritting his teeth, but McDermott stepped from the shadows and put his body into the man, bringing him to the ground. Realizing the moment was not lost, Macleod sped up, arriving out of breath and landed as the larrikin pulled a knife, slashing McDermott. McDermott stepped back and faced off, but Macleod had the larrikin from behind and with his arm around his neck he brought him to the ground, knee on his back and heel of his hand on his head.

"Got you, you bastard," he said.

"You got nothin' copper," he said, pinned to the ground and squirming like a worm. "When my father finds out what you've been up to you won't have long to live."

"Don't threaten me," said Macleod, lifting the man's head by the hair and shoving him to the ground hard, so there was a loud thud and a crack, and the man fell silent.

McDermott stood and lightly kicked the body on the ground in front of him.

"Is he...?"

"No, he's not dead McDermott," said Macleod, irritated at the young constable's naivety. "He's out to it but before he wakes up, I want you to use that rattle of yours and get some police down here so we can get him up to the station. I'll go back and deal with the dead girl."

"Is he the... is he the murderer?" asked McDermott.

"As sure as I'm a Scotsman he's the murderer," said Macleod. "Now get that rattle and get them here."

He stood up and put his foot on O'Malley's back as McDermott swung the rattle, calling in help. Macleod sniffed the air as he heard the footsteps coming and closed his eyes, tilting his head back as he caught his breath.

2

Macleod woke with the sour taste of whiskey and vomit in his mouth. He had drunk too much again, in his room, alone. He stared bleary-eyed at the forlorn empty bottle of whiskey upturned on the floor and the broken glass beside it. He was still in his clothes, his black woollen pants and jacket, boots on his feet. His head was pounding, and an overwhelming sensation of nausea gripped him, so that when he tried to sit, he had to lie down immediately to assuage it. He rolled over and stared at the boards on the floor of his room. His medals were there, the 93rdHighlander medal strewn onto the floor, his uniform trashed and scattered. The army case was open with all of his keepsakes strewn around the room. He knew that *he* had done it. He had done it before in a rage, in his drunkenness, trying to erase his past, breaking and throwing until he was spent.

His landlady had left a basin and water for him and he struggled to stand, staggering over before gratefully taking the towel and washing his face. He rifled through the drawers underneath the basin, until he found a half empty bottle of whiskey and he put it straight to his mouth, drinking as much as he could in one gulp, then another. His mind cleared, and the headache dulled, the nausea retreated.

He glanced at himself in the mirror. His greying black hair tussled and matted, the scar over his right eye red and angry, forcing the eye to droop even more. His black-grey beard was flecked with vomit, and he wiped it roughly. He tried to grasp the whiskey bottle again with the left hand but the missing fingers would not allow it. He shifted to the right, taking another slug before placing it back carefully in its place underneath his clothes. He brushed the detritus off his woollen coat and straightened his shirt. The right leg of his trousers had food matter on them, or perhaps vomit, he could not be sure, but he used the towel and rubbed until it was a smear.

The street was coming to life outside as the clock struck ten. Slumped on his bed, he struggled to piece together the evening's events. He remembered coming back to the Lord Nelson last night after locking up O'Malley and beginning to drink, but beyond that he remembered nothing. He needed to get down to the station and deal with the felon. Looking around for his hat he saw it on the floor, next to the broken glass and the empty whisky bottle. As he picked it up, they were in the room's corner.

They were sitting as if posing for a portrait. His wife in the middle, his three sons and daughter at her side, evenly spaced around her. They smiled at him and beckoned for him to come toward them. Entranced by the vision he took two steps but as soon as he moved, their faces began to change. The spots appeared on his wife's face as the pox overtook her and then his children, one by one. The smallpox burst out all over their bodies and their faces and arms, in their mouths, so they became ashen and shrivelled. He watched in horror as they writhed and slowly died. Their faces became gaunt, eyes sunken and lips pale; the weeping sores covering them. Remaining in their upright position, like a macabre puppet show, they looked at him imploringly, their dead eyes searching him for an answer. He staggered back, covering his eyes. A loud knock at the door shook him from the ghastly vision.

"Mr. Macleod!"

He realized that he had been screaming. The door knocker was relentless.

"Mr. Macleod. You were screaming. Is everything all right?"

"Yes Hetty," he said. "Thank you."

He walked to the door and opened it and she was there. The faithful housekeeper who cleaned, hid his drunkenness and ensured he had food and water in his dingy room, upstairs from the Lord Nelson public bar.

"There was quite a commotion in here last night Mr. Macleod," Hetty said.

"I am sorry Hetty," he said. As he spoke, he waved his right arm to the room. She put her hand up, showing he need speak no more.

"I understand," she said. "I'll clean this up. There is a young constable downstairs who wants to see you. He's been waiting."

"Thank you," said Macleod, as he put his hat on and started out of the room, leaving Hetty to clean up the debauchery from the night before. He descended the winding steps carefully, the dizziness slowly leaving him as the whiskey became effective, dulling his hangover. McDermott was waiting at the bottom of the stairs, his blue police uniform stained with blood from the night before, his hat held in his hands.

"Sir," he said, "I'm sorry to bother you."

"No apologies McDermott. Just do your duty," said Macleod, his eyes closed, trying his best to control his temper.

"O'Malley," said McDermott, "They are going to let him go."

"What?" said Macleod, unbelieving.

"Fosbery says we have to let him go."

"Damn Fosbery!" said Macleod, as he pushed passed McDermott, slamming open the door of the Lord Nelson and stepping out into the street. He strode off down Argyle, McDermott in tow, trying to keep pace.

"They moved him sir, to the water police on Phillip Street."

"What the hell for?" said Macleod. He was irritated and breathing hard, his right leg wound aching.

"Orders from above sir. We had to move him, so we moved him to the water police Station in Phillip Street, to the cells there. That's where he is waiting."

"Have they have released him?"

"Not yet, but the orders are coming."

"Then we'd best hurry," said Macleod. "We don't want that bastard on the street again."

The sunshine and blue sky intensified Macleod's headache as he marched down Argyle, past the vendors and markets with their wares. He ignored their cries as they implored him to buy. The stink of manure and the remnants of empty chamber pots filled the morning air.

"And the girl," he said to McDermott. "Did we find the family?"

"Yes, sir. And the doctor has seen her. The autopsy says the throat slash killed her."

"Anything else the doctor said?" asked Macleod.

"Nothing sir," said McDermott.

The rotten stench of the docks hit Macleod as he came to the foreshore and turned right. He reached the water police station, the sandstone blocks foreboding. Bursting in through the front door with McDermott in tow, he confronted the desk sergeant.

"Inspector Macleod."

"O'Malley. Where is he?" asked Macleod.

"We let him go sir. We had to release him."

Macleod slammed his fist on the desk.

"What do you mean? I put that man in custody myself last night. He murdered that girl!"

"Not enough to hold him, sir. Orders came from above sir."

Macleod felt his anger growing and slammed his fist three times on the counter to disperse his rage, but it stayed with him.

"Sir, there was nothing I could do. The orders came from higher up."

"Where is he?" asked Macleod. "When did you let him go?"

"He went an hour ago, sir. He skulked back down to Reynolds Lane or who knows where, with the other larrikins."

Macleod turned to go after him but McDermott stood in his way.

"It's too dangerous sir. We can't go after him."

"What are we?" said Macleod. "Are we the police or do we let murderers stay on the street? He murdered that girl, and we had the evidence, we had him in the lock-up and they have released him!"

A voice called from the Inspectors room behind the desk.

"Macleod! In here!"

Gallon was suddenly standing at the door and pointed for Macleod to enter.

"Get in!"

Macleod reluctantly entered the room and Gallon slammed the door.

"You stink of whiskey Macleod. You're half drunk and trying to wreak some of your own personal destruction on The Push with no evidence."

"It was his kerchief," said Macleod. "It's him, I know it."

"But we don't have enough to hold him and his father has pull at the top, so we have to let him go."

"On your order?" he said to Gallon.

"Not mine. Higher up."

"Who then?"

"Fosbery has made it clear that we are not to hold people without evidence. New rules."

"Fosbery!" Macleod spat the words. "Bloody public servant politician. He wouldn't know his arse from his elbow. God, I wish McLerie was still alive."

"We all have to adjust Macleod. Fosbery's ways are different and he is not a military man, but you still have to respect him."

"Respect him when he does this? Turns a felon onto the street. We had him Gallon!"

"No more on it and no pursuing him. Orders from the top."

"What are we going to tell that girl's family?" asked Macleod. "That we let the killer go?"

"We have told them that we are investigating and we will find the murderer."

Gallon sighed.

"This is not the London Police Macleod. We can't do things that way."

"In the London Police, we did things properly. We caught people and locked them up and kept the peace. This place is becoming soft."

Macleod turned and opened the door, pushing past McDermott and slammed it behind him, as he went back on to the street. The clattering of horse hooves pulled him up as he stepped back and a carriage rushed past him. He was determined. This one would not get away.

3

In a gloomy mood, belligerent and angry, Macleod made his way back towards the docks. He squinted into the daylight; the bright sunshine shielded by a low bank of cloud. He was feeling hungry, despite his hangover, but thought it best to wait before eating to see how his stomach behaved toward midday.

On the docks, there was a ship disgorging sailors, and he stepped roughly through the throng of excited young men, keen to waste their wages in the dirty streets of harbourside Sydney. Horses whinnied, as their masters loaded rickety wagons, money exchanged for produce. The commissariat had its doors open wide, workers shuffling goods in and out of the bloated storage rooms.

Macleod ambled past the dockyards and Cadman's Cottage, his right leg pain now fierce, his limp more apparent. The morgue was quiet as he pushed his shoulder into the door and squeezed in. An attendant greeted him, hands bloodied as he wiped them on a piece of linen.

"Is Johnson in?" he asked.

"He's finishing up. With you in a moment," said the attendant.

Macleod didn't wait. He burst into the autopsy room as the doctor was closing.

"What are you doing in here Macleod?" said Dr. Johnson, exasperated.

He looked over the top of his spectacles, his large mutton chop side-burns framing his ruddy face. He was wearing a three-piece suit with smears of blood on it, as he tied up the chest on an unfortunate sailor.

"What's his story?" asked Macleod.

"Drunk most likely and fell."

He pointed to his head and a large ugly gash into his skull. Macleod could see pieces of brain.

"Head wound killed him and it looks like his liver was shot anyway," said Johnson. "He wasn't long for this world."

"He's right to go," he said to the attendant. Johnson took a piece of linen and wiped his hands.

"Did you hear about the girl?" asked Johnson.

Macleod nodded.

"The family came to take her this morning. They have arranged the funeral."

"What did you find?" asked Macleod.

"Same as the other ones," said Johnson. "Throat cut to the bone, died of blood loss. No signs of a struggle."

"Was there any violation?" asked Macleod.

"None," said Johnson shaking his head. "The savagery of the cut... it was like whoever did it was trying to take her head off. It bears a striking similarity to the last one, the one from two weeks ago."

Macleod nodded.

"Same killer. I am sure of it and I know who he is."

"I heard," said Johnson, "but I think you'll need more evidence if you're going to keep him in the lock-up."

Johnson finished wiping his hands and threw the linen over on to the bench.

"I have three more dead sailors to look at but I could meet you after for dinner."

Macleod nodded. "Right you are. Fortune of War."

Johnson nodded and Macleod took his leave, pushing past the attendant and walking out the front of the morgue.

Walking back to the scene of the murder at the end of Campbell's Stores, he surveyed the scene. They had washed the pavement; the blood lost, mingled with the endless ocean. He examined the area in the dim light of the cloud-covered day and walked further, along Campbell Stores, to the edge of the harbor. As he reached the end of the stores, he stood overlooking the water and took a deep breath. The salt air assaulted his nostrils, and he sneezed, shaking his head. Gazing across the harbour as the ships rolled and swayed, he tried to focus his thoughts. Abruptly, he turned, walking back along the stores again, searching for clues. But there was nothing he could find that would strengthen the case against O'Malley.

Disappointed, he made his way to the sailor's home, making inquiries along the way. People wanted to tell their stories but none were helpful and at Cadman's Cottage, there was no joy.

Frustrated, MacLeod trudged up Argyle and onto George Street, towards The Fortune. Johnson was already there and beckoned him to sit at a table in the corner, near the street. They sat drinking rum and smoking their pipes. As the mutton stew was served, Johnson broke the silence.

"Terrible thing," he said. "A young girl with life ahead of her."

Macleod lowered his voice so that those around could not hear. "It's the Push," he said. "It's out of control. Those larrikins think they can get away with anything and unfortunately, the people at the top in this police force don't have the courage to stand up to them."

"I tend to the living and the dead," said Johnson, " and many a sailor I have stitched up or mended after their encounters with The Push. Still, they go to Reynolds Lane seeking whatever they seek."

He leaned forward so that only Macleod could hear him.

"Be careful Cormag, that boy O'Malley has a powerful father. Word is already out on the street he wants revenge for two of his larrikins you roughed up."

Macleod took a spoonful of his stew, chewing the gristle as he contemplated Johnson's words.

"Let them come," he said. "I don't fear them."

"Just be careful," said Johnson. "You don't have the back-up like you used to."

They supped their stew in silence thereafter and after a few more rums and idle chat they bid goodbye. Johnson turned to return to his practice and Macleod wandered the streets.

Until the darkness fell he trawled the docks, searching. He roughed up a few at the sailor's home, squeezed a blaggard or two, but no-one was talking. As the moon rose, he began the last search of Campbells' stores. After an hour, empty-handed, he pulled up outside the city morgue and rested against a pylon, and prepared his pipe.

"*A 'bhiast as mutha ag ithe na beiste as lugha*" he muttered.

"They're more scared of them than you Cormag."

He swung around and peered into the gloom.

"I heard you—big fish eat little fish—if I have the Gaelic right."

Macleod recognised Johnson's voice and his shoulders sagged. The doctor was closing for the night, his medical briefcase under his arm.

"What are you, my nursemaid now are you?"

"You know me better, Cormag, but no-one is talking for a reason. Word is the Push will deal with their own. Best to stay out of it lest you get hurt."

"I'm not abandoning this town to those bastards," spat Macleod. "I'll be buggered if I let him get away with it."

"As I said Cormag, please take care, less haste more speed."

Macleod waved him away and strode off up Argyle. He marched along, shadowing the alleys behind George Street and stationed himself inside an alcove. He had a good view of The Fortune and of the street as the revellers poured in.

There he was again, O'Malley, bold as brass wheeling and dealing in the street. He had a brightly coloured kerchief replacing the one that Macleod had retrieved from the body. Macleod gritted his teeth and hissed. He stood watching him for some time, as he pushed sailors around, escorting some to the Canal and then returning to the street, backward and forwards as the night drew on. Macleod slipped along toward Argyle, mingling in with the crowd, waiting for his moment. He waited in silence along O'Malley's route. As O'Malley swaggered his way back from the Canal towards The Fortune, Macleod sprung forward. Grabbing him by the shirt, he swung him into the wall and O'Malley groaned, slumping to the ground. Too late, Macleod realised the ruse, and as Macleod swung at him O'Malley dodged and ran. Quick-footed, he skirted down Argyle, turning left along Campbell's Stores. Macleod pursued, but as he rounded the corner of Campbell's Stores O'Malley disappeared. A familiar voice was at his side.

"Sir."

He turned and there was McDermott beckoning him to come towards him.

"What are you doing here?" he hissed.

"Sir, please. It is my job to shadow you, to keep up with you."

"I don't need a shadow," said Macleod, advancing menacingly towards the boy constable.

"Please sir, I'm only doing my duty."

Macleod was angry. Now they were putting a bloody shadow on him and stopping him arresting those who needed to be in prison. He felt the anger rising in him, broken by a clattering on the roof above them. There was O'Malley, having climbed on to the high roof of Campbell Stores, making his way along the top, like a jack-o'-lantern, leaping here and there.

"The ladder!" said McDermott.

Macleod lurched towards it and went up, climbing to the top with McDermott hot on his heels. He balanced on the pitched roof of Campbell Stores and then lurched along. McDermott got ahead of him, his younger balance helping him traverse the roof with ease. O'Malley faltered ahead of them, slipping and falling sideways. McDermott was on him in a moment, pinning him to the roof as Macleod arrived at his side. McDermott held his hands as Macleod advanced towards him. O'Malley laughed.

"You've got nothing on me, Copper! You put me in prison and I'll be out again. Quick smart! You best let me go, leave me alone lest any harm comes to you and the boy here."

Macleod disliked being threatened. Clenching his right fist he punched O'Malley hard, breaking his nose as blood gushed. O'Malley shook his head and smiled, the blood running down over his teeth, painting them red. He laughed.

"I can taste the metal inspector! But my blood is sour, not as sweet as the blood of those girls!"

He smiled and laughed, digging his elbow into McDermott so that the young constable buckled and O'Malley ran, laughing, along the rooftops. Macleod gave pursuit but O'Malley skipped along, sliding this way and that with Macleod struggling to keep up. A gap in the roof appeared between buildings and O'Malley turned, leering at Macleod.

"Think you've got me?" he called.

Macleod lunged toward him, but O'Malley was too fast.

He spat at Macleod and ran forward, taking a leap. But he misjudged it badly and disappeared between the buildings. Macleod heard clattering and then a deep thud moments later. He reached the edge and McDermott was by his side in moments. They peered over the edge and saw the body of O'Malley, blood pooling rapidly around his head. His neck was at an impossible angle, arms and legs splayed.

4

Macleod waited in the outer office, his foot tapping impatiently. He lit his pipe and took a deep draw, exhaling so that smoke surrounded him. The news of O'Malley's death had spread quickly and riot in Reynolds Canal followed. They had injured police officers and Fosbery wanted someone's head.

The door opened, and the constable beckoned him forward.

"Commissioner Fosbery will see you now."

He walked in and Fosbery studiously ignored him. He continued to read the document he had in front of him, and took his time, as Macleod stood at the desk waiting.

That's right you bastard, keep me waiting as long as you can.

At length, Fosbery signed the document and handed it to the constable. He looked over his spectacles at Macleod, his fine clothes a stark contrast to Macleod's dishevelled woollen suit.

"A fine mess Macleod," said Fosbery. "The murder of a man..."

"The murderer..." interrupted Macleod.

"Don't interrupt me!" yelled Fosbery. "I am in a mind to discharge you completely and set you free on whatever course your disturbed alcoholic mind will take you! We have a dead man; the larrikins are just short of rioting again and three policemen are injured. To make matters worse, that young constable is implicated and is now in grave danger. A fine mess."

"We need to push back at them hard sir," said Macleod. "It's the only thing they understand sir, violence, and brute force."

"This is not the army," said Fosbery. "We are not fighting in the Crimea, you are in Sydney Town. You do not take up arms and march up there and shoot people. My job is to keep the law and to keep order, not to promote chaos, unrest, and anarchy."

"If McLerie was here...."

"McLerie is dead!" said Fosbery. "I know your allegiance to the man was in part because he was military, but he is gone. McLerie built a fine police force in this town and I intend to carry on his legacy in an ordered fashion. I don't know what deal was struck four years ago to transfer you here, Macleod. But let me make it clear, you do not have the free reign you had before! This lawlessness must end."

Macleod was silent. He knew that there was no point in mounting an argument. Fosbery was a politician first and a public servant second. He would not listen to any arguments that Macleod raised.

"I will take your silence as tacit agreement," said Fosbery. "Now to the matters at hand. For your own safety, and Constable McDermott's safety, I am ordering you to leave Sydney."

"What?" said Macleod in disbelief.

"I know that you do not regard your safety as important Macleod, but perhaps you will think about the boy. There is a bounty on both of you. O'Malley's father has put a large sum on both of your heads. It is best for both of you that you leave Sydney."

"And to where?" asked Macleod, gritting his teeth.

"As it happens, an inspector has been requested."

"Where?" said Macleod, dreading the response.

"One of the smaller townships, up past the valley, North of Newcastle. Allynbrook.."

"And to what there?" asked Macleod, "A horse thief, cattle rustling? That is what you will have me do?"

"A murder," said Fosbery. "someone has murdered a wealthy landowner's daughter. They have requested assistance from Sydney in solving the matter and I am inclined to help, given the circumstances."

"But can't the local constabulary handle it?"

"Let me make this very clear," said Fosbery, "you will put all your efforts into investigating that murder. And for his safety, you will take McDermott with you."

"For God's sake," said Macleod, "what am I now? A nursemaid for a wet behind the ears lad who'll be no help?"

"Watch yourself," said Fosbery. He glared at Macleod before continuing.

You will both be on the steamer tonight to Newcastle, then Clarence Town and from there to Dungog. The doctor there, McGilvray..."

Fosbery was shuffling papers.

"Here's the man's details. He will give you the particulars of the murder. And supply you with horses for the journey to Allynbrook."

Macleod took the paper in his left hand, his remaining fourth and fifth fingers clasping at it. He knew there was no use arguing; he was being punished and; they gave him the care of a young man, a task he neither cared for nor wanted.

"Pack your things, the steamer leaves this evening. McDermott will meet you at the docks."

Macleod stood for a moment, preparing a defence. But he was cut short.

"You are dismissed inspector," said Fosbery, waving him away with a flick of his hand.

Fosbery went back to his work, and the constable opened the door. Macleod exited, walking out into the street and clenched his fists. Outside, the sky was grey and rain threatened. Horse and carts trundled up and down the street, creating dust clouds.

Macleod looked at the sky, realising they had outmanoeuvred him. As he was contemplating his situation, a woman darted across the road, dodging the busy traffic. He flinched as she closed on him, clutching his right arm. She was short and slim, neatly dressed, her brown hair tied back, a shawl about her shoulders.

"Keep him safe," she said. "He's my only boy. I have six girls and only one boy. Keep him safe."

McDermott's mother had tears in her eyes, as she beseeched Macleod to safeguard her son.

"Mrs. McDermott..."

"No!" she said, "You got him into this and it is your responsibility to keep him safe and bring him back unharmed when the danger has passed."

For a moment Macleod saw his own wife's face, the steely determinedness, and the fiery temper. He softened and nodded his head.

She wept, bowing her head as she sobbed. Then tightening her grip she pulled him closer, their faces almost touching. She drew him until she had him in her vice-like grasp, weary tear-filled eyes searching his face.

"You swear," she said, "you swear that you'll bring him back safely."

Macleod shook his head. "I can't..."

"You swear!" she said, punching him in the chest, sobbing as she flailed at him. He took her hands and looked into her face. Her lips quivered, and she sobbed, throwing her arms around him. There was naught to do but relent.

"All right, I swear to you I'll bring him back safe. I'll look after him. He'll come back to you."

She grasped his lapels and pulled his face close to hers, searching his eyes. Then abruptly she pulled away, pushing him back roughly as she did.

She turned and went back to her other children who were waiting on the other side of the street and gathered them to her. One of her smallest children, looked over her shoulder at Macleod, scowled and made the sign of the cross, before turning away.

Macleod turned on his heel back towards the harbor as the sun swung low in the sky, making his way back to the Lord Nelson.

5

The afternoon sun was low as Macleod opened the corner door to the Lord Nelson. The conversation at the bar lulled immediately as he entered. He could feel the scrutiny of every soul in the room as he walked slowly across the floorboards. Silence cloaked the mob, their fear and superstition rank as they glared at him. The crowd parted to let him through, patrons arching back lest they accidentally be touched by him. He could feel the dread in that room, seeping from the pores of the drinkers, a heady mix of pheromonal primal fear and rum.

Nuair a thig air duine thig air uile.

He reached the stairs and started up, deliberately slowly, methodically as they surveyed him. Reaching the top, he strode to his room, determined.

The murmur rose downstairs as Macleod rounded the steps toward his room. The door was open and he could see Hetty inside, fussing about, moving things this way and that.

"Don't tidy it up too much," he said. "I won't be able to find anything."

Hetty ignored his comment. "Your bag is packed, Mr. Macleod. You'll need to check if I've put everything in that you need. The steamer leaves at nine bells. The boy, McDermott will meet you here so that you can escort him to the docks."

She met his eyes for a moment to make sure that he had understood and then hurried out of the room. Macleod checked his canvas kit bag. He lifted and weighed, running his hand over his name and rank, neatly inscribed, his hand lifting as it reached the stains of blood and filth. Loosening the rope, he peered inside. Neatly packed were a spare shirt and various other travel items. He saw his cut-throat razor, his spare pipe and tobacco. Nodding in satisfaction he pulled the rope, the canvas drawing tight. Opening the second drawer of the bureau, he took out the bottle of whiskey, taking a hardy swig. The calming effect of the alcohol spread across him, and he took the bottle with him, moving over to sit on his bed as he contemplated the events of the day.

The sun was setting and as the darkness deepened Macleod lit a solitary candle to protect him from the encroaching darkness. As the evening had worn on, the murmur downstairs had become a din, the loud voices spilling out onto the street as the hotel patrons shuffled out into the darkness. Another swig emptied the bottle, and he searched around for another. He found it hidden in the bottom drawer of the bureau and packed it into his possibles pouch before shoving it into the kit bag. A second was under his pillow, and he took it out and looked at it longingly. He was feeling the effects of the quarter bottle he had already drunk and thought it best to keep his wits about him. Reluctantly, he placed the bottle into his bag and sat on the bed to wait. He closed his eyes as the darkness deepened and when he opened them they were there.

The Russian soldier stood in the room's corner, this one with his throat gashed and the blood spattering his uniform, continuing to fall in great gouts as his mouth moved soundlessly. Macleod admonished the apparition. "What do you want?" he asked. He closed his eyes, shielding himself from the hallucination but when he opened them the soldier was still there. His right arm was missing, the stump and ragged flesh mixed with uniform, dripping blood onto the floor. His face was pale, lips blue and his eyes had deep black circles, the large black pupils a stark contrast to the ashen, ragged skin.

Macleod stood in an attempt to banish, to exorcise the spirit from the room. "Leave me!" he yelled. The apparition remained, staring at him, its mouth moving, soundless gestures. A knock at the door broke the moment and Hetty appeared.

"Mr. Macleod..."

The apparition was gone, disappearing into the ether, leaving Macleod shaken.

"Mr. Macleod," repeated Hetty, "Constable McDermott is here."

"Send him up," said Macleod, almost relieved to have company as the darkness deepened. Macleod regarded McDermott; his five foot eight slim frame almost seemed to float into the room. He wore plain black woollen trousers and a linen shirt that was covered by a coat that was too big for him, swimming about him as he shuffled into the room sheepishly. He placed his swag gingerly on the floor.

"We ought to make ready to go soon," said Macleod.

McDermott nodded. He looked vulnerable but Macleod was in no mood to mollycoddle him.

"Shall we go down Argyle Street sir, toward the docks?"

"Well, that would be the quickest way," said Macleod. "We best make haste. The last bell will be soon."

Macleod looked out the window of his small room. On Argyle Street, down near the alleyway under the bridge, he saw four figures huddled together, lit by flint as they smoked. He watched as they stood and were milling about, maintaining the same position. As he scanned the street, he saw closer that there were another two sitting quietly with nowhere to go.

"Shall we leave Mr. Macleod?" asked McDermott.

"Wait," he said, extending his arm behind him pointing his finger at McDermott. He looked out again. They were unmoving, holding their position, waiting for something. Macleod knew they could not go down Argyle.

"We must take the back entrance, through the bar and not the side door."

"What is it, Mr. Macleod?"

"Just do as I tell you!" said Macleod. "We need to move quickly."

They gathered up their belongings and moved out to the corridor where Hetty was waiting.

"We'll need to move through the back of the bar and use the back entrance. There's trouble waiting for us down Argyle Street."

"Right enough," said Hetty, leading them down the stairs.

The bar was empty; the patrons having left early as if a curse had settled over the place when Macleod had arrived. Hetty had locked the front door.

"It's early to close Hetty," said Macleod.

"For safety sir," she said. "Orders from the police."

They descended the steps, turning around and moving to the back of the bar, out through the smoking kitchens and to the back door where a rickety set of steps led to the back alley.

"May God go with you," said Hetty, nodding to them as she closed the door behind them.

"Make haste," said Macleod who was moving quickly. McDermott fell in behind as they moved down the side street, crouching so that they were hidden from Argyle Street, turning right down Lower Fort Street toward The Hero of Waterloo and then scouting around the back way toward the docks. There was considerable traffic, horses and carts and revellers moving up and down the street. Blending in with the crowd, they made their way down and around past the sheds. As they rounded the end of Campbell's Stores, the crowd thinned and soon they were alone on the docks. The stone muffled their footsteps as the gentle swell lapped against the wharf. The dimly lit end of the wharf was deserted. In the distance, Macleod could see the steamer, passengers loading. Pressing forward he urged McDermott to move faster. As they hurried along, two figures stepped out of the shadows. Dressed in the garish garments of the Push, they sauntered toward them.

Stepping forward quickly, Macleod swung at the first, catching him on the jaw so that blood and teeth spattered as he reeled backward. But he was made of solid stuff; the blow stunned but did not disable him, and he staggered forward as his friend drew a knife and advanced.

"Behind me McDermott," said Macleod squaring up to them. The second lashed at him with the knife, catching his coat but not puncturing flesh. He countered, punching with his right-hand square on the man's jaw so that he lurched to the side and fell to his knees, spitting blood. The first was up again and moving toward him as Macleod dropped to the ground, kicking his legs from under him so that he fell heavily. He was on him in a moment, beating him and lifting his head by the hair, smashing it into the concrete blocks. But he had a head like a bull and Macleod could not put him out.

His hands were pinned as the second grabbed him, forcing him to his knees and dragging him up. The first was up again, blood streaming from his nose and face, right eye closed by bruising and blood. He spat on the ground and advanced toward Macleod, drawing his knife. His accomplice grabbed Macleod's hair and pulled his head back, exposing his throat. Macleod struggled but the larrikin's grip was firm. Then McDermott was there, wielding an iron spike that he had taken from the wharves, smashing the first bull-like man across the back of the head so that he fell to his knees and then again twice and a third time so that his skull split open and blood pooled around him. The second loosened his grip and Macleod was up in a moment with an elbow to his jaw and the knife turned on him across his throat. As his hand went up great flows of blood squirted around it as the carotid artery emptied. He fell to his knees, twitched and bled out.

Macleod quickly surveyed the surroundings. No witnesses, no further assailants.

"You all right?" asked Macleod. McDermott was shaking. He backed away in horror, dropping the iron spike. Macleod grabbed him by the shirt.

"You pull yourself together. It was self-defence, they were going to kill us. You did what you had to do. Now get rid of that spike and I'll deal with the knives."

Macleod picked up the knives and threw them into the waiting harbor. McDermott did the same with the spike.

"Here, help me," said Macleod. They took the first, both of them struggling to drag his enormous bulk. They weighed him down with chains and rocks and he crashed into the water, sinking fast. The second was smaller, the job of disposal easier, and as he sank beneath the water Macleod instructed McDermott to wash the blood from his clothes and hands.

As they washed, the boarding bell rang for last passengers.

"Mr. Macleod..." said McDermott.

"There is no time for us to talk son, we've got to move," he said. The last bell continued to toll as they hastened along Campbell's Stores toward the steamer. The gangplanks were just beginning to be pulled as they arrived, out of breath. Macleod drew the ticket of passage from his pocket.

The weathered captain eyes them carefully, his prodigious stomach barring them access to the vessel. He looked at the ticket of passage and back at the two men. "Everything alright gentlemen?" he asked, eyeing the stains on their clothes.

"Yes, I'm sorry we are late," said Macleod. "someone detained us."

The captain nodded, and folding the tickets, he handed them to Macleod before stepping upside.

"Inspector Macleod and Constable McDermott," he said "Get on board. Last bell. Welcome aboard *The Maitland*."

Macleod stepped forward onto the gangplank as it bowed under his weight but held fast. As they boarded the last bell rang, and they hoisted the gangplanks onto the ship. The crowd outside was dispersing, the well-wishers waving goodbye to those standing on the deck; mothers saying goodbye to sons and wives to husbands. Macleod grabbed McDermott by the shoulder.

"Best we are down decks. They need not see us."

As the crew made the vessel ready for departure and the great wheel of the steam engine began to turn, they hurried downstairs into the cabin that had been made ready for them. Horsehair couches were set, and Macleod collapsed on to one, taking a deep breath. McDermott sat opposite, his hands folded between his knees and his head down. Macleod rummaged in his bag and took out the bottle of whiskey and took a deep draught, lolled his head back and sighed as *The Maitland* pulled away from the wharf.

6

Macleod shifted on the rough horsehair mattress, opening his eyes slowly. His hips were aching and his right leg throbbed. He looked across at the saloon and McDermott was staring into one of the looking glasses. His face was gaunt, ashen, and Macleod could see that he had been weeping.

"Time to go up decks," he said to McDermott. "Bring your gear with you. It's best to keep it safe beside you."

McDermott nodded and in silence fell in behind Macleod as they ascended the steps and up to the deck. As the ship moved methodically toward the heads, Macleod lit his pipe and jostled through the other patrons to the side of the ship. McDermott joined him, staring over the edge into the water. Macleod surveyed the night sky, clear ahead and the ocean was calm. He took three deep draws and exhaled, letting the smoke surround him. His head buzzed with the nicotine as he offered the pipe to McDermott. McDermott shook his head.

"Likely a smooth journey ahead," he said to McDermott. "You don't get seasick do you?" he asked.

McDermott pondered the question. "I've never been on a ship before Sir."

"Well then, we'll find out quickly, won't we?" said Macleod, taking another puff on his pipe.

The murmuring of the other passengers filled the silence. McDermott looked up and took a deep breath. "My father killed a man once," he said.

"Your father was a copper?" asked Macleod.

"Yes, in the service under McLerie when they were cleaning up The Cove. T'was a very dangerous place then. He never spoke of it much but sometimes, I'd hear him muttering in his sleep. He died in his uniform you know. He wouldn't be taken out of it, even when he had the dropsy he insisted on wearing it."

Macleod nodded. "And he wanted you to be a copper?"

"I was the only son in the family and there was no doubt that is what I would become, even though my Mamy did not want it."

Macleod could feel McDermott straining to talk about what had happened, but he resisted. That talk was best left for a silence when they were together, not something to be openly discussed when others could hear.

"Well, I am sure you...." Macleod stopped. He was not sure how to finish the sentence, nor was he sure what he was about to say. McDermott continued nonetheless.

"I am not sure I did him proud after what I did today," he said. He lowered his head and took a deep breath.

"Do you think they'll be safe at Parramatta sir?"

"No doubt, "said Macleod, not knowing any of the details but wanting to reassure the boy. "I am sure that the Commander has arranged safe passage for her and he'll get her settled out there, far away from the larrikins. She'll be safe until it's over."

McDermott gazed out over the water as the ship chugged away, now breaching the heads and moving out into the ocean. Someone had set the tables and on them was a mixture of food; ham and dried beef and bread from the docks. Macleod was not hungry, but he motioned toward the table with his thumb. McDermott shook his head. "No thanks, I'm not hungry. How long to Newcastle?"

"An overnight trip," said Macleod. "On to Clarence Town by the Williams and from there by coach to Dungog. We'll be there by this time tomorrow."

Macleod took another deep draw on his pipe as McDermott slumped, shoulders hunched over the railing at the side, his chin resting as he contemplated the sea.

As Macleod lay in his bunk, the deep snoring of the man above him kept him awake. Twelve bunks fitted snugly into the saloon and those that had imbibed on brandy or rum at the outset of the trip were now sleeping soundly. Macleod took a swig from the whiskey bottle under his pillow and contemplated the sonorous beat from the great giant above him. The room was dark, pitch, mercifully black so that he could see very little in the gloom. He could make out the shape of McDermott opposite, lying still in his bunk and he hoped that he was asleep. As Macleod's eyes adjusted, shapes shifted in the darkness, uniform-clad bodies with missing limbs shuffled. He closed his eyes against them and turned to the wall, refusing to acknowledge them or to allow them into his mind.

With his mouth dry and caked from the whiskey, Macleod stretched. Sleep had eluded him for the most part, the vivid visions occupying the small hours until at last as the day was breaking, he had fallen asleep, exhausted. He scanned the cabin and as his eyes adjusted; he realised that McDermott was missing from his bunk. Grabbing his kit bag, he ambled up the creaking steps to the deck. McDermott was there watching the coastline, as *The Maitland* rounded Nobby's Island, Macquarie's pier stretching to the mainland. As they rounded the headland, they entered the calmer waters of the harbor, jostling with the other ships arriving and leaving in the busy port town. Macleod left McDermott alone and did not engage with him. Readily, the waters lapping against the steamer; they shut the engines down and the port staff pulled her alongside. The gangplanks were down and passengers were invited to disembark for a short break before the journey up the Hunter and the Williams.

The seaport was busy, coal and timber moving out of the port as anxious well-wishers thronged the wharf, some waiting for news, some for goods and others to welcome their friends. Macleod slung his bag over his shoulder and beckoned for McDermott. The two ambled together along the wharf until they found an uncrowded inn and sat opposite each other, at a rickety table. Over mutton and eggs they ate noiselessly, neither willing to break the silence.

Macleod felt the pang of empathy for the boy, he was barely nineteen and could not muster a beard if he tried. As McDermott toyed with the food on his plate, Macleod wanted to comfort him, but not able to find any words, he maintained his silence and lit his pipe.

They sat and watched as the crowds bustled up and down the busy wharf, exchanging goods, workers moving backward and forward with coal ships being filled and timber being loaded. Stray dogs yapped and fought over scraps of food on the dusty foreshore as horses jostled with the throng. The unpleasant smell of sewerage was near to them; the bustle and noise of the place began to unnerve Macleod. He was relieved when the Blue Peter went up.

They hastened back to the wharf, weaving through the heavy crowd. The sky had cleared, and wood smoke filled the air, as they reached the dock.

The captain touched his hat as they approached.

"You'll find more room as we travel up the Williams," he said, "we've had a large number of the passengers disembarked."

The gangplanks were up quickly and, as they took their seats on deck, the great paddlewheel began to turn as they stoked the fire, steam pouring from the ship's funnel.

The Maitland coasted along, steam power propelling her up the river. At times the great expanse of untapped land stretching before them; at other times the banks fringed with trees which shadowed every object beyond. Water and woodland, hill and dale, at every turn, and then closed in again by the trees as the river widened and narrowed.

Macleod stretched out on the deck, crossed his legs and put his hat over his face, stealing moments of sleep as the vessel made its way up the Williams River.

"Whoa. Ropes!"

Macleod woke with a start. *The Maitland* lurched as the stern thumped into the bank. He got up slowly, observing the frenzied activity on the shore as ropes were hauled and the vessel brought to the dock.

A short, balding man approached them as they alighted. He had an official-looking piece of paper with him and he read it, mouthing the words first as if the task was more difficult if he did not mime the action before speaking. He looked over the top of his glasses.

"Inspector Macleod and Constable McDermott?" he asked.

"That is us," answered Macleod. "And you are?"

"Jeremiah Steel."

He put out his hand and Macleod shook it. He did not offer his hand to McDermott.

"I have a coach waiting for you to get you to Dungog. We will have you there by late afternoon or early evening. We have accommodation for you at The Settlers."

Macleod ambled forward, duffle bag off his shoulder, slinging it into the cab. He stepped in as the cab rocked towards him and gave as he sat in the far corner, lighting his pipe. McDermott joined him and the cab was closed as Steel leaped on to the top and spurred the horses into action. The gentle swaying and an occasional bump lulled Macleod so that soon he was dozing again, his dreams filled with blood and steel.

7

Macleod rocked back and forth as the coach bumped along the dusty road. Opposite McDermott slept, his head slumped, exhausted by the journey. Macleod put his head out the window holding his breath against the dust. Pastures surrounded them, and as they rounded the turn, he could see a settlement in the distance. The Williams River stretched off to the right, glistening in the afternoon sun, and smoke lazily lifted from the chimneys along the main street.

As they clattered along he was surprised to see evidence of civilisation, a blacksmith, a butcher, a church or two and several inns. But these early signs of development were soon overwhelmed by the lack of gas lamps in the street and the primitive, dusty road, furrowed by carriage wheels and horses' hooves. They settled to a slower pace as carriages passed them on the right laden with goods and travellers and he could hear the driver waving and calling to those he knew. As they journeyed down the street, the Williams river fell away as they turned inland, almost down to the bottom of the town where the buildings gave way to lush pasture land, spreading out to the north and the east. Cows and sheep grazed lazily on the verdant grass where the forest had been felled.

A shout to the horses from the driver signalled they were coming to a stop. The horses pulled up, stamping their feet and whinnying, protesting against the bridle. Their driver leaped from his seat and arrived at the cab door quickly.

"Welcome to Dungog gentlemen," he said.

McDermott was awake and rubbing his eyes.

"Let me escort you to meet the owner of your lodgings."

The afternoon sun was dipping toward the horizon and Macleod squinted into the glare as he alighted onto the dusty street. Stray dogs scuttled around as the inhabitants brought water from the river to their homes for the evening meal. He saw a low flat building with a makeshift post office in the front on the right. There was a short man standing there with a full head of hair, unruly and untamed. He wore an ill-fitting suit and his wife, in a housedress and bonnet, was standing just behind him. The driver introduced them.

"Samuel and Hannah Redman, Inspector Macleod and Constable McDermott."

With the introductions made and handshaking and curtseying completed, Samuel Redman ushered Macleod and McDermott to their rooms.

"Welcome to Dungog," said Samuel Redman, extending his right arm to direct them to their room. "I trust your lodgings will be comfortable. The mattresses are well stuffed and pillows with the finest down we have available in the town. We've brought fresh water up from the river for the evening, candles are there and the privy is down the back. He indicated they were to go out and around the building to locate the small privy, at the rear of the property.

"The floods have made the ground soft back there so watch your step."

"Floods?" queried Macleod.

"The floods came through in early March. Badly affected Patterson and Allynbrook. No lives lost but there was damage to property. All on the clean up now but just watch the ground, it yields. If you need anything during your stay my wife and I would be more than happy to provide. We will have breakfast for you tomorrow morning before you leave and tonight you will eat at The Settlers, just down the track there. I'll let the magistrate know that you are here."

Macleod nodded and motioned for McDermott to have a seat on his bed. The room was small and cramped, the two beds barely fitting into the cramped quarters. Macleod saw that his bed was short and lamented the fact he would spend another night with his feet sticking out, unsupported and hanging slack. He tapped his pipe and took out his tobacco, slowly stuffing and preparing it, before striking the flint as the pipe flared and he took a first draw, the nicotine making his head buzz and the smoke searing his throat. He took out a bottle of whiskey from his possibles pack and took a deep drink, then another, his tremor settling.

McDermott was sitting on his bed, wringing his hands. Macleod sensed that he would have to deal with it before the boy would be of any use to him.

"What's the trouble boy?" he asked as the darkness encroached upon the room.

"I can still see their faces," said McDermott wringing his hands and shifting his feet.

Macleod contemplated for a moment, letting the silence settle on them. He put his hand on the boy's shoulder and spoke softly.

"There is only one way to think of it," said Macleod. "Had we not killed them they would have killed us and we'd be in the harbor now, food for the fish."

"But I didn't mean to kill him," said McDermott. "I wanted to help get him off you."

"God knows you didn't mean to. It was an accident, a simple accident. Accidents happen boy. You can spend your time blaming yourself and worrying about what might have been, but those two were criminals, dirty low life, scum of The Rocks, and all we did was a bit of cleaning to keep people safe. Now you've got a choice, you can keep thinking about it and turning it over or you can let it go. And I'm telling you to let it go."

McDermott nodded. He took his hands apart and placed them on his thighs, pushing downward toward his knees as if he was cleaning his hands of what he had done. Macleod knew it was for show, he could see the deep furrows in the boy's brow, but there was naught else that could be done.

As the darkness was deepening, Macleod lit a candle and then another to brighten the room. The shadows danced on the whitewashed walls and played out on the stone floor. A knock at the door interrupted the silence.

"The magistrate is here Inspector Macleod. Come to the parlour, he is waiting for you there."

"Shall I wait here?" asked McDermott.

"No," said Macleod. "I expect we are going to get the full once over. You will need to come with me."

He left his hat on the bed and led McDermott out along the narrow hallway to the parlour. The magistrate was sitting facing the window, looking out onto the street. The furniture was rudimentary, patched stuffed sofas, a small bookshelf and a bureau with a pitcher and jug. There was a looking-glass over the bureau. Macleod could see in the reflection Samuel and Hannah Redman crouched behind the door listening to the proceedings.

The magistrate stood as he heard the footsteps. He was a portly man, balding with long mutton-chop whiskers and stubble growing on his chin. A large waistcoat squeezed around his ample girth and his suit was ill-fitting, too small for the size of the man.

"Inspector Macleod and Constable McDermott?"

"Correct," said Macleod. They waited until the magistrate indicated that they could sit and they sat facing each other, knees almost touching. The magistrate produced a document and put his tongue between his yellow teeth as he concentrated on the contents.

"93rd Highlanders, Balaclava and wounded at Lucknow..." he looked up at Macleod.

"It's true what it says? Discharged after wounding? Joined the London police as a sergeant and rose quickly to an inspector, H division, meritorious service, bravery award," said the magistrate. He stopped for effect and raised his eyebrows at Macleod.

"It's true. But you need not read it all," said Macleod, "if there is anything you are unsure about please ask me. I do not think we need to review my entire record in front of the boy."

The magistrate clicked his tongue, eyes darting to McDermott and back to MacLeod and then continued.

"Lost your family in a smallpox epidemic in 1872; transferred to Sydney Cove after erratic behaviour."

He looked at Macleod for confirmation.

Macleod nodded.

"Effective clearance rate in The Rocks."

The magistrate continued to read but kept the details to himself as he digested them. He turned page after page, poring over the report, occasionally glancing at Macleod. When he was satisfied, he slowly closed the file.

He turned to face McDermott. "I have little on you."

"No sir," said McDermott. "I joined the force this very day one year ago. My father was a policeman."

The magistrate put his hand up.

"I know that part. There is no need to repeat it."

"So," said Macleod, "you seem to know a lot about us but we know nothing of you, not even your name."

The magistrate gritted his teeth.

"Simpson. I'm the magistrate of the town and that's all you need to know."

"I take it from your tone you are not happy that we are here," said Macleod.

"No-one is happy that you are here," said Simpson, sitting forward so the spittle from his mouth sprayed, some of it glancing Macleod on the face. The smell of the man hit Macleod. He smelled of the fields, manure, and whiskey. He had broken capillaries across his ruddy face, a testament to his habit of imbibing.

"We didn't ask for someone from Sydney to come and investigate this murder. We could handle it very well on our own. The local constabulary here is very efficient."

"And yet they have asked us to come..."

"You've been sent here for your own safety," said Simpson scowling at Macleod. "Let me make it clear that we don't need you here and we don't want you here."

"Point made clear," said Macleod, "yet we are here and we must get on with the task. Can you provide me with details of the case?"

The magistrate sat back and breathed out heavily. Either he didn't have the energy to continue fighting with Macleod or other pressures made him move on.

"Gruesome, terrible, the body was found on the property by the local priest of St Mary-on-Allyn. The church borders the Allyn river in Allynbrook over the way." He gestured with his thumb to the west.

"A pissant place in the middle of nowhere. Mostly farmers, landowners who have been granted land. O'Dell, one of our respected and wealthy landowners here sent his daughter across there to be a schoolmistress for the children of the Shea family. Mrs. Shea did not like her children being taught by the local schoolmaster. O'Dell agreed to send his daughter across as the governess."

He paused and lowered his voice.

"She was fifteen years of age and her name was Emily. They found her in the churchyard. A most dreadful thing."

He looked at the ground as if he did not want to discuss the details and lowered his voice.

"Strangled and then mutilated in the most unholy way. The family was distraught. McKinlay, the local doctor, went with a constable to collect her. The funeral was two days ago. She's buried in the family plot."

"The murder occurred...?" asked Macleod.

"Fifteen days ago this night," said the magistrate.

"Suspects?" asked Macleod.

"None," said the magistrate. "At first we thought it was a local tribe that had come back from the Barrington but it is not something they would do."

He leaned forward, his voice dropping to a whisper.

"The town is so small. We have interviewed everyone. Nothing human could have done this."

Macleod nodded, considering his words carefully.

"And McKinlay... can I speak with him?"

The magistrate sat back, and exhaled, his frustration plain.

"He'll meet you at The Settlers Inn just later. He lives out of town. He won't come here to the Redman's cottage because Hannah pesters him to come to live here in his old age. He is a stubborn old bugger. He lives in that grand house out of town on the river all by himself. He has been the doctor here for years, apart from the time he took a sojourn in Adelaide."

"You trust him then?" said Macleod.

"Yeah, I trust him. More than I trust anyone else around here," said the magistrate.

Macleod stepped out into the darkness with McDermott close behind. The streets were dark. Candlelight in the occasional window and the moonlight were the only guides. They trudged down as the brisk evening enveloped them. On the corner was an inn, the corner door open, and Macleod could see candles inside. As Macleod entered, the publican watched him carefully.

"Evening sir," he said. "Are you the inspector from the city?"

"That's right," said Macleod. "This is Constable McDermott."

"I have fortified wine, sherry, and some whiskey."

"Whiskey for me," said Macleod, "and one for the constable."

"I will bring it to you over there. McKinlay is waiting in the corner."

The inn was empty and Macleod realized they had cleared it out for the special audience. McKinlay was sitting quietly and gazing at the fire as it crackled and popped in the corner of the room. He had a small white pointed beard, his sparse hair brushed neatly across his scalp, his suit neat, general appearance fastidious. As Macleod and McDermott approached he did not acknowledge them, staring into the fire, eyes haggard and empty.

Macleod reached the table where McKinlay was sitting and moved one of the chairs gently. McKinlay broke from his trance and looked up animatedly, greeting Macleod as he stood with a warm handshake.

"Greetings inspector," he said. "And the young constable." He stood and took his walking stick, limping to the fire, his left leg causing him considerable pain as he moved. He stoked the fire and threw on another log of wood, beckoning for Macleod and McDermott to take their seats. As he limped back to his chair, he complained loudly "Damn leg! I was thrown from the buggy last year and injured my left hip. There is nothing for it. I'm sure it will be the death of me one day if I trip over something." He sat down heavily, taking a deep breath.

"Richardson!" he yelled.

"I'm on my way McKinlay," yelled the publican carrying a tray in the dimly lit room, the crackle of the fire punctuating his footsteps. He set down three glasses generously filled. McKinlay picked up the glass and held it in the air.

"Slainte Mhath."

Macleod replied, "Do dheagh shlainte."

They both finished the whiskey and put their empty glasses on the table. Richardson shuffled over to fill them again.

"You've met the magistrate then?"

"Yes," said Macleod.

"Not the most competent of men," said McKinlay. "Ever since the sixties when they changed it over from the police paid magistrate to the local landowners we've had a succession of magistrates who have been relatively easy to bribe or cajole. Some felons in this district that should be in goal are wandering free. If Christopher Lean has his way we will be back to a paid police magistrate and I look forward to it," said McKinlay, downing another glass of whiskey.

Richardson came over to fill the glass again but he waved him away. Macleod downed his whisky and accepted the refill.

"Ordinarily I'd have you down at The Hermitage," said McKinlay, pointing to the south where Macleod guessed his house must have been. "It's a mess at the moment. I'm packing it up. Hannah Redman has been at me to move up to the boarding house after I hurt my hip. I'm old and I suspect soon I will have to accept their offer. So my apologies we meet here rather than at my home."

"No apology required," said Macleod.

As the fire hissed, clouds covered the moon so that the darkness became deeper, the shadows more foreboding.

"And so to the business of the murder," said McKinlay. "A dreadful thing. I've been in this town for many years and knew this young girl. Treated her when she was younger for diphtheria. She survived that awful infection only to be cut to pieces by this monster. I made drawings."

He reached over and out of a saddlebag he pulled papers and shuffled them together.

"They kept her at the magistrate's residence until I got there," said McKinlay. "The local constable had done his job and interviewed all the townsfolk but no clues were forthcoming. They found her at St Mary-on-Allyn, propped against the door. Strangulation the likely cause of death. Dreadfully mutilated post mortem."

McKinlay pushed the drawing towards him. Macleod examined it in the candlelight.

"These are...."

"Bites," said McKinlay, 'here on the chest, arms, face. Savage, tearing bites, the flesh torn away."

"An animal?"

"Human," said McKinlay. "We had the dentist in Paterson examine the casts from the deeper bites."

He reached into his saddlebag and placed a moulded set of ragged upper teeth on the table.

"You're certain?"

"Poor dentition, ragged teeth, but only a human could make those bite marks."

"God save us," said McDermott, making the sign of the cross.

"Anything else?" Macleod asked.

"She wasn't violated, if that is what you mean," said McKinlay.

"And the pieces of flesh?" asked Macleod.

"Never found them. We searched the graveyard and the river but she was buried without them."

"And the constable you went with, is he available for interview?" asked Macleod.

"Ex-convict," said McKinlay. "Irish. Got Spooked and fled. No offence young man but I hope you won't mind me saying that these Irish are a superstitious lot."

"He is not a suspect then?" asked Macleod.

"No," said McKinlay, "I suspect he scarpered so that he would not be asked any further questions. But he is definitely not a suspect."

"And the family?"

"Well known in this district. The O'Dell's have been landowners here for over forty years. They have a large estate out of town. Simpson will take you to meet them tomorrow. They will have horses for you to take the overland track to Allynbrook. It will be a day's journey but faster than going back via Patterson. When you reach Allynbrook, we've made arrangements for you to stay at Reynella, a local inn. The landlady there, Bridget O'Donnell is a fiery lady but true enough. She will provide you with food and board. But I have digressed," he said. "You must forgive my age. The mind wanders."

"The O'Dell family have been here for forty years. They are a large family; five boys and three girls. Emily was the eldest girl. She was well schooled here in Dungog and excelled in letters. Selected to be a governess for the Shea family. Simpson no doubt told you the story. She left six months ago and reports to the O'Dell family were that all was well. And then the murder."

"And the father?"

"Not a suspect," said McKinlay. "Nor anyone else in the family. The mother and father are devastated, the funeral so very sad, shocking."

He stopped for a moment, staring into the fire. Then abruptly, he changed tack and began again.

"She was strangled no doubt, a tight cord. There were ligature marks around the neck. Quite likely the flesh was removed post mortem. Apart from that, I can't tell you anymore. The rest of the examination was unremarkable. Her internal organs were all in good health, there were no signs of violation."

"Any signs she fought back? A struggle?"

"Her hands were clean," said McKinlay. "Her shoes were on. There were no signs she struggled."

A heavy silence came over the room as the fire crackled and popped.

"Richardson!" called McKinlay. He motioned to the publican who brought over the whisky and filled their glasses. They downed them one more time and McKinlay rested his glass gently on the table.

"Whoever or whatever did this... it wasn't natural. Something evil to do such a thing to a human body."

McKinlay stood, teetering on his left leg. "Come, gentlemen, I'll join you back at the Redman's. I'm staying there tonight. It's too far to walk out to The Hermitage."

Sensing the conversation was over, Macleod stood and motioned to McDermott to help McKinlay. As they exited through the door, the clouds broke and the moonlight shone, casting long shadows on the street. In the distance, a distressed cow bellowed, the sound echoing around the valley, stalking the trio as they walked in darkness.

8

Macleod walked cautiously along the passageway. His right leg was throbbing, an old injury complaining after the long hours of travel. He rubbed his thigh, stopping for a moment, and taking a deep breath, continued on, entering the dining area where McDermott was waiting for him. The young man was tucking into eggs and bacon as Hannah Redman fussed around him.

"Good morning Mr Macleod," she said briskly. "Eggs and bacon for you?"

"That would be very pleasing, thank you," said Macleod, taking a seat and drawing himself up to the table. McDermott noticed his superior had arrived, and he stood up abruptly, bone-handled knife and fork clattering to the floor.

"At ease constable."

McDermott sat down, picking up the utensils and put them by his plate, waiting until Macleod had received his food.

"Continue on please. Don't let it get cold," said Macleod.

While they were sitting quietly Macleod took out his tobacco pouch and stuffed his pipe, breathing in the aroma. He lit it up while he was waiting for his breakfast, contemplating the events of the past twenty-four hours. McDermott ate quietly beside him, waiting for Macleod to speak first. Hannah Redman bustled into the room carrying a plate filled with rashers of bacon and poached eggs with soda bread on the side. She placed it down in front of Macleod, wiping her hands on her apron.

"I hope you enjoy that, sir. The soda bread is made right here and the pigs are ours, and the chickens."

"Very good," said Macleod. "McKinlay?"

"Up and left early," said Mrs. Redman. "Down at the Hermitage pottering around and cleaning up. He is resisting, but he needs care. We will get him here, eventually. He's getting old." She added the last sentence as an afterthought, nodding her head to no-one in particular, before bustling out of the room toward the kitchen.

Samuel Redman was out on duty that morning, Macleod had seen him leaving earlier in the day and so he did not expect to see the master of the house. The dining room was empty, apart from the two, and they enjoyed their meal in silence. Whilst they were eating Hannah Redman brought out a large pot of tea, black and steaming, and poured it for both of them.

"Mr. O'Dell has had two stock horses brought for you. They're saddled and out front. You can ride them out to the property and then tomorrow when you leave you can take them with you across to Allynbrook."

"We are well cared for then," said Macleod. Hannah smiled and nodded, not giving anything further away.

"This evening Mr. Lean has requested your company for dinner. I will serve dinner at six. Salted pork if it is to your liking? Mr. Lean is a local landowner and likes to have his say on law and order. He'd like to speak with you before you leave for Allynbrook."

"Of course." Said Macleod, not wanting to refuse an invitation and seeing the opportunity to gather more information.

Completing their breakfast they stowed their belongings and walked out into the brisk autumn morning. The sun was at a quarter height in the sky and the street was busy, the clank from the blacksmith mixed with the bustle of those purveying their goods, the butcher and bakery, sulkies trundling up and down the street carrying passengers and goods, bullocks trudging along, hauling the valuable cedar foraged from the forest. The dust from the road was kicking up as Macleod spotted their horses. He took the first he came to, a large chestnut mare, sturdy with a splash of white down her nose. The second smaller horse he motioned for McDermott to take. It was a dappled grey mare, and it nuzzled McDermott as he took the reins. The horses had been fully equipped with saddle blankets in place, stock saddles, and bridle.

Macleod patted his ride gently, running his hand up and down the nose and stroking her cheek. She was settled and friendly and he watched as McDermott did the same with his mare. Taking their horses they eased into the traffic on the road, keeping to the left, away from the carts and sulkies. The horses clip-clopped at a gentle pace and soon they reached the outskirts of town, past the Settlers Arms and down towards the Williams River on the bend. The directions gave them about a mile to travel out of town to the O'Dell's, and as they ambled along, the dust of the town faded and the air became clearer, magpies cawed in the distance, crows hopping here and there throughout the trees.

The dirt road out to O'Dell's was a bullock track, uneven and lined heavily by trees. They rounded several curves and Macleod was beginning to wonder that they had gone too far and missed the turn, but a track appeared to the left and he could see in the distance the O'Dell homestead. A fence line surrounded the property and they let themselves through, urging the horses up the hill to the homestead. The large building was foreboding in the mid-morning light; the curtains drawn in mourning. A solitary windmill turned slowly in the gentle morning breeze. The gardens were well kept, wisteria growing along the wide verandas around the property with a rose garden in the forecourt.

A stable hand greeted them, and as Macleod alighted, he saw a large man standing on the veranda. Taking off his hat he walked towards him, ensuring that McDermott was two steps behind.

"James O'Dell," said the large man, his well-fitting waistcoat and pocket watch a testament to his wealth. A large beard surrounded his ruddy face with red-rimmed eyes betraying his grief.

"Inspector Macleod and Constable McDermott."

"Thank you for coming," said O'Dell. "Let's sit outside if you don't mind. My wife is not taking visitors, and it has hit the children hard. The two girls won't come out of their room. The older boys are at work on the property."

"Mr. O'Dell," asked Macleod carefully. "Would it be possible to speak with the boys? I could have my constable attend to it."

"I'm not sure what they could tell you," said O'Dell, "but if you think it will help?"

Macleod nodded to McDermott. McDermott was up and moved away quietly.

"Such a horrible thing," said O'Dell, looking out over the pastoral land. "I can scarcely bear to think about it. We sent her over there in good faith. She was doing well, thriving and her family loved her. Who would do such a thing?"

He looked at Macleod, beseeching him for an answer.

"That is what I am here to find out," said Macleod. "I am very sorry for your loss Mr. O'Dell."

"Thank you," said O'Dell, leaning forward, his elbows on his knees, his hands clasped together, wringing slowly. "She was fifteen years old and a bright beautiful girl, chestnut hair and green eyes, a light in our lives. She wanted to spread her wings, talked of going to Sydney and the like but we managed to keep her close by, at least in Allynbrook, thinking that she would be safer."

McLeod waited a moment before speaking, allowing O'Dell a moment to ponder, to be at one with his grief. When he spoke, it was almost in a whisper.

"Does anyone bear any grudges against you Mr. O'Dell? Anyone with a score to settle?"

"Some people around town are envious I suppose, but no-one would do this sort of thing. If they wanted money, I would have given it to them... land... whatever they wished!"

"No enemies of your sons? She had no courtiers?"

"None. She loved teaching, and she loved the family she was with and the children loved her. We hoped she would marry at some stage soon but she was still young; when we last saw her two months ago when she came to visit, she had never been happier."

"May I see her room?" asked Macleod, knowing he was pushing the boundary.

O'Dell was obliging. He staggered momentarily and Macleod caught him. Regaining his balance O'Dell led him through the front door and into the large opulent parlour and down to the left wing.

"We have the boys over here to the right and the girls down here in their own private area. They shared a room the three of them, they wouldn't be separated."

The room was neat, tidy, everything in its place. Emily's two sisters, frightened by the advancing footsteps, scuttled from the room and ran off down the corridor. Macleod surveyed the bedroom with the three beds in an orderly line, unfinished sewing on one of the beds; shoes, a hairbrush, nothing out of place.

"May I?" he asked.

"You can, "said O'Dell. "I'll wait at the door here if you don't mind." Macleod walked carefully into the room, his footfalls on the floorboards reminding him how empty the room was. Macleod touched the books. They were neatly aligned, and he stooped to survey the orderly collection. As he ran his gaze along, he noticed one book, bulging, straining; out of place in the surrounding symmetry. He took it out and opened it. Inside there was a heart-shaped token fashioned from wheat sheaves, small and delicate, a keepsake. He examined it carefully and placed it back where he found it. Finding nothing else untoward he left the room, walking solemnly with O'Dell, passing room upon room where the curtains were drawn, the house in a permanent state of mourning.

"Would you like tea Mr Macleod? I am sure I can get one of our servants...."

"No thank you," Macleod said. "I won't trouble you any further."

McDermott was back, standing on the front porch, pensive. Macleod knew that it was best not to tarry, best not to wade in this man's grief. As he shook hands with the homeowner, O'Dell searched for something to say but could find nothing and let it go.

"I'll do my best to find them. I'll bring them to justice," said Macleod, anticipating O'Dell's statement.

O'Dell nodded, eyes brimming with tears, nodded and turned away, hiding his face from them.

The stable boy brought their horses, complete with saddlebags for the journey on the morrow. As they turned from the house Macleod looked back over his shoulder, watching as the stricken father slumped in the chair on the veranda.

As the horses wandered along, and when they were out of earshot, McDermott addressed Macleod.

"The older son, Manus, says he thought Emily may have had a gentleman friend, the oldest boy in the O'Malley family, Eamon. The O'Malley's are landowners in Eccleston, just out of Allynbrook. He said they had spoken of it when she returned home two months ago. She had not told her father fearing that he would not approve as Eamon was below her station."

"Had they planned to elope?" asked Macleod.

"As far as Manus was aware they had planned nothing."

"Had Manus ever met Eamon?"

"No," said McDermott. "I have no more information on him. The rest of the boys were grief-stricken, but they concurred with what Manus said. A terrible thing is it not Mr. Macleod? What sort of person are we looking for?"

"I don't know yet," said Macleod.

Thereafter they rode along together in silence, down the dusty road back into town. When they reached the boarding-house Simpson was waiting for them.

"Before you get off those horses," he said, his waistcoat bulging where one button had fallen off, "they found the constable that went to Allynbrook with McKinlay. He had scarpered."

"Where is he held?" asked Macleod.

"At the lock-up. Thomas Cook, the Chief of Police, has him there."

"Then we best go over there," said Macleod.

"I'll come with you," said Simpson, moving awkwardly towards his sulky. He rolled awkwardly into the driver seat and grasped the reins. Then the sulky lurched off, gathering speed, Simpson apparently intent on winning the race to the lock-up. What reason he had Macleod could not fathom, but he made a comical picture, his tubby form struggling to reign in his pony as it dashed down the road.

Macleod set off at a slow pace with McDermott. By the time they reached the lock-up on Dowling Street Simpson's sulky was parked and he was well inside. The Chief of Police, Thomas Cook, was waiting for them as Simpson fawned around as if he was beholden to the man. Cook was a no-nonsense policeman, and it was clear from the interaction Macleod could see that he had little time for Simpson. As Macleod and McDermott entered the lock-up, he looked up from the desk, took off his spectacles and placed them on the counter. He sat in his chair for some time regarding them, taking them in, sizing them up. At length, he stood and did not offer his hand in friendship but bid them welcome from a distance.

"Inspector Macleod, Constable McDermott."

Macleod replied. "Chief Constable."

Simpson made to interject but Cook waved him away, asking him to wait outside. Macleod glimpsed disdain on Cook's face as he spoke to Simpson and ordered him out of the premises. When he was gone, Cook spoke slowly. Macleod noted that he carefully avoided any mention of the murder in Allynbrook and concentrated on the facts of what they were dealing with in Dungog.

"We caught him on the run over on the McClellan property. He was trying to thieve chickens, no doubt hungry after several days on the run. He was talking gibberish and we could not make any sense from him so we brought him in here. He was talking all sorts of strange things that have occurred, ghosts and hauntings. The Irish are very superstitious."

Macleod nodded. "Yes, they are. McKinlay said he was a felon, released..."

"No," said Cook. "His father was a felon, given his ticket-of-leave by Charles Boydell over in Gresford, years back. They granted him a small parcel of land for his service and thereafter he made his way over here to Dungog where he lived and worked. His son joined the constabulary. The boy has always been skittish; I've had to discipline him several times, but he has never gone absent without leave."

"What was the sequence of events?" asked Macleod.

"Well, we only have McKinlay's report but they had the body with them, on the road to Patterson, and just before Patterson, O'Brien takes flight, leaves the company and is not seen until now."

"May we question him?" said Macleod.

"You'll need to be in my presence. He is still part of my constabulary and he is under my jurisdiction."

"Understood," said Macleod.

Cook measured him again and then led him through to the cell. O'Brien was sitting in the corner, knees drawn up with his chin pulled in, as if he was trying to make himself the smallest target possible. His eyes darted about the room. The keys to the cell clanked loudly as Cook turned them and admitted Macleod and McDermott to the cell. Cook remained outside, watching proceedings carefully. Macleod eyed the boy thoughtfully. There was no doubt something terrified him. Terrified of something he had seen or something he had done.

"Should we try to get him up?" asked McDermott. "Should I try to talk to him?"

"It won't help I don't think," said Macleod. "He's traumatised. He's seen something. Let's leave him where he is and try to converse with him there where he feels safe."

They moved over closer to him and dropped to their haunches with Macleod's knees popping loudly as he knelt. The boy looked up at them as if he was seeing them for the first time and shrank back; then relaxed as McDermott put his hand on his shoulder.

"O'Brien," said McDermott. "Do you know where you are?"

"In the lock-up, Dungog. I know where I am," said O'Brien.

Macleod observed that McDermott had a way with him and he let the questioning resume, nodding to McDermott that he should continue.

"Can you tell us anything about what happened?" McDermott asked.

O'Brien put his right index finger to his lips and spoke in a low whisper. "I saw him. Saw him plain as day. He was there, in Allynbrook, and then he followed us. That's when I left."

"Who?" asked McDermott.

"The spirit," he said. "Spirit with fire around his hair. He was there."

"Tell us what happened," said McDermott.

"I went with McKinlay over to get the girl. I didn't want to go anyway but the Chief Constable, he said I had to go. I never like seeing dead people and I saw her, you know, cut up. It made me sick, but I said I'd stick with McKinlay and bring her home to her family, so I stuck with him. That night at the magistrate's, where she was... they left her lying there see... covered overnight, until we could get the hearse organized to put her in, to get her down through Patterson and home. That night I was in the back room and I looked outside and he was there. It was hard to make out at first like he was hiding, then I saw him behind a tree staring at the building. He was pale-faced no doubt with fire around his head. He disappeared as quickly as I saw him but then he was there again later. Later in the morning, I heard a bird calling or some such noise, and I got up to look out the window and I swear I saw him moving there again with fire around his head and pale ghostly skin. It's a Banshee, I know it, an evil thing. Evil on evil."

"And then what happened?" asked McDermott.

"Well, the next day the sun was out, and we got her into the wagon and started down toward Patterson and the road was rough, chopped up, and we had to stop lots of times but I saw him in the bush, just following us, real stealthy like. I saw his shadow, but I knew he was there. When we got close to Patterson, I knew I had to get out so during the night when we were near Patterson I took off. I knew as long as I stayed with that body he'd be there, following us, and I knew he meant to get one of us, or both of us, so I wasn't sticking around."

"So you left McKinlay?"

"He had a driver. He was safe. He's old anyway. The Banshee wouldn't want him. It was young blood he was after."

"Have you seen it again anywhere here?" asked McDermott.

"No," he said. "No, it's gone. The body is buried. There is nothing to be here for. She's dead. She's gone." He wept, putting his head in his hands. "I'm sorry," he said. "I shouldn't have left here. Mammy always told me if I saw one I should get out of its way or it would come for me. I'm sorry I left here." He wept as he said the last words and put his head down.

McDermott patted him on the shoulder as he and Macleod stood and turned to leave the cell. Cook nodded as they left and turned the heavy key, the lock turning.

"What will you do with him?" asked Macleod.

"I don't know yet," said Cook. "The constabulary here is a fine constabulary. I can't have him as part of it if he is like this. I suspect I must discharge him back to his family farm and they can look after him."

"What's he talking about? Does her really mean to say he saw a Banshee?" asked McDermott.

"Like I said," said Cook. "The Irish are superstitious. He thinks he has seen something. He has seen nothing. It's just the wild imagination of a young boy."

"But he is so terrified," said McDermott.

"They are all terrified, the Irish. I was never sure the boy was quite right in the head, anyway. I took him on as a favour."

They walked back to the front of the lock-up and they could see Simpson outside, leaning toward the door and listening intently for any morsels of information. Cook shut the door of the lock-up against him.

"Can I ask you about where we are going?" asked Macleod. Cook nodded, seemingly distracted.

"The magistrate, William Boydell, one of the Boydell brothers. He is a good man with a good head on his shoulders but they've only got a court of petty sessions there. They don't deal with murder. That goes to Patterson."

"And the constabulary?"

"There is one, Forrest, another dependable man by all reports, mostly used to breaking up fights and petty stealing over there. I think you'll find they will not be trained in a murder investigation. You may have to take it from the beginning and gather all the facts yourselves."

"Thank you," said Macleod. He put his hand out to shake Cook's hand but Cook hesitated before bringing his hand up and shaking Macleod's hand firmly, looking him squarely in the eye.

"You best be careful over there Inspector. Whatever did this is still out there. You be careful turning over too many stones in case you don't like what you find."

Macleod nodded and motioned to McDermott to move toward the door. As they opened the door Simpson fell inward, landing heavily on the concrete.

"Get up Simpson for goodness' sake!" said Cook. "Be off with you!"

Macleod and McDermott remounted and made their way back to the boarding house.

The day was wearing on and Macleod knew that they would be scrutinised again tonight by another town dignitary, Charles Lean. After tethering his horse and ensuring they were fed, he sat in front of the boarding house and lit his pipe, watching the traffic pass, contemplating the events that had occurred.

The sun was low as Macleod heard the call from Hannah Redman for dinner. She came to the door of the room and knocked quietly so as not to startle the occupants. McDermott had been out attending to the horses, making sure they were ready for the journey in the morning. Macleod had been resting, dozing uneasily in the afternoon's warmth. He sat up abruptly on his bed, thanking Hannah Redman for retrieving his coat.

"I will serve Constable McDermott's meal in his room. Mr. Lean wants to meet with you alone."

"As he wishes," said Macleod. He made his way to the dining room, which was empty save for an imposing man sitting at the middle table. He was well dressed in waistcoat and suit with chain and fob watch fastened neatly. He had sharp features and a full head of well-groomed hair. His green eyes scrutinized Macleod as he walked into the room. He held out his hand. "Charles Lean," he said.

"Cormag Macleod."

As they sat Mrs. Redman fussed around serving fortified wine. Lean talked and Macleod listened. In two hours, over a dinner of salted pork and spotted dick, Lean spoke at length, pausing only occasionally to gain Macleod's approval. Macleod listened, nodding occasionally, gleaning information about the district and various tribulations of the shire. What he garnered most was Lean's disdain for the gentleman magistrate who had replaced the police magistrate. As they sipped whisky and smoked, Macleod felt that Lean had measured him effectively. Although he had talked non-stop throughout the dinner, Macleod knew that Lean had been scrutinizing his every move, evaluating him.

"The investigation is important," said Lean. "We must have an answer otherwise it will drive settlers away. The future of this shire and settlements around it hangs in the balance inspector. If we cannot provide a plausible explanation and bring the murderer to justice, then we cannot reassure anyone in this district that they are safe. Who would come here knowing that a murderer was loose, and that we failed to apprehend them? Settlers will leave and take up elsewhere in the Hunter and all that is built here will be dust."

Macleod knew that he was not being dramatic. A turn of events such as this could change the outcome in a small settlement.

"I want to convey to you the utmost importance of your investigation," he continued, "that you find the one responsible, and he is brought to justice, and the justice is public so that all know the region is safe. And finally," said Lean, finishing his whisky, "ensure any findings are not reported to Simpson. He is not trustworthy and verily within the next year, if I have my way, he will be replaced with a police magistrate once again, someone who can be trusted. Any findings of note should be communicated to Thomas Cook and I, and anything that you require for the investigation should be requested from me, not from Simpson. He is to be kept out of this at all times."

"Understood," said Macleod.

Lean stood abruptly and took his hat. "Thank you Mrs. Redman," and he nodded to Hannah as she stood next to the kitchen with her hands folded in front of her.

"Safe journey for tomorrow."

Macleod stood and shook his hand, then Lean strode from the room, disappearing into the night.

Macleod sat back in his chair and finished his whisky. As he was sitting, Samuel Redman entered the room and approached him carefully. "Inspector Macleod," he said. "I have a map for you." Redman produced a piece of parchment with a rudimentary map drawn on it detailing the district of Dungog through to Allynbrook. It was hand drawn, showing the various allotments throughout the Dungog area, a suggested route on horseback through to Allynbrook. Redman traced a line with his finger.

"You'll head west and meander along this way," he said whilst tracing the map, "through these allotments. Some are cleared and some are not. You may find yourself in deeply forested areas on occasions but there is a way through. You will reach the Allyn river and once you do, turn Norwest, and soon after reaching a bullock track. Take it to Reynella. It is on the road out of town. Bridget O'Donnell and Edward Bird will expect you. They are the proprietors."

"They have different names?" queried Macleod.

"Second marriage for Edward. His first wife died. She fell from a horse. O'Donnell is fiercely Catholic and wants to be known as Mrs. O'Donnell. She runs the place."

He folded the map and handed it to Macleod who took it gratefully.

"Safe journey tomorrow, Inspector."

Redman left the room and Macleod stood, his balance affected by the whiskey and wine, and he stumbled his way down the hallway to the shared room with McDermott. McDermott was already there, fast asleep, or pretending to be asleep, as Macleod collapsed onto the bed, staring at the ceiling into the darkness.

As he turned onto his side, just outside the room, he saw the shape of the Russian soldier, an arm missing, the limb shredded above the elbow. He was joined by a comrade, his face missing and a terrible cacophony of blood and gore. Macleod closed his eyes and turned his back to them, refusing to acknowledge their presence.

The gentle call of whip birds, punctuated by the warble of a magpie, accompanied McDermott and Macleod as the stock horses carefully wound their way along the uneven ground west toward Allynbrook. Hannah Redman had made a breakfast meal of maize cakes and hot tea ready for their journey and they set out early after arising before the town awoke. Unseen, they travelled north down to The Settlers and then to the west, skirting the O'Dell property in the distance and moving across the unfenced land into the bush.

Their hosts had supplied them with enough damper and salted pork to see them through the day. Macleod was satisfied that their water supplies would last easily.

The early autumn morning was chill but there was no frost on the ground. The eucalypt and ghost gum trees provided dappled shade as they wound their way through them. The rains had brought new shoots of grass and more often than not the stamping of the hooves of the horses sent snakes slithering off out of harm's way. They were forced to double back several times where a watercourse had blocked their way or a tree had fallen, slowing their progress.

They stopped mid-morning; trees and a bullock carcass, bloated and maggot filled, blocking their way, and they doubled back to the valley floor. Here they appreciated the maize cakes and tea, as the morning bird calls fell silent, and the subtle sounds of the bush enveloped them. Macleod's hangover was lifting, but he was in no mood for conversation, keeping his head down as he sipped the hot tea. Fire ants coalesced at their feet as they sat, and Macleod signalled to McDermott that it was time to move on.

By midday they had completed half the journey and, choosing a clearing beneath the shade of eucalypts, McDermott cleared a space, brought kindling and lit a fire to brew the billy for hot tea. The fire was crackling, and he warmed the damper that Hannah Redman had given them, distributing the food when it was warm with the salted pork. Macleod gratefully accepted it, regretting his silence during the morning. The hot tea warmed him and taking out the bottle of whisky he offered it to McDermott who put up his hand and declined. Macleod poured a large amount into his metal cup full and drank it, the spirit warming him further; he felt the muscles around his scalp and neck relaxing as he rested back against a large eucalypt, rummaging for his tobacco pouch and pipe. As McDermott sat staring into the fire, the smoke lazily rose through the gap in the trees, the horses whinnied and stomped their hooves.

Macleod looked up and on a fallen tree to their right, an enormous raven had landed. It croaked three or four times and cheekily hopped closer to the food. McDermott shooed it away but it flew into the air only a short way before landing down again close by. It cocked its head and called, the wail and warble splitting the silence as it hopped closer, testing the opposition to see whether it dared another attempt. In time it stopped calling and stood still, titling its head to display its hackles, the pale left eye fixed on Macleod.

"Is it true what he said?" asked McDermott as Macleod stared back at the raven.

"What about?" asked Macleod.

"The Banshee, the spirit. You know, the evil."

"From my experience McDermott, most of these things are in men's minds only. No doubt he saw something but his imagination made it more than it was. Perhaps he saw what he wanted to see."

MacLeod took a swig of whisky and drew on his pipe, squinting as the smoke from the fire drifted toward him.

"Do you believe in ghosts Mr. Macleod?" asked McDermott.

"Do I believe in ghosts?" asked Macleod. He sat back against the tree. "When I was growing up in the highlands, my mother always told me never to go out at night, lest we be taken by the spirit in the woodlands. She said it waited for stray children, and when it got you, it would eat your soul and condemn you to hell. It scared us, but it never stopped us staying out late. Until one evening a child went missing, a sweet young lass, seven years old. She disappeared on dusk while collecting berries in the forest. The townspeople searched and searched but could not find her. My mother said the spirit had taken her. That stopped us all going out at night, convinced the Banshee was abroad. For weeks, we lived in terror, the sounds of the forest haunting our sleep."

Macleod took another draw on his pipe, letting the exhaled smoke drift out slowly, savouring the taste.

"Eventually they found her though. Strangled, the body hidden deep in the forest. They got a local boy for it and he hanged."

MacLeod sighed, taking a long draught from the whisky flask.

"So, when you ask me if I believe in ghosts McDermott, and particularly in evil, my answer to you is that we need to be wary in being afraid of things that exist on the edge of reality. Most of the evil in this world is in men; we don't need spirits for evil to be close to us."

As he was finishing the raven wailed again, a sad, mournful cry, and hopped on the ground, closer to McDermott. Macleod pointed toward it, raising his chin to the bird as he addressed it.

"In the highlands, these are a bad omen. They are always around when there is death. My grandfather used to say a raven like this, staying so close, meant that you and I would be in danger and we would soon face death." McDermott looked at Macleod uneasily. Macleod grinned and laughed softly. Realising he was unnerving the young constable he stopped laughing and waved his hand as if to erase the entire conversation.

"It's a bunch of shite, tales meant to scare children," he said, "we best stick to the facts McDermott and leave the superstition behind us."

Picking up a rock and throwing it at the raven, he struck the bird, and it staggered to the side. Awkwardly it took flight, croaking as it soared across the treetops.

"Best we clean up and get moving," said Macleod.

The steady motion of the horses pacified them as they traversed the other side of the mountain, coming at length to the Allyn River as it turned and meandered along its course. Turning Norwest they followed the bush path and after a time came to a rough bullock track, furrowed and uneven. Macleod led McDermott along single file as the horses trod warily amongst the potholes and cartwheel ruts. An hour later, as the sun was low on the horizon, to their left they reached a low-roofed slab building with a bullock train laden with cedar pulled up at the front. A large clearing area, away from the road, provided ample room for bullocks and horses. Wisteria wound its way around the bark thatched roof that covered the veranda. Someone had scratched a sign on a piece of wood, mounting it upon the entrance, *Reynella.*

The horses ambled in and after dismounting they tethered them away from the bullocks, on a low crossbeam over a water trough. Over to the left, under a great elm tree at the entrance to the inn, an unruly looking man was reclining as a younger man clipped his whiskers and went about making his disorderly hair look neat. Standing behind them, in the tree's shadow, was an older man, sipping from a pottery mug, watching the activities intently. Macleod and McDermott's boots kicked up the dust as they went over the gravel-strewn ground toward the men. The older man looked up and, seeing them, strode toward them with his hand outstretched.

"Edward Bird," he said. "Ned."

"Inspector Macleod and Constable McDermott."

"Ah, yes, we've been expecting you," he said. "This is my son Patrick. If you need a haircut or shave while you are here he'd be happy to oblige!"

Patrick acknowledged Macleod with a nod and continued on with his work. The customer opened one eye and, satisfied that he was safe, went back to dozing as the barber continued his work.

A kookaburra's laugh echoed in the distance as Ned led them inside. Off the wide veranda, through a door at the side of the timber slab building, there was a bar. It was bright enough inside, the westerly sun shining through the open windows. They had placed seats and tables along the left, leading up to the rough timber bar, well stocked with fortified wine. There were bullock drivers seated scattered around the room, murmuring, smoking and drinking as a young lady moved between them, serving and talking. They knew her well and laughed with her as they exchanged stories.

"Nell," called Ned. "Come here."

Nell Bird walked over and bowed her head to Macleod and McDermott.

"Pleased to welcome you gentleman," she said. "Can I get you something to drink or something to eat?"

"It's early for that," said Ned. "We'll fix them up later."

Their conversation was broken as a screech came from the kitchen.

"Nell! Nell! Get out here!"

A woman dressed in black appeared, her hair tied neatly back in a bun, fiery green eyes darting around the room as she launched into the bar.

"Nell Bird, get out there into the kitchen and stop talking to those men! If you talked less and worked more you'd be at least halfway useful!"

Nell smiled sweetly and bowed to the men and walked to the kitchen. The woman in black watched her with gritted teeth as she walked past before striding over confidently to greet the two men.

"Bridget O'Donnell," she said, curtseying to them. At five foot two, she was short but nevertheless an imposing woman. Macleod could see that she ruled the place with an iron fist. The bullock drivers had stiffened in their seats when she had walked into the room, all of them sitting upright as if in a classroom and the schoolmistress had entered. Even Ned seemed to straighten, and he hid the pottery mug behind his back.

"I can see that Ned Bird. A bit early isn't it?"

"Right you are Bridget," he said.

"Right," she said, "inspector and constable." She pointed to them in turn. "That's correct."

"Do you have any idea how long you'd like to stay gentlemen?" she asked. "We are very busy at this time of year with bullock drivers but I can allocate you a room off to the side for a longer stay if you wish?"

"I'm uncertain exactly how long," said Macleod. "Until the job is done."

"Yes, well, I know better than to ask what it is about," said Bridget. "Come with me and I'll show you to your lodgings."

She led them past the stiff-backed bullock drivers, all wary as Bridget brushed past them, moving out the front door toward the cedar tree and pivoting right. As she turned, she called to her son Patrick.

"Very nice job Patrick, well done."

He smiled and nodded back. She turned to the right down a narrow corridor and then to the left. There was a small room with two beds and a wooden table. The floor was timber, clean and neat. A pitcher and bowl stood outside the door with two pieces of cloth.

"This will be yours for as long as you need it. The inn can get rowdy some nights from the bar but I'll keep them quiet for you. We stuff the mattress with corn husks and you'll find them to be the most comfortable in the district. The pillows are down. I have extra coverings if you need them although nights are mild at this time of year."

She gave them a moment to survey their room and then placed her hands in front of her, feet together as if she was giving a sermon.

"Some ground rules gentleman: we say Rosary every night at five; dinner promptly at six. The inn stays open as long as we need to, some bullock drivers arrive late. Fighting will not be tolerated. So you do not have to suffer the embarrassment of enquiring, I'm Ned's second wife. His first wife Catherine, was killed after she fell off a horse and broke her neck. Not an easy job taking over five stepchildren and then we had Patrick together. He is such a sweet boy. He always does as I ask him. Ned's children on the other hand... It's best not to mention Catherine around Ned. With the mention of her comes the black dog and then he drinks again. You will see some of my step-children working around the inn on an odd day and I will introduce you if I have the time. I'll expect you at six this evening; corned brisket and Nell's quince dumplings. It's about the only useful thing she does around here. I'll send her in to show you to the privy. She will have to go down to get water. Questions?"

Macleod realised that it would be of little use trying to gain information from this strong-willed woman and he held his tongue.

"No, thank you, Mrs. O'Donnell. Well explained and all clear."

"Very good," she said.

She walked to the door of the room and then turned toward them. "I'll leave you to get comfortable. The dreadful thing that happened." She made the sign of the cross twice. "What sort of person does that?" she asked. It was a rhetorical question and Macleod let it lie as the afternoon sunlight peeped through the entrance, casting long shadows in the hall.

"You are welcome to join us for a drink before dinner, and for the rosary, if you like. I will lead it with Ned and his children in one of the other rooms off to the left."

"Thank you, Mrs. O'Donnell but we will take the opportunity to rest," said Macleod, "but we will join you for dinner."

She nodded, fixing her gaze on him and then abruptly turned and left the room.

The smell of tobacco drifted from the tavern and the murmuring from the gathering dipped as Bridget O'Donnell's footsteps passed through the bar and out to the kitchen. Macleod could hear that after she had left the crowd's spirits lifted again, the conversation becoming more boisterous.

He was sitting on his bed when Nell appeared. Her hair was tied neatly, her housedress covered by a pinafore and she was carrying two large buckets. She beckoned them towards her. "Come with me please gentlemen," she said smiling, "I'll take you down to see where the watercourse is and show you the privy."

She led them out, past the elm tree where Patrick was finishing his barbering duties. He nodded to her, and she smiled, turning to the right and down along the fence line. McDermott struck up a conversation with her.

"Mrs. O'Donnell tells us you are making quince dumplings this evening."

"Yes," she said blushing. "My specialty. We get the quinces from Hancock's farm over the back. I'm embarrassed to say they are popular. I really don't know why. Such a simple recipe."

"Mrs. O'Donnell seems a tough lady."

"Oh, she's had her share of rough times. I can only expect it was very hard taking over a family after Ned's first wife died. She's good enough. She just has a fiery temper. You best keep out of the way."

She turned to McDermott and smiled. They reached the bottom of the property and there a creek wound its way around the back, babbling quietly. There was a small lean-to next to it.

"The privy is there," she said. "There's a water bucket near it. Be careful at night time and make plenty of noise when you walk down here to scare the snakes away. Summer is gone but some of them will still be hanging around."

Macleod nodded.

"The bullock drivers are a rowdy bunch," he said, as Nell filled the buckets with water from the creek.

"They are good enough. Most of them have good hearts unless they get drunk and then they can be a problem. But they still have enough respect; they will quiet down if I ask them."

"Anyone different coming through in the last week?"

"The same traffic as always," she said. "I haven't seen any new faces. It's a busy time with the cedar logging going on. I know little about what goes on beyond here. I'm up at dawn and in bed at dusk. This place provides enough work for all of us. I like to get out to Ravenscroft to visit mother and father when I can."

"Ravenscroft?" asked Macleod.

"It's my family's property, The Kenny's and the Doohan's, out at Eccleston. It is a lovely place, sitting high atop the hill with the river winding around it. When I married Patrick I came here to live at Reynella and work for Bridget. I get to go home occasionally but Bridget prefers that I walk, she doesn't like me riding the horses."

She finished filling the buckets and then heaved them up, her tiny five-foot form struggling to lift the enormous water receptacles.

"Here, let us help you," said McDermott stepping forward.

"No, no..." she said, "if Bridget sees you helping me then there will be hell to pay. You are guests."

"At least let me carry them up the hill," said McDermott. "You can carry them from there."

Reluctantly she handed them over to McDermott, very grateful that he took the weight for her and he carried them dutifully to the bottom of the course, out of the sight of the building. Nell took them from there, thanking him gratefully.

"If you need water, there is always some in the kitchen, just behind the serving area. Or you can come down to the creek here. For hot water, for tea, there is an urn that sits on the fire out the back. I can always get you hot water if you need it. There is a bell on the bar; if you need anything, just ring it. I'll come as quickly as I can."

The sun was setting, and she turned and left them, walking back through the bar as bullock drivers arrived. The crowd was getting noisy, and Macleod signalled to McDermott that they should make the way to their room and prepare for dinner.

The dinner bell roused Macleod, his mouth dry from the whisky he had imbibed during the afternoon, and his head felt thick. The room was dark with a solitary candle in the hallway to light his way. McDermott had left, his bed neatly tidied and his luggage stowed on the bed. Macleod stretched, his shoulders popping. His thigh was aching again, and he shook the leg as if to ward off the pain. He took another slug of whiskey, noting that his supply was low.

Putting on his hat, he walked toward the front of the building. Three more bullock trains had arrived whilst he had rested and the inn was rowdy. Full to capacity, there were men crammed at makeshift tables with hot food being delivered from the kitchen.

Bridget stood in the middle of the room, barking orders to her stepchildren and to poor Nell, who ran up and down at double time delivering wine and food to the tables. The air was thick with smoke as men enjoyed their pipe after a long day on the trail. Some were becoming raucous and he could see Nell urging them to quiet down lest they draw Bridget's ire.

McDermott was seated at a corner table, talking to a stranger. Macleod crossed the floorboards and pulled out a chair. As he approached McDermott stood, and the stranger remained seated, as Macleod removed his hat.

"Inspector Macleod, this is Constable Thomas Forrest."

Forest stood as he was introduced and put his hand out and Macleod shook it. The man had a firm grasp. He jerked his thumb toward McDermott. "I see they are making the constables younger in Sydney these days."

Macleod smiled. "He can hold his own. He is a sturdy young lad."

Macleod saw a glint of a smile on McDermott's face, quashed immediately as McDermott did not allow himself the emotion.

"Mr. Forrest has just been informing me of the events."

"It is probably best we retire to your room after dinner to discuss the more confidential details further. There are too many ears in this room and it's getting too damn loud."

In the corner, one driver had brought out a fiddle and was playing as rowdy singing broke out in different quarters. Most of the men joined in, the raucous singing filling the room. Macleod had to lean forward to hear Forrest over the din.

"You'll meet tomorrow with William Barker Boydell, our magistrate. The property is just up from Reynella, Caergwrle. It's next to St Mary's-on-Allyn, the church where the body was found. Boydell has been the magistrate in town for years. They tried to oust him back in the sixties but when he went they couldn't wait to get him back. He is in his late fifties now but is still sharp. He lost his wife Mary Phoebe several years back and it almost broke him, but he endured. He lives out at Caergwrle with his sons and daughters who run the property, tobacco mostly. He came here many years back now, following his brother Charles, who emigrated here and was granted a parcel of land years ago. The Boydell's are good people. I am sure he will give you every assistance he can."

"The church?" asked Macleod.

"Bishop Broughton built St Mary's-on-Allyn. Mary Phoebe was his daughter who married William. It's a beautiful church with new sandstone; such a horrible spectacle played out there."

As they were speaking, Nell came to the table with a tray with steaming corned brisket, mashed potato and carrots.

"I hope you enjoy it, gentlemen. We grow the potatoes and carrots here on the property."

They thanked her as she bustled off, eager to serve the straining hoard as they drank and ate their fill.

The brisket was tasty, well salted and the three men ate in silence as Macleod eyed the room, looking for troublemakers. The fiddle player continued and the room was becoming more raucous as more of the travellers finished their dinner and concentrated on heavy drinking. Bridget kept their glasses filled, the till turning over. Ned and Patrick assisted in encouraging the imbibing under Bridget's watchful eye. Forrest broke the silence as they completed their main meal.

"You are a military man then Macleod?"

"I was," he said. "93rd Highlanders, like my father."

"A noble calling," said Forrest. "You left the service?"

"Wounded," he said whilst holding up his hand showing the missing fingers and pointing to his face, his drooping eye and scar testament to his war injuries. "They discharged me after the uprising in Lucknow. Bloody business."

Forrest seemed to sense that he shouldn't go any further and he let the matter lie. A dark cloud came over Macleod for a few moments and McDermott struck up a conversation to fill the gap, allowing Macleod time to recover.

"No suspects?"

"None," said Forrest. "In this town, I deal with fights. There is the occasional rustling from gangs from Patterson and land disputes. We have a court of petty sessions but we don't deal with murder in this town."

The conversation faltered again as Ned took their plates and Nell proudly brought out the quince dumplings. They were steaming and hot and she placed them on the table in front of the men, smiling with pride.

"Nell," yelled Bridget. "Hurry, these men need wine!"

Her moment of pride short lived, she shot off behind the bar, grabbing more bottles and filling up those who were asking. The din of the song continued, becoming louder and louder, stifling further conversation. At that moment, as the cacophony reached its peak, there was a sound of a whinnying horse and rider, clad in full riding gear bursting into the inn. He was intoxicated, whooping with glee as he rode the horse in. He fell off and landed heavily on the floor, Ned taking the mount and dragging it outside. "Peter Collinson you are a fool!" yelled Bridget, picking him up by the ear and dragging him over to the corner. She stood there for some time admonishing him as the crowd looked on and the song stopped. He was offered a drink. The horse was tied up outside, and the singing resumed. The smoke-filled air became oppressive and Forrest suggested they retire back to Macleod's room to discuss matters further.

Nell bowed to them as they left and they thanked her and Bridget for the meal, Macleod leading them out and around the corner along the candlelit hallway and back to the room. Inside he lit two tallow candles and took out the last of his whiskey. He offered it to Forrest who gratefully took a drink and to McDermott who respectfully declined.

"I'm not sure I can trust a man who doesn't drink," said Forrest, looking squarely at McDermott.

"He is under orders," said Macleod, taking a large swig from the bottle. Forrest sat in a chair in the room's corner, Macleod and McDermott on their respective beds. The noise from the inn wafted into the room but was sufficiently dampened by the walls so that the three could speak. Forrest continued.

"Father Martin found the body. He is the priest at St Mary's-on-Allyn. He opened early on Sunday morning for the service and there she was against the doors. To mutilate someone like that......."

"You investigated the scene?" asked Macleod.

"I was first on scene and she was still there. We searched the grounds and removed the body back to Caergwrle. We don't have a doctor in town so I had no one to examine her, so we kept her cool there with water in the room until McKinlay got here. McKinlay and that sorry excuse for a constable."

"O'Reilly?" asked McDermott.

"Yeah... out of his mind when he got here. Talking about ghosts and banshees. The Irish are so superstitious. Spirits, ghosts... Irish superstition," said Forrest. "It's the same for the Gringai, the local people. They talk of bad spirits and the like. It's all bunk."

"What did you find?"

"Well, Martin was a mess, blessing himself over and over, quoting biblical versus. He kept watch over her until I came and Boydell was there. She was sitting upright, head laid back against the door with her feet out in front. There were ligature marks around her neck and, as you know, she was bitten all over, the flesh torn in great chunks."

"Did you know the girl?" asked Macleod.

"I'd met her a few times when she was in town getting things for the family. She was sweet and a very nice girl. She was always very polite. Everyone in the town knew her and liked her."

"Did she have any suitors?"

"There was talk that the young son in the family and her had goings on but nothing was ever proven. I spoke to him after and he seemed innocent enough."

"Anyone else? Anyone you can think of?"

"Look, Mr. Macleod, what you've got to understand is this town is small. If there was anyone I could think of I'd have them by now in the lock-up. They'd be on their way to Patterson to be hanged. I can't think of anyone from within this town that would do such a thing. And her being with child even makes it worse."

"With child?" asked Macleod.

"When McKinlay did the post mortem, she was pregnant. He didn't tell you?" asked Forrest.

"He told us everything except that," said Macleod.

"The O'Dell's are a powerful family," he said, "and information has likely been suppressed. I imagine it is not something he wanted to report to the family, a child out of wedlock you see. I expect it is a fact he has hidden from them, and from you. It's not news I have discussed with anyone, except you, even Boydell does not know. Such a matter is best-kept secret for now." Forrest eyed them both carefully. Macleod could sense that he knew he was in danger, having divulged information that was meant to be kept secret, that might incur the wrath of a powerful family from Dungog.

"We will keep it safe," said Macleod. "Thank you for telling us."

"I best be off," said Forrest. "I'll collect you tomorrow morning after breakfast. The priest Martin, Boydell, and his sons will be at Caergwrle. We can walk across to St Mary's-on-Allyn to examine the scene."

"Thank you," said Macleod, "we will be ready."

Forrest took his leave, exiting the room as the tallow candles cast dancing shadows about the room. Macleod took another swig of whiskey, preparing to light his pipe. McDermott lay back with his head on the pillow, his hands behind his head, looking at the ceiling in the dim light. Macleod lit up as the songs in the adjacent inn quieted. He could hear Bridget O'Donnell ushering men off to their beds before there was too much trouble.

"Why would McKinlay have withheld that information Inspector Macleod?" asked McDermott.

"As Forrest says, he wanted to spare the O'Dell's. The poor girl murdered and in such a way, I suspect it did not seem to him it added anything to the case to mention that she was also with child."

"But it could be important." said McDermott.

"Sometimes importance is placed on different things, depending on your perspective," answered Macleod. "You had best get rest. We will need to be up early for breakfast and will need our wits about us tomorrow." McDermott got up and blew out the candles and the only light was Macleod's pipe burning occasionally as he drew the smoke in and contemplated the information he had been given. McDermott's breathing became regular as he fell into an exhausted sleep.

As Macleod removed his boots, in the corridor a Russian soldier was standing, bleeding slowly from a large wound in his stomach. A sepoy joined him, his face slashed so that his jaw bone laid on his chest, his right arm missing, blood oozing slowly onto his white uniform. Macleod regarded them and willed them away but they were insistent, standing and staring at him accusingly. He lay back on the bed and closed his eyes, willing them away, his eyes opening and shutting as he approached sleep but they remained there, keeping a vigil as he struggled to sleep.

10

Forrest greeted Macleod underneath the great elm tree after breakfast. McDermott was close behind as Patrick Bird hailed them, their horses in tow, bridled and saddled ready for the journey.

"Fed and watered for you Mr. Macleod, ready to go," he said.

"Thank you, Patrick," said Macleod, taking the reins of his horse. He patted the horse softly on its nose and looked around in the morning light. The bullocks were still grazing in the paddocks as the bullock drivers slowly arose from their rum infused slumber. The chickens were clucking quietly as they moved around the paddock, cocking their heads as they foraged. Whip birds called in the distance as pigs snuffled in their feed troughs. Orange trees, largely stripped but still bearing fruit from the summer, afforded a green and orange patchwork to the fields below. The smell of wood smoke was in the air but as the breeze changed direction, the smell of the pigs struck Macleod.

"You'd be right in thinking those pigs stink," said Patrick. "I'm going to shift them further down the back. We've had complaints from a couple of the bullock drivers."

Macleod nodded.

"Best you be on your way before the bullock drivers get going and clog up the road."

Macleod mounted his horse and Forrest did the same, with McDermott falling in behind. As they were turning to leave along the dusty furrowed road, they heard a voice calling from behind them.

"Mr. Macleod!" Nell Bird was running towards them holding a small cloth bag. "Scones," she said, "for Mr. Boydell. He likes them."

She handed them up to Macleod, and he caught them, gratefully smiling. Bridget O'Donnell appeared as she handed them over.

"Nell, get back in here! There is cleaning up to do. Half of the gents still haven't had their breakfast! Patrick, get in the kitchen as well!"

She turned on her heel and walked inside without a goodbye to Macleod and his company.

Nell shook her head and smiled. "We'll see you for tea," she said, waving goodbye as they encouraged the horses along and walked up the narrow track.

The early morning was brisk with the sun rising in the sky, warming the farmlands. The horses dutifully meandered along the road and McDermott and Forrest made polite conversation. Stretching out along the way Macleod observed the fields of tobacco, the St. Michael oranges, the occasional dairy cow and the surrounding fields teeming with life. Starlings darted across their path as they wound their way along the narrow road to Caergwrle. After three quarters of an hour they made good progress and, winding through a hollow and round to the left they saw the English Oak that marked the entrance to the property. A man in working clothes approached them as the horses came to a halt.

Macleod dismounted from his horse and made to shake the man's hand but he moved quickly away, taking the reins of the horse and turning the horse to the side. After McDermott and Forrest dismounted, he took their horses, leading them off and tethering them on a wooden post near the entrance to the property. He refused to make eye contact or speak with the company, keeping his head down as he tethered the horses. Out of earshot, Forrest spoke in a low voice.

"The stable hand is Seamus Sullivan. Not entirely trustworthy but his family has been in O'Dell's service for years. He's not capable of murder, just to put that thought to rest."

Macleod nodded, watching Sullivan carefully as he tethered the horses.

He took a moment to survey their surroundings and noted the tobacco fields stretching out as far as the eye could see; orange trees and wheat. The main residence was stone, with wattle and daub attached buildings, hidden behind English elm trees. A second separate building with smoke pouring from the chimney he guessed was the kitchen.

A well-dressed man approached them and put out his hand.

"John Boydell."

"Inspector Macleod and Constable McDermott."

They exchanged handshakes and Forrest and Boydell acknowledged each other.

"My father is up at the church. We can join him there. George Hancock and William Collison are there. Please follow me."

Forrest filled Macleod in as they walked along. "George Hancock is a local landowner with a vested interest in what has happened here. He has eleven children and a large property to protect. William does a lot of good work around this town, just like his father. We don't have a doctor in the district but William has saved many a life, particularly children affected with diphtheria. Both are gentlemen."

They walked along the dusty road with St Mary-on-Allyn visible in the distance, surrounded by English elms with the morning sun imparting a soft glow to the uneven sandstone of the walls. As they approached, they could see two men standing and then a third appeared from inside the church.

"That's the priest, Martin," said Forrest.

Macleod studied the church carefully as he walked towards it. The English elms shaded the warm colours of the sandstone, still in full green leaf, the yellow leaves of autumn a month away. The stone of the church was rough and uneven. A long building without a transept, the stone was neat but not geometric, rough-hewn stone from the riverbed and overhanging cliffs. As they approached John Boydell went out ahead as if to warn the men of the approach of strangers. Macleod slowed his pace to allow John Boydell to converse with his father and allowed Forrest to step forward, as the familiar face in their company.

They exchanged pleasantries. The priest, in his white frock, and with black hair and unruly eyebrows regarded the men carefully. William Boydell was well dressed in a neat waistcoat and woollen suit, his full head of hair immaculately kept. George Hancock was thin and wiry and Macleod thought he looked like a hare ready to spring from a trap. William Collison was reserved, tall and stocky; he greeted the men in a friendly manner but then retreated to the rear of the group.

"It's not often we see men from Sydney here," said William Boydell, beginning the conversation.

"Well, we are pleased to be here to help and we will give any assistance we can," said Macleod, realizing that his remarks must have sounded perfunctory.

"Gentleman I will ask you to treat this place with respect," warned William Boydell.

"We understand and we will," said Macleod. "May we begin?"

William Boydell nodded his acquiescence, and they moved through the two large green elms, to the large flagstone at the front of the church. The cedar arched door was shut, the handmade nails, wrought iron bolts and hinges closing the inside away from prying eyes. Macleod stood and surveyed the surroundings. To the left, the building sat on the edge of the plateau and below the Allyn river, swollen from recent floods, surged around. On the right, the doorway turned on a corner before leading around to the paddock beyond. The priest Martin spoke. He spoke quickly as if he needed to impart all of his information without hesitation, lest it sit with him too long and cause him harm.

"I found her here," he said. "I came to open the church in the morning and to check everything was in order."

"Regular routine?" asked Macleod.

"Yes it is, I come every day, there are valuables inside, to make sure they are intact."

Macleod nodded.

"Anything else unusual on that day?"

"Nothing," said the priest. "I got up, as usual, came here by horseback, rode past Caergwrle early in the morning at first light. I did not see her at first. The dark shadows were hiding her but as I tethered my horse at the front, I saw her sitting there. At first, I thought she must have been asleep but then I saw...."

He could not go any further. Macleod understood what he had meant and nodded as if to let him know that he did not need to take the thought any further.

"Her hands? Her feet?" Macleod asked.

Her feet were out in front and someone placed her hands on her lap as if she was praying. Her head was down to one side. It was only then I realized what he had done to her."

"Was there blood on the dress or around the area?"

"There was none," said the priest.

"Did you see anyone? See any movement around?"

"Nothing," said the priest. "Just her, here, in the stillness of the morning."

"What did you do?"

"I went straight to Caergwrle and found John, told him, raised the alarm."

"We came straight over," added William Boydell. "Such a terrible thing. When we lost Mary Phoebe last year, I thought I could not feel any more grief but to have this monstrous act committed here, at this church, I cannot comprehend it."

Macleod allowed the silence to settle for a moment before speaking again.

"McDermott, check around the outside. Go to the left. Constable Forrest, would you mind taking the right? Look around the perimeter of the building and look carefully."

Hancock spoke rapidly.

"Be careful on the left constable. Marquat fell there. He died and fell into the river on the left side there. The river is swollen. Be careful."

Macleod looked to Boydell, hoping for an explanation.

"Marquat worked for me. Johann Christopher Marquat. He died two years back. He fell asleep on the ledge. He was probably drunk, and we had to drag his body out of the river. It is dangerous there constable. Watch your step."

McDermott looked down the hill to the river and then stuck close to the side of the building, searching as he walked. Forrest dutifully moved off to the right.

"May I see you inside?" asked Macleod to Boydell and Father Martin, who stepped forward, taking the large iron key out from under his cassock, and then wrestling with the iron lock. It gave way with the door reluctantly swinging open. Macleod walked through on the flagstones, watching them extend all the way to the middle part of the church. The Eastern stained glass windows filled with light and the blue glass was vibrant as the morning sun shone through. The cedar lectern and pulpit stood forlorn as Macleod strode into the middle part of the church before taking a seat in one of the cedar pews. From where he was sitting he could hear the river, a low roar. The pew creaked and groaned as he looked around and up at the magnificently crafted roof. The priest stood beside him as if to ensure he took nothing nor did any damage during his visit.

Macleod took a deep breath. He could feel nothing, couldn't get a sense of what happened. He walked back along the flagstones, his footfalls heavy, reaching the cedar doors and moving back to the outside. He looked carefully at the place where she had been, saw no blood stains or anything else that gave him clues to what had happened or why. Father Martin still stood stock still in the middle of the church, his white cassock illuminated by the morning light, as he contemplated the evil that had befallen the church. William and John Boydell regarded Macleod carefully and George Hancock made to ask a question but thought better of it and stepped back. Macleod measured the number of steps from the cedar doors to the elms at the front, turned and looked back and then walked forward again. McDermott was returning from his scout to the left and Forrest from the right.

"Anything?"

McDermott shook his head, Forrest the same.

"We did a full scout after we found the body and they had taken it away," said William Boydell. "We found nothing then and you won't find anything now."

Macleod nodded.

He turned back and paced toward the two elms at the front and turned back again to look carefully at the flagstone and the door. Martin had made his way to the front and was shutting the door to the church and locking it. As the priest wrestled with the door, Macleod saw it. On the left, between the lower sandstones, it was stuck, fastened. He walked toward it and bent down on one knee to look closely. Taking out his knife he levered the stones apart and gently eased it out.

It was a small leather brand, no larger than a penny. Macleod put it to his nose and the smell of leather was strong but there was another smell - the unmistakable metallic smell of blood.

"What is it?" asked Boydell, stepping forward. The men crowded in as Macleod held it toward them.

"It's from a saddlebag," said Boydell. "But how did it get there?

"I suspect it has fallen from someone close at the time of the murder. There is blood on it.."

Martin's face was white as he looked at the brand. "I know that brand," he said. On the middle of the brand was the outline of a bird.

"I know that brand too," said Boydell.

"Would you like to share it with me?" asked Macleod.

"Ravenscroft."

Midday approached as they made one last sweep of the grounds, McDermott returning from the river to report that he had found nothing. After the finding at mid-morning, they had made a thorough sweep of the grounds and the church, Macleod scouring the inside with scrutiny of the priest. Hancock had made to leave but Macleod had insisted that he stay, he wanted no warnings being sounded throughout the district. Their searching finished and fruitless, Macleod eyed the small leather disc, the raven now obvious to him, sitting above the dark stain of blood.

William Boydell suggested lunch and Macleod agreed, content they would find no more by continuing to search. As they trudged back along the dusty road to Caergwrle, Macleod was in deep thought. There was an animated conversation around him but he wasn't interested in it, his mind was focused on the killer. As they ate salted pork and bread for lunch, Macleod carefully questioned William and John Boydell, as Forrest looked on.

George Hancock continued to look agitated.

"Are you sure it's the brand for Ravenscroft?" asked Macleod.

"I am certain," answered William Boydell, "it's the brand they use. I have a record of it somewhere, I'll bring it to you."

He came out with parchment and put it on the table, spreading it in front of Macleod. He pointed to the brand at the top.

"Ravenscroft use it on their pigs and on their property. It's protection against rustling and stealing. There are the others there. All the families in the region have a brand issued."

"What's it doing here then?" asked George Hancock, agitated.

"Eccleston is a quiet part of the world, they have just opened the school out there with what's-his-name, ah, Mr. Buschell, the teacher. It's a civilized place," said Boydell. "We don't get any trouble from out there."

"Who lives there? At Ravenscroft?" asked Macleod carefully.

"It's the Kenny's place. Jessie and Eugene Kenny owned it after Jessie's father Alexander Norrie bought it years back. He's dead now, and Jessie died this last year, but Eugene is still there, his son Andrew and his wife Ellen. You've met Nell at Reynella."

"Nell Bird?" asked Macleod.

"Yes," said Boydell. "She is the eldest of their eleven children. They still have nine of them at home working the property; tobacco and some oranges, mostly pigs. I was last out there about twelve months ago. They were faring well. Ellen's sister and family, the Doohans, have to come to live on the property to help them work the farm. Up the road, near to their property are the Shea's, Victoria and Richard with six children. And the O'Malley's are further along. All God-fearing people and hardworking."

"Anyone new who has come into Eccleston?" asked Macleod.

"I'd know about it," said Boydell. "We'd have it on the register. I don't know what that brand was doing there but know that no one out there would be responsible for this murder."

"Perhaps they saw something," re-joined McDermott.

Boydell nodded, finally understanding the line of questioning.

"How long on horseback to get there?" asked Macleod.

"Eccleston is a way out but if you set off soon you'd be back by nightfall. It's a job best left for tomorrow when you have most of the day to attend to the questioning you need to do there."

"I prefer we get to it today," said Macleod, looking across at Hancock who was still agitated. "I suspect this news will travel swiftly in a community such as this. If we have a suspect in the district, I would not like someone to alert them to our findings."

"I understand," said Boydell.

"Then we best be on our way," said Forrest. "The bullock trains will be on their way through and we will have to stop here and there. I'll come with you so a familiar face greets the families there. If we leave now, we should be able to make it back by nightfall."

Macleod nodded and stood, thanking Boydell for the meal. Outside Sullivan was holding their horses and as they mounted, he nodded to them before stepping back in a bow. Kicking up dust, they trotted off, out on to the main bullock track and north, along the winding road through to Eccleston. The sun was high in the sky and the day was warming as they moved along. The road meandered, cutting backward and forwards along the Allyn River. The conversation was at a minimum, all the companions contemplating the events of the day.

Within two hours they had reached the chapel of the Eccleston bridge. They were forced off the road as two bullock trains were moving through, kicking up enormous amounts of dust as they hauled the cedar prize along the track. They waited inside and Macleod, realizing he had neglected to give the scones to Boydell, decided it was best not to let them go to waste and offered them to Forrest and McDermott. They took them gratefully and as Forrest and Macleod smoked their pipes, McDermott stood at the entrance to the chapel watching as the Bullocks' trudged past. When they were through McDermott hailed them and they were back on their horses, ambling along the narrow road, the surrounding fields filled with wheat and tobacco.

The sun was tilting to the west as they came over a rise. "Here it is," said Forrest, "Ravenscroft."

Up a narrow track on a plateau, sitting high above the valley below, a slab hut was visible with the entrance obscured by two large elms. The Allyn river wound around the alluvial plains at the bottom of the house, like a medieval moat, isolating Ravenscroft from the fields beyond. A second slab hut was off to the right and two larger barns were at the side. Pigs trotted here and there, chickens scattered as their horses meandered up the road.

They approached the house, and the horizon darkened with storm clouds forming. They obscured the sun so darkness covered the landscape in the early afternoon. A man dressed in farm breeches came towards them with a suspicious look on his face.

"Mr. Forrest," he said. "Do we have an occasion to see you here for any reason? And who do you have with you?"

"Inspector Macleod and Constable McDermott."

"I thought as much," said Andrew Kenny. "The boys will take the horses. You had better come inside."

As they dismounted, there was a low rumbling in the west as the thunder built and the rain-filled clouds advanced toward the homestead.

11

As the clouds gathered above, Andrew Kenny led them toward the two elm trees marking the entrance to the timber slab hut. As they entered the low door, the sheets of bark covering the roof brushed against Macleod's head. The earthen floor was clean and Macleod could see smoke rising from the fire in the kitchen at the back of the building.

"Margaret!" he called. "Get those shutters up on the windows. There's a storm coming."

Two or three children appeared and placed slats of wood into the open windows, against the oncoming rain. They worked in double time, practiced at the art.

As Macleod stooped to walk down the hallway, he surveyed the primitive residence. Sheets of bark-covered timber trestle beds were crammed six to one sleeping area. A jute bag sewn together served as a mattress and Macleod could see the straw poking out the end as part of the filling. Each of the beds had a jute bag at the bottom, sewn together to serve as a blanket.

"Ellen," yelled Andrew. "We have visitors!"

As they walked along the narrow entranceway, they entered a slightly larger area with an open fireplace. A large pot hung over the fire with boiling water inside. A woman dressed in working clothes bustled in from outside and Macleod guessed from the kitchen to the back of the house.

"This is Inspector Macleod and Constable McDermott and you know Constable Forrest."

"Could I get you something to eat?" asked Ellen Kenny. "Or perhaps tea?"

"Tea would be fine," said Forrest. Andrew Kenny beckoned them to sit on the few rickety wooden chairs, placed around the room. In the corner, an older man was sleeping beside the fire. "Don't mind him," said Andrew, "that's my father Eugene. He sleeps a lot nowadays."

As they sat, Macleod could hear children outside, pigs squealed as thunderclaps rolled in.

"What brings you all this way out?" asked Andrew Kenny, looking directly at Thomas Forrest.

"The gentlemen here are investigating the murder in Allynbrook."

"Ah, yes," said Andrew, "we heard snippets. A terrible thing."

Macleod took up the questioning.

"Who lives here on the property Mr. Kenny?"

"Well, there is me and Ellen my wife. My father Eugene," he pointed to the man in the corner, "and then we have nine children left with us here on the property. Nell married Patrick Bird and moved down to Reynella and one of our other children, Eugene, has gone to work in Gresford. The other children have been home a lot on account of the typhus outbreak. Mr. Buschell, the new schoolmaster is none too pleased. But we dread typhus in these parts and it is best to keep the children away from school until it passes. It started with the Shea family over yonder."

He pointed over his shoulder to the south.

"One of their children, Richard, was very ill from it."

"Anyone else here on the property with you?"

"Ellen's sister Mary Doohan and her husband William Doohan, live over in the house around the plateau with their six children. Their older children are a great help here on the farm with the pigs and tobacco crops."

"Can we speak with them?" asked Macleod.

"They'll be back soon," said Andrew. "William is down at the river with his eldest son Alexander fishing for herring. I imagine they will be back soon with the storm approaching."

He called Margaret, one of his children. "Margaret, go across and get Mary and William and Alexander, bring them over here."

Margaret dashed out the front door, eager to do as she was asked. There was a low rumbling from outside and in the distance ravens wailed, echoing the approaching storm.

Ellen broke the silence, entering the room with a wooden tray with mugs for each of them, black tea brimming. "Sorry, I don't have any sugar," she said, "not until we go to market in Gresford in a week."

"That's all right," said Macleod. "It's fine as it is." On the tray, a damper, steaming and hot, was presented, with a small dab of butter on the side. Macleod appreciated the gesture, butter was precious and Ellen had done her best to provide what she had.

"Thank you very much, I appreciate the butter."

She smiled and acknowledged him before retiring from the room, leaving the men to talk.

Andrew Kenny filled the silence. "Not much happens out here that you'd need to know about inspector," he said. "We run pigs and grow tobacco and some wheat. We live from day to day. I can't see how we would be connected to what happened in Allynbrook."

Macleod thought this was the opportune time to introduce the evidence. He took it from his waistcoat pocket and held it out. "We found this at St Mary-on-Allyn, under the door where the body was discovered. Do you recognize it?"

Andrew examine the disc closely, a frown appearing on his forehead.

"Surely that's our brand," said Andrew Kenny. "But I've never seen it on a piece of leather like this. It's the sort of extravagance we couldn't manage. Found at the church you say? It makes no sense. Why would our brand be on this disc of leather? I don't understand it."

"You've never seen it before?" asked Macleod.

"Never. Well, the brand is ours, but the piece of leather, I've seen nothing like it. We wouldn't have any use for it out here. We brand the pigs with an iron. If we need to brand on to anything else, we burn it on. We would not have any use for something such as this."

"Would anyone else in the area have something like this where your brand might have mistakenly been used?" asked Macleod.

"I can't see that the Shea's would have them. Kitty Shea is all high and mighty and thinks she's better than all of us, claiming her heritage is from a good line in England. But they would produce nothing like this either. I don't see how our brand would get on to it, anyway."

The fire crackled in the corner as lightning flashed outside and the storm clouds obscured the sun and darkness descended. Ravens groaned at the approaching storm and the livestock went quiet, with the countryside seeming to sense the impending rain.

Macleod heard footsteps approaching from outside and Andrew stood, beckoning those in the hallway to come through.

"William and Alexander Doohan," Andrew announced. "Inspector Macleod and Constable McDermott and you know Thomas Forrest."

"What's this all about then?" asked William Doohan, folding his arms in defiance. His son Alexander was a strapping lad, taller than his father but he stood behind him in deference, mirroring his father's folded arms.

"Herring on the run then are they?" asked Andrew.

"That they are," said William. "A fine catch and we'll have enough for dinner and the next few nights."

"Well done," said Andrew.

"Ellen," he called, "the herring are on the run."

Ellen called back, a shout of approval but unintelligible otherwise.

"What brings you all the way out here?" asked William Doohan, suspicious of the out-of-towners.

"Investigating the murder in Allynbrook," said Macleod, standing, so he stood opposite William, measuring the man.

"What would it have to do with us?" asked William. Macleod showed him the leather disc with the raven stamped on it. William dropped his guard for a moment, his hands falling to his side as he examined the disc. "That's our brand all right, but leather? We'd never come by such a thing."

Macleod looked behind William, watching Alexander's face as his eyes widened.

"I've seen nothing like it before. What is it? From a saddlebag or from a saddle?"

"It's leather," said Macleod, "with your brand stamped on it. Would you have any idea how it got there?"

It completely disarmed William.

"I do not understand," he said, acquiescing to Macleod's questions. "It makes no sense. Andrew?" He looked at his brother-in-law imploringly.

"I've no idea either William. It's strange to me it should end up at the site of the murder."

"My God," said William, "I don't know who or what put it there but I can tell you it would have been no one from here."

Macleod nodded, watching as Alexander shifted behind his father.

"Alexander? Do you know anything about it?"

"No sir," said Alexander quickly. Too quickly thought Macleod. At that moment a lightning bolt flashed across the sky and a deafening peal of thunder. Eugene Kenny awoke, startled, looked around. His left hand twitched, then his arm, and as the convulsion marched on, his body arched in the chair before flailing to the ground, foam spewing from his mouth, his face contorted..

"Ellen!" called Andrew. "He's taking a fit!" Andrew dragged him to the ground in front of the fire, supporting his head as his body shook violently. The children crowded into the room to see what was happening, as Andrew tried to shoo them away. The old man shook violently on the floor, soiling himself, blood flowing from his mouth as he bit his lip, staining the dirt. At length, the seizure passed and Eugene rested quietly on the floor. Ellen wiped away the blood from his mouth as Andrew cradled his head.

"He takes fits," said Andrew, "often brought on by the storms. He will be all right now. You children out of here, shoo!"

The children disappeared as quickly as they had appeared. There was only one thing amiss, Macleod noted. During the diversion, Alexander Doohan had left the room.

Lightning flashed across the sky again, multi forked as thunder peeled out and hail fell. It clattered for a moment before turning to heavy rain, dousing the fields around. Drips of water came through the roof and Ellen bustled around, putting receptacles here and there for the water as it soaked through. Macleod and McDermott dashed up the hallway to the door and looked out into the pelting rain. Alexander was making his way across the field as quickly as he could. McDermott did not need to be asked twice before he was off after him in a flash, Macleod preferring to let the younger man do the legwork. He remained in the doorway and watched as McDermott sprinted across the field after him. They disappeared over the edge of the plateau down towards the river. Not being able to control the situation any further from that point of view he moved back inside.

Eugene Kenny was waking up and being helped back into his chair, his bottom lip bleeding, Ellen bustled about finding a fresh pair of trousers.

Thomas Forrest was questioning William closely. Macleod listened to the conversation.

"He has taken off quickly William. Do you know anything? This is important."

"He's a good boy, he wouldn't have anything to do with it. He's just frightened because the police are here. You know what it's like these days, young men get blamed for anything. That's why he has taken off. I can tell you he would have had nothing to do with it."

"Well, we will see when McDermott brings him back," said Macleod.

The rain poured down outside as the darkness encroached even further.

"Ellen" called Andrew, "I think we will have three extra men for dinner." He nodded to Macleod and Forrest.

"Much obliged," said Forrest. "I don't think we will head back tonight in this. If you could see your way to giving us accommodation?"

"We have room in the barn. You can sleep on the straw in there if that is acceptable to you. I agree that heading back to Allynbrook tonight would be treacherous with all the roads flooded. When the storm has passed, you will be able to travel back in the morning safely."

"Agreed," said Forrest.

Realizing that there was nowhere to go, Macleod took out his pipe and sat next to the fire. Eugene Kenny nodded to him, blood trickling down from his lip, as they both enjoyed the warmth of the fire and the storm raged outside.

True darkness was cloaking the property as McDermott finally returned. The rain was falling heavily, and he appeared out of the gloom sodden, drenched to the skin, alone. Panting, he apologized as Macleod greeted him. "I'm sorry sir, I searched everywhere for him but he got away. He went down by the river. I thought I had him down there but he slipped away. I searched and searched but wherever he is, whatever hiding place he has, I can't find him."

"It's all right," said Macleod, "he knows the land better than you. Come in. We'll get you dry."

Ellen Kenny bustled towards him with a dry set of clothes and beckoned that he move to one room and undress. He emerged in clothes that were too big for him, a somewhat comical figure, working clothes that swum around him. Ellen took his sodden clothes and hung them by the fire while Eugene snored loudly, the blood on his bottom lip drying into a dark smear.

Forrest joined Macleod and McDermott, forming a huddle as they spoke in low voices; Andrew Kenny and William Doohan strained to hear them.

"He slipped down over the edge of the plateau and down to the river and wound through the trees. I kept with him for a long time. He crossed the river and got to the other bank but then I lost him. I searched backward and forwards but I couldn't find him. No trace."

"You did your best," said Forrest.

"The question is," said Macleod, "why would he run?"

William Doohan, listening intently, broke into the conversation. "As I said to you Inspector, I am sure he has nothing to do with this. Young boys are blamed in this district for all manner of mischief. He has seen the police and scarpered, that's all. He'll turn up tomorrow and be able to explain himself. I will make sure of that."

Macleod nodded. "Have you any idea of where he would have gone?"

"My guess is Shea's property, up beyond. He knows the boys there well. I expect he is hiding in their livestock shed. He is not foolish enough to stay out in this," said William, yanking his head toward the rain outside. "He'll be undercover. We'll go to Shea's and find him in the morning."

"You sure he won't come back tonight?" asked Macleod.

"In this?" asked William, "Not a chance!"

A bell rang, signalling that dinner would be served and Eugene woke immediately, struggling out of his chair with the promise of food on the way. They dashed across between the buildings, from house to kitchen, collars up against the rain. Steam and smoke were emanating from the fire as freshwater herring were served. Mary Doohan had joined her sister Ellen in the kitchen. Initially shaken and tearful after her son's sudden flight, she now seemed to have recovered her composure. They had set the rough wooden table log with seats and Eugene Kenny took his seat quickly, obviously afraid that he might miss out with the visitors handy. They had farmed the children off to the Doohan's residence for dinner while the adults sat and ate. They crowded around the small makeshift table, sharing the implements amongst them around the table as Ellen distributed clay platters to each of them. Steaming fish was brought forward and served to each plate with a flett cake, the lard oozing from the cake onto the side of the plate. Macleod thanked the women for the dinner, standing as he did, and Eugene Kenny said grace. Thereafter they ate in silence for a time, the lard cake warming Macleod's empty stomach, the fish flesh soft and juicy. They provided fortified wine and Macleod drank his fill, calming his tremor. In front of the women talk of the crime and Alexander's disappearance was mooted, as they discussed the weather and other matters.

"The Shea's?" asked Macleod, "Have they been there long?"

"Kitty Shea is all airs and graces," said Ellen, "she's a cut above us. All her children are brilliant of course. With all her fancy show, saying she comes from high-class family in London. I don't believe it. I don't believe any of it. Her older boys are Alexander's age and they are the same. They often go to market together and exchange goods for us."

"They run the same as us over there," said Andrew. "Pigs, a bit of tobacco. We trade what we can in town. The eggs earn a good price per dozen. Often we can exchange them for a bit of cream or butter if we are lucky. We don't get it very often out here."

Macleod nodded, showing his understanding.

The rain was easing outside and the rivulets around the house dissipating as they drained down toward the Allyn River, coursing its way around the plateau and into the darkness. The torrents of water coming through the bark roof in the kitchen settled to a drip as the storm began to pass.

After dinner, Mary produced some St. Michael's oranges. William looked surprised.

"Well, this is a luxury," he said. "From Boydell's farm? These would have cost a pretty penny. What did we have to give up to get these?"

"Quiet down," said Mary. "Alexander brought them back after his last visit."

"What did he pay for them?" asked William. "Boydell charges a kings fee per dozen?"

"Well, he got a half dozen," she said. "I don't know how he got them and I didn't ask but I'm sure he did it by legal means," she said, looking at Macleod. "He likes to help his mother where he can."

Macleod took the quarter of the orange they offered him. It was juicy and sweet and he spat the pips out on his plate.

With dinner completed, Mary and Ellen cleared up and the men retired back into the main house. Fortified wine was offered around and all took part. The conversation was slow as the evening drew on and as the rain stopped Andrew Kenny suggested that he show the gentlemen to their lodgings for the night.

"It is comfortable out here," he said. "The straw beds we have set up for travellers who come through every now and again. We charge them just a small amount to stay."

They walked in the dark night, the cloud-covered sky causing no shadows; he darkness closing in around them. The light of the tallow candle was the only mark as they walked across the rain-sodden yard, avoiding the puddles and the mud. Macleod ducked his head as he moved into the low shed, with Andrew Kenny careful to keep the flame outside.

"I'll shut the door for you," said Andrew. "It should be warm enough for you tonight. There are jute bags there if you need them. With the cloud cover, the temperature should stay at a pleasing level."

Macleod lay back on the straw, his hands behind his head with his boots still on. Forrest and McDermott had settled in.

"What do you know about the Shea's?" he said to Forrest, knowing he could now ask away from prying ears.

"Not much liked around here," said Forrest "on account of Kitty being so high and mighty but good people. I've had no trouble with them. They work hard."

"And the boy? Alexander?"

"Probably as his father says, he has scarpered because he thinks he is in trouble for something but not knowing what. I suspect we will find him up there hiding out."

Macleod grunted. He lay quietly in his bed, staring into the darkness as the heavy breathing of Forrest and then his loud snoring punctuated the night. McDermott was breathing regularly, a sure sign he was in a deep sleep after his escapades earlier in the day. Macleod drifted but sleep evaded him and two Russian soldiers appeared, standing at the bottom of his bed, bent over in the gloom. The one with his guts open was back, his intestines spilling out on to the bottom of the straw, just narrowly missing Macleod's shoes. A sepoy joined him, a gruesome duo, the sepoy's face and his left arm all bone and blood. Macleod closed his eyes tight and as he opened them, they had faded. But soon they materialised again; he closed his eyes tight and willed himself to sleep, to escape the spectres. But he could not sleep, and lying awake until the early hours, one after another the other grisly phantoms visited him.

The cock crowed just on dawn, waking Macleod from an uneasy slumber. He had finally found rest just before dawn. He could see a blue sky, the sun waiting to rise to dry out the ground from yesterday's torrent. He pulled himself up out of the bed as the dawn light suffused the landscape. He pushed open the door, bowing his head, emerging into the day, taking a deep breath and stretching his back. His back cracked and popped as his old bones groaned at him from the night on the straw.
McDermott walked towards him from the main building, now back in his usual clothes, looking less the comic and more like the constable he was. Forrest was stirring behind him and he could see smoke rising from the kitchen as he assumed that breakfast was being prepared.

Pigs wallowed in the mud as it covered every inch of the ground, the sodden unsheltered chickens were clucking and strutting, flapping their flightless bodies to ward off the rain from the night before. Rat-kangaroos, bodies nimble, darted about, foraging in the early morning light. Macleod looked up and saw ravens sitting in the large trees surrounding the property, silent and mournful.

"I don't like straw beds," said Forrest, stretching his neck.

"Not good for old backs," said Macleod agreeing.

McDermott, knowing better not to add that he had slept well, informed the gentlemen that breakfast was being served. They trudged across the open ground, through the mud and around to the kitchen. Eugene Kenny was sitting up, as usual, awaiting food, and he greeted the three men as they entered the room.

Ellen beckoned that they sit, and she served them thick slices of bacon with flett cakes. The flett cakes were from the same tasty lard as they had enjoyed the night before and MacLeod appreciated the meal, thanking Ellen for her efforts.

"William and Andrew?" asked Macleod.

"Securing one of the chicken enclosures. They'll be here in a moment." The two men appeared after she spoke with muddy hands, a testament to their work on that early morning.

They sat down to the table and Ellen turned and tut-tutted. "No time to wash," said Andrew. "We've got a lot to do. There is a lot of damage out there from the storm."

He picked up the bacon with his muddy right hand and swallowed it in one gulp. Hot tea was served, and they made plans to travel to Shea's property. They agreed that William would join them. With the work they were doing on the farm, Andrew decided to stay behind to supervise the children in helping him get the farm back to order.

They set out with the sun just above the horizon, magpies calling in the early morning and the life of the bush returning after the heavy storm. The stock horses had been saddled and fed and William joined them on his mount, a black stock horse that was fidgety and feisty. He reined it in and then led them back down the trail. The weather had damaged the track and Macleod could see the rivulets turning into furrows of water; the mud engulfing the road. He guessed there would not be many bullock trains running along the way today.

At length, they reached the chapel and turned right, across a cleared paddock and up to a rise. There in the distance was a small house with smoke rising from the kitchen at the back. A livestock shed and chickens, in every way mirroring the Kenny property. Macleod could see figures moving here and there around the buildings and as they drew up at the front, a young man dressed in worker's clothes took their horses.
"Thank you, Thomas," said Constable Forrest. It was clear that Forrest did not intend to introduce the young man but Macleod guessed he was one Shea son.

Dismounting into the mud they trudged across the yard and up to the house where a plump lady wearing a housedress was standing, her brown hair pulled back in a tight bun with a pinched face and pursed lips, her hands folded in front of her.

"Kitty Shea," said Thomas Forrest.

"What brings you here Constable Forrest?" she asked. "William, so nice to see you come over this way."

Macleod saw William wince as she said this and he replied with gritted teeth and raised his hat. "Kitty."

"Inspector Macleod and Constable McDermott," said Forrest, undertaking the perfunctory introductions.

"From Sydney, I hear," she said. "So pleased to have cultured men from the city here. Perhaps you will, at last, solve this most dreadful crime. Such a beautiful girl, a wonderful governess. Goodness knows the constabulary here has made no progress. Please come in. I have tea ready. I can answer questions you have about the O'Dell girl. Such a shame, such a horrible, horrible shame."

Macleod sensed that the sorrow she felt was for her family's loss of a governess, rather than for losing Emily O'Dell. He resisted the urge to question her.

"A moment," said Macleod. "We are looking for Alexander. You know the boy?"

"I know the boy," she said. "He's not here. I saw you travelling into the Kenny's yesterday and I thought if there was any trouble out here they would be sure and point the finger my way."

"Now, that's not fair Kitty," said William.

"You very well know," said Kitty, "that any trouble in this area and you are very quick to point to the Shea house."

Macleod sensing the disquiet, attempted to break the argument.

"We'll join you for tea," he said. "And may I request thereafter that we be able to look around the property?"

"Of course, "she said. "I have nothing to hide."

As they walked inside a small beaten looking man was standing there, his hat in his hand. He was turning it nervously as he greeted the men with a soft handshake.

"Richard Shea," he said, "pleased to meet you." He was dressed in soiled workmen's clothes, covered in mud and manure, and his wife waved him away after the introductions.

"Richard, you will need to see to the livestock shed after the storm."

"Yes, Kitty," he said, leaving the men and walking out of the room.

It was clear to Macleod that Kitty Shea held court, formidable and unyielding. They sat in the kitchen at a natural timber table. Kitty poured tea and offered them sugar. "Take as much as you like, we have plenty of sugar here," she said. She looked at William Doohan and smirked.

She brought out damper and Macleod noticed that the amount of butter she offered was almost three times that on the Kenny property.

"We trade well," she said, "to ensure we have the finest for our family." She looked at William again and as he made to interject Thomas Forrest took up the conversation.

"Thank you, Kitty," he said, as he supped the last of his tea, "but we must get out and see the property. If Alexander is here, these gentlemen need to find him and speak with him."

"Can I ask what it is regarding?" asked Kitty.

"It's police business," said Forrest. "Just let them do their job."

"Of course," she said. "I would not want to pry."

She led them out as they inspected the livestock sheds, picking up her skirts so they didn't drag in the mud. At length at the rear of the property, they came to a small rise. Beyond the rise, there was a steep hill leading down to the Allyn. McDermott knew without being asked.

"I'll go down there and search," McDermott said.

"Careful," said Forrest. "That hill is treacherous after the rain."

McDermott inched his way down the hill, finally reaching the bottom and waving to say he was safe. He scampered off toward the river.

Macleod turned back and took a deep breath, looking around the property. Several older boys were helping their father push a sulky that had become stuck. They bent their backs to it as he urged them on.

"Thank goodness for strapping young sons," said Kitty. "I am so proud of them. They help their father every day here. I've schooled them myself you know before the governess arrived."

As they were watching, there was a shout from the river.

"Sir!" they could hear McDermott's voice faintly on the wind. "Sir, quickly!" Macleod and Forrest ran to the edge of the plateau and, leaving Kitty behind, they inched their way down carefully. Macleod stumbled occasionally, so he felt he would fall to the bottom and break his neck. He managed it with difficulty and on reaching the bottom moved as quickly as he could over the sodden earth to where McDermott was standing beside the river. William was hot on their heels, realizing that they had found something but mercifully, several yards behind the policemen as they came upon the body.

Alexander Doohan lay on his back beside the river. He was on his back, body facing the sky, dead eyes half open. There were bruises around his throat, bite marks covered his face and arms, his shirt had been torn off and torso mutilated.

Unable to stop him, Macleod stood mute as William Doohan fell to his knees over his boy and thumped his fists on the ground, weeping loudly.

12

The mid-morning sun was climbing toward its zenith as Macleod listened to the sobs of Mary Doohan from the adjoining kitchen. He could see William with her, his arm around her, as they mourned for their son; cold and dead on the kitchen table. In the sitting room Eugene Kenny sat by the fire, mumbling and fidgeting.

"What's to be done?" asked McDermott.

Forrest thought for a moment. "When you found him, was there rigor?"

"Yes, the rigor was on him when we found him," replied Macleod. "It means he must have died anywhere from midnight to two o'clock in the morning. Very little blood at the scene, I suspect strongly that the tearing of the flesh and other abominations occurred post mortem. He was strangled first and then the killer waited, at least one or two hours, before biting the body."

"We've searched the property," said Forrest. "I don't have any more clues to report back."

Macleod looked at McDermott, visibly shaken and haunted by the events. The young man's usual rosy complexion was grey, his eyes sunken.

"Do you have any suspicions at all about the Shea's?" asked Macleod.

"I have suspicions about everyone in this community at the present time," said Forrest, "but to answer your question, no, nothing definite. I questioned them at length after their governess was killed, and I am convinced they are not part of the crime."

"And questioning them this morning I gleaned no useful information. We agree however that the murders are related," said Macleod. "The same method and almost identical mutilation."

"Agreed," said Forrest.

"And the procedure from here?" asked Macleod.

"I must go back into Allynbrook and speak to Mr. Boydell, report to him what has happened and he'll authorise the burial. We'll need the body in the ground quickly. With the typhus spreading recently we are all feared of disease."

Macleod nodded his assent before speaking again.

"There is something else I need to check before you go back to Boydell. Would you accompany me, please?"

As they rose, Macleod indicated to McDermott that he should remain in the other room, a guard of sorts from intrusions from family members while Forest and Macleod inspected the body. McDermott nodded and stood at the doorway.

The young boy was lying flat on his back where he had been placed, his clothes removed and his body covered in a piece of cloth. Macleod brought the cloth down off his face so he could examine his upper torso and head. "There," said Macleod, "the mark around the neck, identical from the drawings I saw from McKinlay on the other girl. A rope or similar used to strangle first and then the biting and removal of flesh, post mortem."

He picked up the boy's hand from under the sheet. "Nothing under the nails except for some dirt from the farm. No blood, no scratches, and no clues. No evidence of a struggle."

"Who are we dealing with here Macleod?" asked Forrest, recognizing the older man's experience.

"Sadistic, driven, a fury," said Macleod. "To bite and mutilate like this..."

"But have you seen anything like this before?" asked Forrest.

Macleod hesitated before carefully giving his answer. "Nothing exactly like this."

Forrest stared intently at him and then let the moment pass, staring back at the boy's face.

"Do you believe in ghosts Mr. Macleod?" asked Forrest.

"I believe in the living," said Macleod. "It would be our mistake to assume this was done by anything other than a human being, an evil one at that. To presume a spirit had done this, or some other evil we can't describe would be our mistake."

Forrest nodded. Macleod could see the superstition creeping into the policeman's investigation.

"Tell me," asked Macleod in an attempt to break the fear, "the O'Malley's are the only other family in this area? How much do we know about them?"

"They are a good family, as I told you before," said Forrest. "Three sons, three daughters, and Catherine and Patrick are God-fearing people. They work a property just out of Allynbrook, an hour's ride from St Mary-On Allyn. "I need to speak with them," said Macleod. "They are a piece of this puzzle I can't fit in."

"I should come with you," said Forrest. "They will suspect someone from out of town."

"Well, they will need to be suspicious. Can you give me something I can take them, to vet me, so I can talk to them."

Forrest thought for a moment before reaching into his coat and taking out a piece of paper. "This is a letter of introduction from Boydell. I carry it in the event I have to investigate any new settlers that come to town. It will do just as well."

Macleod glanced at the paper.

This document introduces the bearer as a representative of William Boydell, Magistrate of Allynbrook and Eccleston.

"That will do enough," said Macleod and tucked it into his pocket.

"We'll ride together," said Forrest. "I can show you the way to O'Malley's and I can peel off to Boydell's. I won't be back until tomorrow but I'll bring the priest for the burial. Could you check on the horses for us? I'll talk to the family."

Macleod nodded as he covered the boy's face and Forrest moved off toward the other homestead. Macleod watched as he stooped to enter the front door and went inside. In the anteroom, Eugene Kenny was sleeping quietly in his chair as the fire crackled.

Macleod spoke to McDermott outside out of earshot of Eugene Kenny.

"I need to speak to the O'Malley's and Forrest needs to get permission for the burial tomorrow. You will need to stay here, keep guard over the place and preserve order."

McDermott was frightened, nodding quickly as a child would who takes instructions from an adult, but they do not want to hear. His brown hair was matted together and the dark circles under his eyes were deepening.

"You stay with me now boy," said Macleod, "I can't have you losing your nerve."

"No sir," said McDermott.

"You've seen more death in the past two days than you have probably seen in your entire life," he said, "but you have to compartmentalise it, put it away so you can do your job. Push it into the background."

As he said this Macleod squeezed the boy's right shoulder and McDermott stood tall and nodded his head firmly. "You can rely on me sir," he said.

"I know I can," said Macleod. "I've never doubted you."

Macleod strode off to where the horses were tethered. He patted his horse, and it nuzzled against him, stamping on the ground three times as it shook off the flies that buzzed around. As the morning pushed on the flies became more numerous, the constant buzz mingling with the warbling of the magpies. Above him in an old gum tree, a great raven sat, staring intently at Macleod, its head cocked, pale white eye watching him as he moved.

"Be gone with you!" he yelled.

The raven flapped and wailed, lifting itself into the air, and gliding away. Forrest appeared readily, leaving Mary and William Doohan behind. He watched as Ellen took a large bowl across and guessed that she was preparing for burial.

"They'll be safe now. I'm glad you are leaving the boy behind." He approached and took the reins of his horse from Macleod.

"He'll keep order," he said.

"Is he all right?" asked Forrest.

"As right as can be," said MacLeod.

They mounted and kept their horses to a walk as they negotiated the muddy track leading down to the road. The Eccleston bullock track had become more furrowed with the hard lumps of mud beginning to dry. As a result, it kept the horses to a walk for the most part until they reached the chapel. They rode in silence with the sounds of the bush filling the background as both men contemplated the recent events.

As they reached the chapel the road bent up, and there was less damage. Macleod broke the silence as they took the turn.

"At the Shea's, did you see the jute bag bed in the animal enclosure?"

"Under the lean-to?" asked Forrest.

"Aye," said Macleod.

"A lot of families in the district have those. Sometimes they rent them to travellers or bullock drivers coming through if they don't make it through to Allynbrook. They give them bed-and-breakfast for a small charge. It is common practice."

"I can't see how any bullock driver could have used this one, not with the rain that came through. But it had definitely been used recently."

"How can you tell?" asked Forrest. " I did not see any boots showing anyone had been there."

Macleod grunted. "I wasn't expecting to see boots but there were fresh food scraps. Someone had been there recently sleeping under that lean-to. And there are enough beds in that house to account for everyone. There is someone at the Shea's who is not accounted for."

"It makes little sense," said Forrest. "Why would they hide the information from us for God's sake? I think you are mistaken, Inspector."

"I'll be guided by you," said Macleod, "you know the people of this area better than I. But if you could indulge me. When you are with Boydell, ask him if there have been any arrivals in the village. He will have the records. Or if there any reports from Paterson of illegal movement around the area."

"I will. We can telegraph the chief constable in Paterson if Boydell thinks it necessary." said Forrest.

Macleod nodded his approval.

The sun had passed zenith by the time they reached the turnoff where they would part ways. They stopped for a moment, grinding beef jerky in their teeth. Macleod was shaking. The alcohol was wearing out of his system.

"I won't get back tonight," said Forrest. "I have business to attend to in Allynbrook; should I let them know at Reynella that you will stay tonight without McDermott?"

"No," said Macleod. "I'll go back tonight."

"Watch your way," said Forrest. "The track is dangerous at night. Many a horse has stumbled in the dark."

"I will be careful and I intend to be back before sundown," said Macleod. He bid the policeman goodbye and turned left, guiding the horse along around the furrows in the dirt road as the flies buzzed around him and starlings swooped across his path. He reached into his saddlebag and took out the fortified wine he had taken from the Kenny kitchen. He tilted his head back and took a long swig, and then another. Within moments the tension in his neck was gone, and the headache subsided. With the tremor in his hands settling he felt he could concentrate again. He looked at the bottle and calculated there was enough to get him back before the evening. The going was slow, and he took a full hour in the afternoon sun to reach the outskirts of the O'Malley property. He dismounted from his horse and led it along by its lead as he approached the homestead, taking the time to examine the surrounding from the ground. The dirt track led up to a small wattle and daub house and next to it a larger residence. A barn to the right held tobacco, and pigs were grunting in the mud behind sturdy fences. The dairy cows grazed in the afternoon sun. The property sat on a peak overlooking the valley and Macleod turned back, able to see The Allyn winding around as it came behind the property meandering back toward Eccleston.

A young man approached him. "Can I help you?" he asked.

Macleod took out the letter from Boydell. "I need to see your father, son, and be quick about it."

The boy backed off immediately and ran to the house, "Da!" he called, "Da!"

A stout man appeared dressed in working clothes and behind him, a woman in an upmarket house dress and white pinafore appeared. Macleod saw children peeking through the wooden shutters of the windows as he approached the house. The man was holding a musket and Macleod put his hands up as he walked closer.

"I mean you no harm," he said. "I have a letter from the magistrate." He held it forward with his right hand.

"Stop right there," said Patrick O'Malley as he got within ten steps. "Put it on the ground and step back from it." Patrick pointed the musket at Macleod. "Unless you want to lose more fingers off your hand," he said, nodding to Macleod's disfigured left hand. The boy that had stopped Macleod when he arrived ran forward and picked up the document and ran it to his father. Patrick examined it closely, turning the seal of Boydell back and forward in the light. "It's authentic," he said while he unclicked the musket and shouldered it. "Who are you that comes with the authority of the magistrate?"

"Inspector Macleod," said Macleod, as he handed the reins of his horse to the boy who took it away to give it water.

"Ah, the Sydney interlopers," said Patrick. "We heard you were in town investigating. I thought you'd be here, eventually. Word was there was two of you."

"My companion is undertaking other investigations for me at the moment," said Macleod. "May I approach?"

"Come and sit," said Patrick. "This is my wife Catherine. She will get us some tea."

He pulled up two crates, and they sat on them outside the house as the cicadas buzzed in the distance.

"The devil is at work," Patrick said. "That poor girl Emily, such a sweet thing, to be cut to pieces by that monster. I tell you, it's never been good in this town since they let too many people in. It brings the bad eggs."

"Could you tell me about her?" asked Macleod, careful with his line of questioning.

"A sweet girl. She would visit us often on her way back from the markets in Allynbrook and we came to know her well. Kitty Shea did not want her children going to school at Allynbrook and when she hired Emily as a governess my wife shared the costs. My wife did not like the youngest girls being taught by a man so we hired Emily from Kitty Shea to teach the girls and to help our sons to learn to read and right. They also had things to do on the farm so they weren't advancing as quickly as the girls."

Macleod thought it prudent not to share any information about the recent events at Ravenscroft hoping it would help Patrick focus and provide him the information he needed. Catherine appeared at that moment with a tray with tea and set it in front of the men. "Sugar?" she asked. "Cream? The cream is made on the property here from the cows."

"Thank you," said Macleod, taking both.

"Have any of the children said anything?" Macleod asked.

"What would they say?" said Patrick. "Children are to be seen and not heard."

"Now Patrick," said Catherine, "the children loved Emily and were very close to her. Eamon has been most affected."

"Eamon?" asked Macleod.

"Our eldest. You can see him down there working." Down to the right was a large strapping lad tilling the earth behind a bullock pulling a plough. "He hasn't been right since she died. He blames himself."

"How so?" asked Macleod.

"Well, Eamon used to go into Gresford with Emily. We let him take her, to get supplies and things. The night she was killed he had taken her into town as usual and he came back without her. That wasn't unusual; her father was friendly with Charles Boydell and sometimes she stayed overnight with the Boydell's in Gresford. Then they found her."

"And Eamon and Emily? They were..."

"How dare you suggest such a thing!" said Catherine. "We run a proper house here and we would never allow anything like that to happen out of wedlock. To suggest such a thing Inspector is unholy!"

"My apologies," said Macleod, putting his hands up. "I only meant..."

"I know what you meant," said Patrick, "and the answer is no, there was nothing between them apart from a responsible young man who took a young girl on occasional trips to the market."

"If you want to really find out what is happening in this town, you should ask those Shea's! They hired Emily and then couldn't afford it so they started having boarders there all the time to make money. They have bullock drivers from here, there and everywhere," said Catherine. "They are bad blood those men. They let them stay on their property making money out of them. Who knows who they are and what they bring to the town? The boarder they've had for a few months now; I've heard stories about him. He is strange and roams the hills at night, howling at the moon!"

"Now come on," said Patrick, "they are just stories."

"No, it's true! The Flanagan boy said they saw him one night wandering the hills."

"What do you speak of?" asked Macleod.

"They are rumours," said Patrick. "Rumours from people talking too much. Making up stories. There is no wild man roaming the hills."

Macleod thought it best to let it go rather than risk turning the conversation into wild speculation.

"May I see where Eamon sleeps?" asked Macleod.

"Why would you want to do that?" asked Catherine.

"We've got nothing to hide," said Patrick. "Go in, look around if you think you can find clues in there but you won't find anything inspector."

"Thank you," said Macleod.

Catherine pursed her lips and huffed before leading him through the low door into the house. There were pine boards on the floor and strips of beef hung inside in front of the fireplace drying. Catherine led Macleod into a small room where there were three stuffed mattresses on the floor.

"This is where he sleeps with his brothers."

She stood and watched as Macleod surveyed the small room. The room was barely large enough to stand in, with jute mattresses stuffed with corn husks taking up much of the room.

"Which bed is his?" asked Macleod.

"In the corner there, underneath the window." The window was boarded with wooden shutters, closed against the afternoon sun. Macleod kneeled and ran his hand along the bed, keeping his back to Catherine. He lifted the hessian bag covering and underneath there was a small heart-shaped wreath. Macleod moved it gently and, deciding against identifying his discovery, he put the hessian back and turned to face Catherine.

"Nothing to find, as I told you," said Catherine.

Macleod nodded and went outside the house and moved to where Patrick was waiting with his hands on his hips.

"I'll need to speak to Eamon if I can."

"As you wish," said Patrick. He moved to the verge of grass leading down to the fields and screamed loudly. "Eamon! Get up here!"

Macleod watched as the boy obediently handed the plough to his brother and ran up the hill. He smelled of sweat and dirt and Macleod noticed he was nervous and agitated.

Eamon was tall, well over six foot, an imposing and muscular young man. He had black rings under his eyes, the hallmark of someone who had not been sleeping, and he was jittery. The noise of a crow nearby made him jump.

Macleod's conversation with the eldest O'Malley son followed the same path as the conversation with his parents. He was evasive and the details of his stories were scant.

"So when you took her into Gresford, you left here there."

"At the market. As I always did," said Eamon. "Then I would go fishing for herring down on the river. After fishing, she would come and meet me there and we would return."

"And that afternoon she didn't meet you." Macleod prompted.

"No. I had a good haul of fish and was waiting for her to come back with the produce but she didn't arrive."

"And you didn't think that was strange?" asked Macleod.

"No, sometimes if she had a lot of produce she stayed in town overnight, with Charles Boydell and his family."

"And you didn't think to go and ask them?"

"I didn't want to pry," said Eamon. "We had an agreement. If she didn't arrive at the time, I would come home. That meant she was staying at the Boydell's and I would pick her up the next day when I came in."

Macleod nodded, noting Eamon looking worriedly at his father as he recounted the details.

"And you wouldn't know anything about this wild man roaming the hills at night, would you?" asked Macleod.

He went out on a limb with the question and Eamon was taken aback.

"What do you mean?" asked Eamon, taking two steps back and looking at Macleod intently.

He knows something, thought Macleod.

"The story your mother told me about the boarder at the Shea's."

"As I told you, Macleod," said Patrick, "it's all just bunk. Isn't it Eamon?"

"Yes Da," said Eamon, "that's right, nothing in it. It's all just made up. Bunk."

Macleod saw the line of questioning close and nodded his head.

"Now Mr. Macleod," said Patrick, "if you are heading back to Allynbrook you best head off soon as the sun is setting. You best not be on these roads at night. They are treacherous for a horse."

"Understood," said Macleod, as the second O'Malley son brought his horse to him.

"He's had food and water sir," said the boy, handing the reins to him as Macleod patted the horse's nose, rubbing his hand up and down as he surveyed the property.

"Well thank you," he said.

"Safe travels," said Patrick.

Catherine said nothing, turning on her heel and taking Eamon with her up to the house. Patrick stood at the edge of the small track that led to the property, watching as Macleod wound his way down to the main road. Macleod stole a look backward and saw that Patrick was still watching, so he took the left-hand turn to make it look like he was heading toward Allynbrook. After he had ambled along for a short time, he turned the horse around and, noting that Patrick had left the hill, he headed back out toward Ravenscroft.

The sun was touching the horizon as the stock horse carefully wound its way along the road. The Magpies were signalling the end of the day as the fly population diminished with dusk approaching. The shadows deepened as Macleod rode along, sinister shapes forming within the undergrowth. He ignored them, keeping his head forward and taking out his bottle to calm his nerves with a deep draught. He finished the fortified wine, feeling immediately settled, and urged his horse on. By the time he rounded the chapel the darkness was well entrenched. The clear sky afforded a full moon so he could find his way. The horse carefully stepped along the furrows, rounding the chapel and on to the deeply furrowed road. A bullock train had been through during the day, evening the road out and the going was a little easier on the way back.

Macleod was beginning to nod in the saddle, exhaustion trying to claim him when he heard a low growling in the bushes. The sound emanated from his right and he peered into the undergrowth. The growling stopped as soon as it began but Macleod, now on high alert, scanned the bush on both sides of the road, trying to discern what was making the noise. The only noise in the still night was the soft clip-clopping of the horse's hooves as it ambled along the road. Macleod heard a stick break near him and looked across sharply, seeing a shape dart across the road in front of him. In the darkness, he could not make it out fully but he was sure that whatever it was it was moving very quickly. It darted across the road, right to left, a flash of red plunging into the bushes on the opposite side of the road ahead of Macleod. He pulled the horse to a halt and dismounted, unsheathing his knife and held it in his good hand. His left disfigured hand held the reins, bringing the horse along slowly behind him. He stepped softly, peering into the bushes, listening intently. There was another soft thud, and he stopped, scanning the eucalypts and high grass. Something hit him hard from behind, jumping onto his shoulders and arms around his throat, cutting off his breath. He let go of the horse, dropped the knife, trying to turn. Macleod brought his right elbow up from under him and slammed it into the ribs of his assailant. It released the arm grip for a moment and he took a deep breath sensing a piercing pain as teeth sunk into his flesh around his neck. He roared with pain and brought his elbow around again, striking the thing in the head. It released its grip and rolled off him but as quickly as he turned it was gone, scampering off into the bush.

Macleod put his hand to his neck where blood was flowing fast from the bite and he took out his kerchief to put over it, applied pressure to staunch the blood flow. He was shaken; the horse had wandered back up the road and he went to collect it, remounting and deciding to stay in the saddle until he made it, or if he made it, back to Ravenscroft. At length, the bleeding slowed from the bite and he could tie the kerchief around his neck, keeping the knife in his right hand as he rode along scanning the bush. But whatever it was it had disappeared. The horse faithfully trod the path to Ravenscroft, and it was with relief on the moonlit night when Macleod found the path up to the property. Turning in with the bush cleared around him he felt a great sense of relief and exhaustion. He urged the horse forward up the path and to safety.

Macleod emerged from his makeshift bed, bumping his head as he ducked to get out of the shed. He cursed under his breath and walked out into a mist-covered landscape. A thick fog had rolled in overnight and the morning sun was straining to break through. Ravens hopped here and there, searching for carrion across the ground, brazen and unheeding of the humans, traipsing backward and forward between the Doohan and Kenny houses. There was a chill in the air and Macleod pulled his coat around him, rubbing his unshaven face, the bristles yielding against his hand. McDermott was walking across to him, carrying a hot cup of tea and a plate of food.

"Morning sir," said McDermott.

"You were fast asleep when I came back last night," Macleod said as he gratefully accepted the damper and tea. McDermott nodded as Macleod sipped the tea, grateful to taste the alcohol that McDermott had slipped into it.

"All right?" asked McDermott.

"Good enough," said Macleod, nodding his thanks. "How are things here?"

"I am sorry I was asleep last night when you returned," looking at the mark on Macleod's neck but knowing not to ask. "I spent the day at the field across the road. William and I dug the grave. We took most of the day as the earth was hard. They buried Alexander Norrie, the grandfather, over there; we had to be careful not to disturb his grave." McDermott made the sign of the cross quickly as he peered into the mist. "When this fog clears, we can get started."

Macleod sensing McDermott's gaze on his neck, pulled his coat around it so the lower part of his shoulder was hidden and the bite mark obscured.

"Forrest is back, just arrived, with the Martin, the priest," said McDermott. "Boydell has given his approval for the funeral to go ahead. When the fog clears, they will start."

"Anything else?" asked Macleod.

"It's a desperately sad place, sir," said McDermott. "The mother is grievously wounded. She sits and rocks all day. Her sister prepared the body and wrapped it in cloth, Mary couldn't bring herself to do it. There is no coffin. We will lay him in the earth as he is."

Macleod nodded, wondering how far he had come from civilisation. He bit into his damper, the salted loaf tasty despite the lack of butter. The sun began to break through the fog and the ravens scattered, scampering to the trees for safety. As Macleod was finishing his whisky laden tea, Forrest approached them.

"Boydell has given his acquiescence for the burial. Martin is here. He is with the family. The family has requested our help in carrying the body. He is a big boy, and there are not enough men here to lift him."

Macleod nodded.

"Any news?" asked Forrest. "The O'Malley's can be a prickly bunch. How did you find them?"

"Prickly," said Macleod, agreeing with Forrest. "Eamon, the eldest, went often into Gresford with Emily O'Dell?"

"Often enough, but it's not uncommon in these parts. Families usually send their eldest with any female that goes into town for protection."

Macleod nodded, not pushing any further. He thought for a moment and decided to withhold the episode that had occurred on the road until later in the day after the funeral.

"The branded leather, can you shed any light?" asked Macleod.

"Boydell has never seen them before," said Forrest.

Macleod filled in the gaps with McDermott and then Forrest continued.

"But they are certainly made at the tannery he uses. He is investigating as we speak, his men have gone down to speak to the tanner. When we're back there later today we should have news. Do you think they are connected to the murder?"

"I don't know," said Macleod, "but I will take any information I can glean."

Forrest nodded, sipping from a mug of hot tea. "The fog is lifting quickly," he said. "We best straighten up and be ready. Martin will want to get this over so he can get back into Allynbrook. He is terrified. I had to almost drag him out here by his ear to conduct the funeral."

"Right you are," said Macleod, handing his mug and plate to McDermott who nodded and took them from him, walking back towards the main house and kitchen.

"He straightened up all right?" asked Forrest.

"He seems all right," said Macleod. "But he's running along the line. I think if he sees too much more it may send him over."

"He seems a strong lad," said Forrest, "good stock."

"I promised his mother I'd keep him safe," said Macleod. "That includes his body and his mind."

Forrest looked quizzically at Macleod, not understanding what he had said but let the comment ride, throwing the rest of his tea on the ground. "It's bitter without sugar," he said, spitting on the ground.

Within the next hour, the fog lifted rapidly, and the sun shone brightly on a cool crisp morning. The Doohan and Kenny families gathered outside the Kenny hut; William Doohan, Andrew Kenny, Macleod, McDermott and Forrest inside. The priest was standing next to the body muttering prayers. He looked startled as the men entered. He composed himself quickly. "Are we ready to begin gentlemen?" he asked.

William Doohan was too distraught to speak, tears falling down his cheeks, but he nodded. The six men gathered around the cloth-covered body, the cloth fastened with muslin. Forrest guided them as they placed their hands underneath and on his mark, they lifted together. The body sagged and Macleod felt the weight at his shoulders as they took small steps toward the door through the sitting room and out where the family was waiting. Mary Doohan sobbed immediately on seeing the body, comforted by her sister Ellen, her arm around her.

They brought the body to a makeshift cart and laid it carefully on the straw that had been put there. Ropes were placed on the cart with the body and Andrew Kenny moved around to the front to lead the stock horse down the road. Martin fell in behind the cart, leading the funeral procession as the family followed with children at the rear. Mary Doohan was supported by Ellen, as the cart bumped down the dusty track. Macleod placed his hand over the body to make sure that it did not move about nor topple out of the cart.

They reached the road and crossed over. Andrew Kenny led the stock horse up a narrow path and then onto grass cleared land. Large boulders here and there meant their way to the graveside was winding, but Andrew Kenny knew his way and led the horse expertly along as the dour procession filed up the hill. A small stone marked Alexander Norrie's grave and beside it, a mound of earth marked Alexander Doohan's final resting place. The cart pulled up and under Andrew Kenny's direction, the six men reached in and lifted the body, carefully guiding it over to lie beside the grave. The family gathered around. Mary Doohan could not stand and knelt weeping at her son's feet, her husband William with his hand on her shoulder. The children stood back frightened, in a huddle, well away from the graveside. The prayers lead the family through the process as they grieved for their lost son and brother. Once the short ceremony was complete and the holy water distributed over the body, three ropes were placed underneath and they lifted the body over the grave. Mary Doohan was held back by her husband as she grasped at the body and on Andrew Kenny's signal, they lowered the cloth-covered body into the grave. Andrew Kenny took a mound of earth and threw it on the body, signalling the end of the ceremony.

McDermott and Macleod stood back as the family members threw a handful of dirt each into the grave, the children's tear-stained and terrified faces haunted as they grasped the dirt and dropped it in. They walked as a group with their arms around each other toward the house, bracing each other against the anguish. The priest walked with them, his head down, and Andrew Kenny took the horse and cart, nodding to Macleod and McDermott as he turned and walked away.

"I'll meet you back over there," said Forrest. Macleod nodded. They waited until the family had moved down across the bullock track and were winding their way back up to Ravenscroft. Then, taking an implement each, they shovelled dirt into the grave, mechanically and in silence, neither of them wanting to sully the boy's memory with unnecessary speech.

After returning to Ravenscroft with dirt-stained hands and sweat-soaked shirts Macleod and McDermott drank the river water as Father Martin prepared to leave after spending time with the family. The hills were darkened as the midday sun was obscured by dark clouds, rolling in as the afternoon progressed. Father Martin made haste to leave and bid Macleod and McDermott goodbye, taking his horse and moving as quickly as he could back toward Allynbrook. Forrest made to leave but Macleod signalled to him and Forrest understood, waiting until the priest had left.

"Bid the family goodbye for us," said Macleod.

"I will," said Forrest, "I think it is best you not come inside."

"I understand," said Macleod.

Forrest left to walk back into the house as Macleod and McDermott retrieved their horses and walked them down to the top of the property, ready to make the journey back into Allynbrook.

McDermott patted the side of his horse softly, humming to himself.

"How are you faring?" asked Macleod.

"It is the first funeral I've been at," said McDermott.

"What?" said Macleod. "Even in your younger days?"

"Ma kept us away from family funerals. It was bad luck to be there. I guess I got my fair share of bad luck now."

He looked across at where they had filled the grave.

"Now you don't want to start believing all that superstitious stuff," said Macleod. "You'll send yourself mad. A good policeman sticks with what he knows and if he starts straying into bad luck and superstition, then he is lost. "

McDermott nodded and managed a smile.

"I'm all right," he said to Macleod, keen to reassure the older man he was not losing his mind. "I'm all right."

Forrest joined them and they mounted their horses, bidding goodbye to Ravenscroft as the cloudy afternoon hid the sunlight. There was a chill in the air as they ambled down the hill on horseback, with a breeze coming from the west. The Magpies had stopped calling and the only sound was the groaning of the Ravens as they reached the road at the bottom and turned back toward Allynbrook. As they were riding Forrest, riding on Macleod's left, halted.

"What in hell's name happened to you?" he said, noticing the deep gouge in Macleod's shoulder. His coat and shirt had slipped back to reveal the gaping wound which oozed serum mixed with blood. The edges were puckered and Macleod could feel the tightness, signalling that the wound was festering.

"I got this on the way back from O'Malley's last night. Something attacked me in the bush. There are things I have not told you, which I can only tell you now. When you asked me before Mr. Forrest whether I had seen anything like this I wasn't completely truthful."

LONDON

AUGUST 1869

13

"Be quick about it," called Sarah, "or you'll miss the horse tram."

Macleod nodded agreement as he looked at his daughter. Emily was sitting on his knee, examining his left hand.

"Will they never grow back?" she asked.

"No, they are gone forever I'm afraid," he said.

"But we learned in school that sometimes animals can grow their tails back," she said, looking earnestly at him.

"Well, I'm afraid humans can't grow fingers back, but my hand works well nonetheless," he said.

"But I wish they would grow back," she said.

"Well, now, we can't have everything we want," said Macleod, looking at her fondly.

"If you two could stop talking and join us for breakfast I would appreciate it," said his wife, bustling about the kitchen as sons Peter and Andrew set the table.

"Jonathon not joining us?" asked Macleod.

"He went to work early today. They needed him early on the docks."

As Macleod walked to the dining room, he noticed it was busy outside as people made their way from Bow to their places of work.

"It's ten minutes until the tram arrives," said his wife. "Sit quickly." She poured tea rapidly, serving fresh bread with bacon.

"Sit with us," he said.

"In a moment," she replied, returning the kettle to the fire.

"No school again today?" he said, sipping the tea and biting into the fresh oven baked bread.

"Benthal Green advised closure again," his wife said. "The smallpox epidemic is worrying."

"But the vaccinations should cover everyone," said Macleod, shaking his head.

"I understand." Sarah gave him a look that indicated to him she was modifying her story for the sake of the children that were present. "They are saying this type of smallpox is a little more wily," she said, choosing her words carefully. "It has come over from Europe, from the French soldiers. So, it is safest to keep the children at home. And they don't mind. Do you?"

Andrew, Peter, and Emily nodded. The two boys were growing into fine young men and at twelve and ten would finish their schooling soon and enter the workforce. At eight years of age, Emily was still experiencing the wonders of childhood.

Macleod watched as his wife directed the children as she ate. Her chestnut brown hair was tied back neatly, small busy strands falling over her forehead. His heart swelled. She was as pretty as the day he had married her and the children were a testament to the life they had built together. He cast his eye over the boys. They had his brown eyes but Emily had her mother's green eyes, sharp and quick. Her brown hair was fastened back from her face, mirroring her mother's, the small strands falling over her face in an imitation of her larger self.

"Will you be late today?" Sarah asked.

"I think not," said Macleod. "There is just one essential duty I must perform today."

Sarah nodded to show that she understood.

He pushed back on the wooden chair, wiped his mouth with a napkin and stepped forward to kiss Sarah and Emily on the forehead. The boys grasped his right hand in a masculine show of emotion. He moved toward the entry hall, bidding his family goodbye.

"Well, have a good day at home," he said. "I expect we'll see Jonathon tonight for dinner Sarah?"

"Absolutely. He knows where the food is served," she said, smiling.

Macleod put on his hat and coat and walked out into the street. The chill of winter was cloaking London streets as summer turned to autumn. He gathered his coat about him, dodging horse manure scattered across the street. The traffic was busy with hansom cabs running up and down the street; riders on horseback and horse trams filling the gaps. There were paupers here and there selling their goods but he waved them away as he walked toward the tram stop. As he waited, he mused on how the horse tram had made his life easier and harder in one fell swoop. His journey to White Chapel and H division was shorter by far and more convenient, but it made the decision to change from H division more difficult. He had not spoken to Sarah about it or any of his colleagues, but the work of policing in White Chapel was beginning to wear him down and he needed a change. The horses noisily pulled the tram to a stop, waiting patiently as the passengers boarded. The tram was half empty at the Bow suburb and Macleod found a seat easily. Sitting quietly he watched out the window as the tram jerked into motion as the horses pulled them along.

As they left Bow and moved east toward the darker streets of London, the scene changed. Human refuse and filth lay in the streets. The street sweepers in Bow were absent and rubbish was plentiful and scattered. The street hawkers were more ragged and the grime thicker as they entered White Chapel.

Alighting at White Chapel he made his way to H division headquarters. Sweeney was waiting for him and greeted him warmly.

"Good morning Inspector," he said.

"Inspector," nodded Macleod.

"Aberline wants to see us," he said.

They made their way two abreast together to the front door, greeting the on-duty sergeant who was manning the desk. There was a somber tone to the police station this morning as they made their way up the steps to Aberline's office. Sweeney knocked.

"Come," was the reply.

They let themselves into Aberline's office. Aberline sat behind a large wood paneled desk, perusing papers. He looked up as the two inspectors walked in and waved with his hand for them to sit, as he concentrated on the document in front of him. Setting it aside his hand went to his face as he twirled his large handlebar moustache and ran a hand through his sparse hair. He took up the cigar that was sitting on his desk and took a deep draw from it before placing it down as he blew the smoke up into the air.

"Well," he said. "I need not reiterate to you gentlemen the importance of keeping these murders from the public view. Not only from the public but from our friends in the newspapers."

Aberline took the piece of paper he had been perusing and brought it back into his view so he could read from it.

"Bite marks and flesh removed! What sort of monster would do such a thing?"

"Well, we have him up at Newgate. The monster is chained, awaiting the noose," said Sweeney.

"Gone deadly wrong," said Aberline. "Four murders, all with the same gruesome aspects of bits and pieces removed, bite marks. Bites! God save us! I put a suppression order on it. With a smallpox epidemic looming we want no more alarm in the streets."

He paused for a moment and picked up his cigar, taking another deep draw.

"If we were to release these details, there would be panic. Are the all the ends tied up; was there an accomplice?"

"We have no real proof that there ever was any," said Macleod. "One witness said they saw someone with the suspect but this was never corroborated. And there were no other reports."

"So we are satisfied that he is the sole murderer?" asked Aberline.

"Satisfied enough," said Sweeney. "At his execution today we should be able to put the matter to rest."

Aberline continued to scrutinise the papers in front of him, shifting them around methodically.

"So random. A street seller, a prostitute, an inn owner, and a market girl; none of them connected."

"None," said Sweeney. "Random acts of violence committed in a violent area."

"Nonetheless, "said Aberline, "the details of these murders stay locked in this room. All involved in the investigation will not speak of the details. I have warned the sergeants not to speak of the details on pain of dismissal. If I find any of this has been leaked to the newspapers, there will be dire consequences. Am I understood?"

He took another puff on his cigar as he waited for a response.

"Understood," said Macleod.

"Of course," said Sweeney. "I don't see any point in releasing these details. It would only panic the masses."

"Do you intend to travel out there today?" asked Aberline.

"We will go and see that the job is done," said Sweeney. "I'll take Macleod with me."

"Good. Report back when it is done," said Aberline. "You are dismissed."

He waved them out of the room, studying the paperwork with the details of the cases as Macleod and Sweeney shuffled along the dusty wooden floor through the creaking door and down the steps to the street.

"Put us out at Newgate," he said to the sergeant at the desk. "We'll be back later today."

"Sir," he said, nodding to them.

They walked out into the street as the low clouds brought darkness to the mid-morning. Grime covered the buildings, horse manure and human excrement filled the streets. As they stood to wait for a Hansom, bobbies squeezed behind them, off on their beat, tipping their helmets as they walked past the inspectors. The Hansom arrived readily and Sweeney flagged it down. They climbed in, closing the wooden slats over their legs to protect themselves against the mud and filth that would be thrown up. Sweeney opened the trapdoor above his head and spoke to the driver.

"Newgate prison," he said, then shut the trapdoor. There was a crack of a whip and the horse took off along the street, the driver expertly maneuvering the cab into the passing traffic.

Drizzle fell as they travelled, making the dark day even murkier and the grime stickier.

"The new smallpox is a concern for you?" asked Sweeney, lighting his pipe.

"The vaccinations have been undertaken but this new smallpox has something in it. They say the French are bringing it over from the Prussian war. A high fatality rate they say. My children are at home."

"And mine," said Sweeney. "It's best to keep them away. I thought we had seen the end of it but it has returned."

"Let's hope it passes quickly," said Macleod.

"I hope so," said Sweeney. "I attended a house the other day where two had died. A most dreadful thing. They were covered in the pox, their bloated bodies had been lying rotting where they had been left upstairs. No one dared enter."

"It is ghastly," said Macleod, looking out the window as the drizzle became heavier.

The driver steered the cab along the streets as they wound in and out along alleyways, finally making their way to Newgate Prison. The remnants of the public hanging place were visible as Macleod and Sweeney presented their credentials to the gaoler and were allowed access to the prison. The Warden was there to greet them.

"Has he said anything?" asked Sweeney.

"Nothing," said the warden. He was a portly man aged in his fifties, spectacled and bald, beleaguered in a thankless job.

"We'll see him then," said Sweeney.

"Of course," said the warden, "I'll make the arrangements. Please take a seat for the moment."

They sat on a wooden bench in the dark corridor awaiting the prison guard to escort them to see the prisoner. With his execution date being set for today he was chained below the keeper's house in the sewers of Newgate. The warden arrived quickly with a prison guard who escorted them along to The Keeper's house and then down a narrow set of stairs. The stench was awful. Macleod put his hand over his mouth as the smell of excrement and rotting meat assaulted his senses.

The prisoner was the only man for execution that day and he was chained by his neck, arms and feet and ankles, deep in a cesspool of water. His head was bowed, and his fiery red hair hung over his face.

"McCoy," said the prison guard, grabbing the prisoner roughly with his baton and pulling his head up. His face was bloody, his ragged teeth blackened. Saliva pooled in his open mouth and he drooled, his pink eyes piercing the darkness, penetrating, all-seeing. He recognized Macleod and Sweeney and smiled. The smile turned to a snigger and then to a laugh.

"What? Here to make sure I swing properly, are you?" he said.

"Watch your mouth!" said the guard and punched him in the nose so that gouts of blood dripped into the cesspool below.

"Easy," said the warden, "we want him conscious when he hangs."

"Leave us with him," said Sweeney.

"But our policy..." said the warden.

"I know your policy. You leave us with him, both of you. We will call you when we are finished."

The warden reluctantly left with the guard, closing the steel door behind them with a thud. Sweeney stepped forward, grabbing McCoy's hair so that his head lifted. The man smiled at him, an evil sardonic smile, his bright pink eyes a stark contrast to his red hair and his albino face.

"You are a strange-looking man," said Sweeney.

McCoy laughed.

"We need to know whether you had an accomplice," said Sweeney.

"I acted alone," said McCoy, his laughing stopping abruptly. "I acted alone with the devil inside me. I did it because they deserved it. They who committed such wrong will see, hear and speak no evil again."

He laughed again and Sweeney released his hair.

"There is nothing we will gain here," he said to Macleod.

They stood for a time as McCoy stood spread-eagled with his head bowed.

"I'm tired of waiting." Macleod turned to the door and wrapped on the iron as a signal for the guard. As the guard came to open the door McCoy called.

"Macleod," he said.

Macleod turned to face the prisoner, as McCoy spat blood on the ground and then licked his lips, slowly, methodically. The fiery red hair framed his pale face, the pink eyes ethereal in the gloom.

"You think it's finished?"

He growled, a low guttural sound, exposing his ragged teeth.

"I know what you are Macleod, you can't hide from me. I will see you again, I'll come to you, in the dark, in your dreams."

He smiled, the gaps in his teeth oozing blood.

Macleod spat on the ground and turned.

The door slammed shut

"You can wait up here," said the warden, showing them to his office. "We'll call you down when the executioner has him on the scaffold."

Macleod and Sweeney lit their pipes, both contemplating the moment.

"His family?" asked Macleod.

"His wife has consumption," said Sweeney. "She probably won't last long. There are two boys that have fled north and I don't know what will become of the daughter. She will probably end up in an orphanage or on the street once her mother dies."

"Are any of their children afflicted?" asked Macleod.

"One boy and the girl. They are albinos. Strange looking and frightened of the light lest their skin burn."

"Did she know do you think?" asked Macleod.

"Who knows what passes in a marriage," said Sweeney. "Whether she knew, I cannot say."

"And the children?" asked Macleod.

"I can only pray that they were shielded from what he did."

"Gentlemen."

Their conversation was interrupted as the warden motioned for them to follow him. The priest had been called, but the prisoner had declined and therefore his movement to the scaffold was swift.

Macleod and Sweeney stood below the scaffold as they brought him forward, hands bound behind his back, the hangman adjusting the noose around his neck. As he stood on the scaffold, the clouds parted and the sun shone for the moment, the prisoner wincing as the light touched him.

A low animal sound emanated deep within his chest as the shaft of sunlight struck him and he howled, recoiling from the light. Screaming he threw himself forward, straining the rope, choking. And then the sun was obscured, the darkness returned, and he was quiet again. Dark clouds closed over the sun as spatters of rain fell. The priest stood beside the prisoner, reading a prayer, and as he finished, the hangman moved to put a hood over the prisoner's head. The prisoner lunged to bite him, jaws snapping, spitting blood and saliva. A punch from the guard quieted him. The hood refused, they brought close the noose.

The prisoner stared at Macleod as they brought the noose over his neck. He growled again, his white face turning into fury as the pink eyes blazed, his wild red hair seeming to float around his head. There he stood, a monstrous apparition, with the rain falling hard as if he had summoned the storm.

The growling reached a high pitch and then the hangman released. The prisoner dropped and bounced, his neck snapping in a moment. Macleod watched underneath as his body hung slack, the last moments of his life ebbing away. The doctor moved in and pronounced him dead.

"Done," said Sweeney, nodding assent.

"A moment," said Macleod, moving toward the body. It swung slowly, his body twisting, the head, and neck at an impossible angle, the face contorted in the mask of death. MacLeod got as close as he dared, staring into that face, the open eyes bulging in death, his tongue protruding slack from the mouth.

Satisfied, he turned and walked back to Sweeney.

And the rain poured down.

14

They rode in silence, before Forrest spurred his horse ahead and then turned it in front of Macleod so that he could go no further.

"And your purpose in keeping this secret then?" he asked Macleod accusingly.

"To avoid panic," said Macleod.

"And you recognized the similarities as soon as you arrived?" Forrest asked.

"As soon as I heard McKinlay's description of the murder when I was in Dungog," he said.

"So you suspected but kept silent."

Macleod answered, grim-faced.

"What purpose would there be in panicking the people in this area? What would I tell them? That the ghost of a man I saw hanged in London over six years ago is haunting them? How do you think that would settle with the townsfolk, Forrest? What do you think would have happened? I'd have had no credibility."

"If not a ghost, then what is it? Who could copy in such a way?"

Macleod glanced at McDermott. The events of the last few days had taken their toll, and he was reminded of the promise he had made to the boy's mother, to keep him safe. He decided to finish the conversation with Forrest quickly so he could dismiss McDermott.

"I have revealed it to you now because I think it may have a bearing on the case. We need to know of anyone new who has entered the area. One thing I am sure of is that this is no ghost. These murders lie in the land of the living and whoever it is, whatever it is, it is not the ghost of McCoy."

A raven cried as Macleod spoke, a solemn testimony to his revelation about his family and the smallpox epidemic that claimed them.

Forrest stopped for a moment. "I am sorry for your loss," he said. "All of them?"

"My wife and my family," said Macleod, stony-faced. "Afterwards I succumbed to despair, and I was not the man I once was."

Forrest watched him carefully for a moment, weighing Macleod's testimony. Macleod sensed Forrest wanted to press further, to uncover more of his murky past, but mercifully he relented.

"Enough said," said Forrest. "Will you join me at Boydell's? I am eager to hear his report of any new settlers that have come to town."

"Of course," said Macleod. He turned to McDermott. "Go back to Reynella. Rest up for now."

He looked into the boy's eyes and saw they were blank. He looked exhausted.

"Go there and let Bridget O'Donnell know that we are safe and we'll need a few more nights. Say nothing else."

"Understood," whispered McDermott, turning his horse off to the south, walking it slowly down the road toward Reynella.

Macleod and Forrest spurred on towards Caerwgle. A stable hand was waiting for them, taking their horses as they dismounted. Forrest led Macleod into the building, his pace brisk, his manner more urgent.

Macleod's shoulder was burning and he could feel tightness and the beginnings of a fever but he put it aside. There was nothing to be done. As he rubbed his hand over the bite mark, he felt the edges puckering, tender and swollen.

Boydell was waiting for them inside at the large kitchen table. The pine board floor echoed their footsteps as they walked in.

"The situations worsens," said Boydell. "I have alerted the magistrate in Paterson of our progress and he will send a party to take over the investigation."

Macleod knew best not to protest.

"As you see fit," he said.

"They would have come tomorrow but they cannot spare men at the moment because of riots. He has given me his guarantee."

Macleod realized that Boydell had lost faith in his ability to prosecute the investigation and he felt diminished.

"If I may," said Macleod, weighing Boydell's reaction as he spoke, "I have related to Forrest that the murders here have a similarity to those that I witnessed when I was in the police in H division in London. The mutilation is similar. But the man who committed the murders hanged. I saw him hang in Newgate. He is dead, and that is certain. Whoever, or whatever is committing these murders is someone new to the township. Do you have any information on any boarders or migrants that have come to the village recently?"

Boydell did not answer his question but pressed him further.

"Did the man have relatives? Anyone else who could be responsible?"

"He had a wife," said Macleod. "She died of consumption. There were two boys, but they disappeared. They sent the daughter to an orphanage after her mother died and she later perished."

"No one else related?"

"None we could find," said Macleod.

Boydell thought for a moment before turning a page on the table in front of him. "We have been able to identify several people who have entered the district via Paterson but none who have come directly to Allynbrook, save one. We had difficulty confirming because it is based upon the evidence of the wagon driver who says he brought the individual here after receiving payment in Paterson."

"He or she?" asked Macleod.

"The driver could not be certain," Boydell answered.

"What, he could not see properly?" asked Macleod, unbelievingly.

"A cowl always covered the face. He could only give a limited description. The individual had pale skin, but that was all."

"Where did he take them?" asked Macleod.

"He says he took them directly to the Shea's farm."

Macleod was taken aback. Forrest looked at him and nodded.

"We thought they had an extra boarder when we were there," said Macleod, "but Mrs. Shea denied it."

"As well she would," said Boydell. "If it is true, what she has done is illegal. She has accepted an individual as a permanent lodger, has kept the border secret, and has not sought permission from the correct authorities. In addition, it is likely that she has received an illegal payment for doing so. It is no mystery why she wants to keep it a secret. The chief constable in Paterson is investigating further and will telegraph as soon as he has further information. "

The darkness was spreading in the room and Boydell's servants placed candles to disperse the gloom. Macleod could feel his shoulder tighten more and more and a chill went through his body. He shook it off.

"It's too late to go back tonight," said Forrest. "It would be dangerous to go along that road."

"First thing tomorrow then," said Boydell. "Macleod can take two men out to the Shea's and find out the truth."

"There is something else," said Boydell. "These leather brands." He took one from his fob pocket. "My tanner made them."

"At your direction?" asked Macleod.

"Certainly not," said Boydell. "Under duress, I gleaned from him he has made several of these."

"For what purpose?" asked Forrest.

"My instinct says smuggling," said Boydell. "But if there is any link to the murders we need to uncover it. There was another like this one discovered today between the sandstones at St. Mary-on-Allyn. My estimation is that whatever will happen will happen tonight."

"Then we should remain here on guard," said Forrest. "Then we can catch the perpetrators and we can have more information regarding the murders."

"Agreed. You will need food but after dinner has been served I will leave it to you and Macleod to decide where your vantage point should be," said Boydell.

"Within the church, if it is permitted," said Forrest. "It would be the safest place to observe without being detected."

"I have a key," said Boydell, "and it is permitted. I will facilitate your entry once you have eaten."

Following a minimal supper of bread and cured pork, Forrest and Macleod made their way with Boydell to the church by candlelight. On approaching the church they doused the candle and walked in the moonlit darkness. Macleod was feeling the bite on his shoulder more and more, as tingles crawled down to his upper back and over to the front of his chest. The area was tight, and he rubbed it as it itched and pulsed.

"You all right?" asked Forrest.

"I'm well," said Macleod. "Let's do what needs to be done."

Boydell turned the key, and the lock clicked ominously, the door creaking on its hinges as it swung open. Forrest entered first with Macleod close behind.

"I'll leave the door open. I shan't lock you in," said Boydell. " Let's pray that something will come of this."

Macleod nodded and thanked him. Boydell turned and walked swiftly away. They listened as his boots crunched across the gravel outside and then faded into the distance. Macleod reclined on one of the pews within the church and Forrest took up a position of equal length on the other side. The only light was the dim moonlight that penetrated the stained glass, drawing long shadows along the flagstones of the little church. Macleod was feeling a fever coming on, little drops of sweat beading on his brow. He wiped them off.

"I'll take first watch," he said. "You rest."

Forrest agreed, unwilling to challenge Macleod.

Macleod watched as Forrest laid himself down on the pew with his boots on and paced slowly as Forrest fell into a deep slumber. After an hour he felt drowsy, but the fever was abating. The chill in his bones remained, but he convinced himself that the worst had passed and he would not fall to a gangrenous wound. As he sat in the silence, he heard the wind rustle in the elms outside but otherwise, there were no sounds. Then he heard it, a child's voice, laughing, over in the church's corner. He stood, seeing a small figure standing near the altar.

"Who's there?" he whispered. There was no reply.

He walked toward it slowly, making sure that his footfalls did not wake Forrest. The child stood, regarding him as he walked toward it, and then abruptly turned and ran, disappearing into the darkness.

"What manner of..." He stopped as more figures appeared over towards the edge of the church behind the altar, a boy and a woman, along with the child. The child was giggling again as he walked towards them. In the darkness, he could barely make out their faces. There was a woman, three boys, and a girl standing close. As he drew near, he recognized them and his heart filled with dread. They stood smiling at him, his wife and children, before their faces turned. One of them coughed as he backed away and put his hand towards them, in a vain attempt to ward them off, as they walked toward him, their faces beginning to break out in spots of the pox, as he stumbled backward against the pew. He closed his eyes and looked away and held his forearm over his eyes. When he took his arm away, they had vanished. He looked left and right and behind him, the only sound now the deep regular breathing of Forrest in the darkness.

I must be mad.

He sat on a pew, suddenly feeling exhausted. Two pews up from him a Russian soldier appeared and regarded him, turning his head this way and that, the left side of his jaw missing and his tongue lolling obscenely through the open wound. Another soldier joined him, both arms missing, bloody stumps dripping onto the flagstone. Then a sepoy, dragging himself along the floor, his entrails behind him. A headless torso turned on the pew to face him. Macleod felt the fever grasp him, a chill running through his bones, he shook uncontrollably, as the grim apparitions multiplied in number, surrounding him.

Someone was shaking him. He opened his eyes and saw Forrest as the cold light of dawn was creeping through the stained glass windows. Forrest held his finger to his lips and pointed to the door. Outside there was the sound of stone moving. Macleod tried to move but his bones ached. His clothes were wet with sweat and he realized he had lost the watch long ago. There was no time to ask Forrest how long he had been unconscious or what had happened. The perpetrator was at hand.

Forrest signalled for him to take a place next to the door as Forrest knelt and looked through the keyhole. The sound of the stone moving stopped. Scuffling and the sound of the stone being replaced.

The wheels of a cart turning on the river side of the church, the clink of a bridle. Urgent whispers, scuffling, footsteps up and down the river bank. Forrest put his index finger to his lips.

They waited. The footsteps continued back and forth, the methodical, practiced movements of those who worked outside the law. After a time, the footsteps retreated down the river bank, murmurings at the water's edge. Forrest eased the door open, just a crack. In the morning light, Macleod could see Seamus Sullivan, by the water's edge, next to a boat on the Allyn River. The loading of the stolen goods completed, he was accepting payment as the recipients prepared to shove off.

Realising that they were too late, Forrest and Macleod surged through the door, the sudden movement startling the horse at the back of the church. It reared and bolted; the cart careening behind it as it galloped off. The commotion alerted the perpetrators, and the boatmen pushed off, easily drifting into the fast flowing current of the Allyn, as the boat and its contraband raced away south. The sun broke the horizon as O'Sullivan raced off north, along the river bank, Forrest in pursuit. As Macleod ran down the river bank his chest hurt, the pain radiating across his chest and down his arm and he staggered before tumbling into the dirt. As he lay there, panting, he watched as Forrest pursued, his vision blurring and fading. Forest gained, and O'Sullivan leapt into the fast-flowing waters, disappearing quickly in the raging torrent. Macleod's head throbbed, the world swimming with haziness all around, obscene shapes from the trees merging with the morning fog.

Macleod woke on his stomach. There was a searing pain in his shoulder and Collinson the bush doctor was there.

"That's a nasty bite Inspector," he said. "I've seen nothing like it from an animal. Teeth marks... I can't explain them."

"Nor should you try to," said Macleod, trying to sit up.

"Please rest easy inspector," said Collinson. "I drained the wound, but it's still proud and inflamed. I've put castor oil and alcohol on it and you will need to have it dressed again tonight."

"I'm all right," said Macleod, pushing himself up, feeling dizzy but shaking it off. He sat with his legs over the bed as the world swam and then everything became right and he looked up. His shoulder was hurting but the pounding and thumping that had been there the night before had gone and his head felt clear. He looked at Collinson who was wiping his hands and he saw in the corner a bloodstained dish lined with bloody bandages and instruments. His shoulder had been dressed and bandaged and Collinson held his shirt for him.

"Let me help you," said Collinson.

"I'm all right," Macleod repeated. He took the shirt from Collinson, easing his right arm into it, groaning as he did. He had trouble doing up the shirt but managed and put on his coat. The events of the night before came to him in a rush.

"Forrest? Where is he?"

"They are waiting for you in the adjoining room," said Collinson.

Macleod seized his hat and burst through the door into the parlour room where Boydell and Forrest were waiting.

"How goes it?" asked Forrest, standing, obviously concerned for him.

"I'm well enough," said Macleod. Boydell was looking at him with sympathy.

"What's happened?"

"That bite you sustained, it gave you a fever. You are lucky Collinson was here. You collapsed on the river bank."

"How long have I been..."

"Well, it is afternoon..." said Forrest. "You are expected at Reynella for dinner."

"The perpetrator?"

"Dead, we dragged his body from the river downstream," said Forrest.

"And the boatmen?"

"We caught them on the river near East Gresford. Paterson thugs, riding the Allyn until it joined the Paterson."

"Sit," said Boydell, offering him a glass of whiskey. Macleod gratefully accepted it and drank it in one gulp. Boydell refilled it and he eagerly drank the second. Boydell stood and put the bottle back on the shelf.

"My people," he said, "I can hardly believe it."

"What of them?" asked Macleod.

"Stealing from me," said Boydell. "They were using the leather brands. My stable hand, Sullivan. He was exchanging my crops and produce for money."

"The Ravenscroft leather brands?" asked Macleod

"He bribed the tanner to make them. The Ravenscroft brands were used as a ruse, in the case that they were discovered. To throw the blame on the Ravenscroft property, but they had naught to do with it. When the buyers were coming from Paterson, they'd send a rider to leave the brand at St Mary's-on-Allyn beneath the flagstone, in the hidden place where you found it. Sullivan would check each day at sundown and when the brand was in place, that was the signal. They would meet for an exchange of the goods the next day at dawn. He would load the wagon during the early hours and meet them by the river. They would take the goods back to Paterson via the river and sell them off."

"Any others involved?"

"I'll be questioning all my staff but I think he was working alone. We will hand the Paterson thugs over to the magistrate in Paterson, he can deal with them. And I'll ensure that all the brands are destroyed and a clear message goes to the area that Sullivan has been found out."

He looked at Forrest. Forrest shook his head.

"No connection we could find to the murders. Simple theft. That is all it is. There's no connection to the murder and no connection to the boarder."

"Damn them!" said Macleod.

"Indeed, "said Boydell. "Now that wound Macleod, you need to tell me how you got it."

"As I told Forrest, something attacked me on the road on the way back to Eccleston. I can't describe it. It attacked me from behind and disappeared. Whether it was an animal or human, I cannot be certain."

"Collinson says human," 'said Boydell. "Those bite marks were not made by any animal. I have friends I want you to meet. The Gringai. They've come back early this year from The Barrington. They have news that may be of interest."

"Friendly?" asked Macleod.

"They have been very helpful," he said. "When I first came here, they told me where to find the best permanent water. That's how I selected this homestead site. We have a working relationship with them. I speak their language or some of it, and we should hear what they have to say."

Boydell opened the door and an elderly man came into the room. He nodded to Macleod and Boydell spoke to him in a language that Macleod did not understand. Despite his short stature, he stood proudly, unafraid of the men in the room. His thick black hair picked up the sun rays in the afternoon light as he conversed with Boydell. They spoke at length before Boydell turned to Macleod.

"They have seen this thing that haunts the mountain. It has fiery red hair and white skin. It has roamed the mountains this year. One of his brothers saw it here around St Mary's-on-Allyn at around the time that young Emily disappeared. They have seen it elsewhere roaming along the countryside."

The Gringai man interrupted Boydell, speaking to him quickly.

"He says it is a fire spirit, more animal than human. He says it is very dangerous."

"Can he describe it more?" asked Macleod fearing the worst.

"He says the face is all white like a ghost. The eyes are pink. The hair floats around it, like a spirit. Fire. Fire all around. He says it is an evil thing."

Boydell and the man spoke again at length, engaged in deep conversation. His task completed, the Gringai tribesman turned to others in the room and spoke directly to them. As he spoke he pointed to each of them, the weight of his gesture and the tenor of his speech conveying the gravity of the situation. When he had finished, he turned and spoke to Boydell, and then silently left the room.

"What did he say?" asked Forrest.

"He wanted you to know of this evil thing that has come here. He told you to be careful."

"You think what he says is true?" asked Macleod.

"I have no reason not to trust him. I have known him and his people for many years and he is one of their elders. Does what he says make any sense to you?"

"No sense at all, except the description he gives is that of a ghost."

"What do you mean?" asked Boydell.

"He is describing the man I saw hanged in London long years ago. There is no way that man could be here."

Boydell turned and opened a side drawer, taking out some papers. He brought them over and put them in front of Macleod, offering him another whiskey. Macleod acquiesced, downing the third as Boydell opened the written pages.

"There," he said. "I received this from Paterson this afternoon. The chief constable has made this a priority."

He handed the telegram to MacLeod.

Confirmed Illegal transfer to Shea's property, Eccleston, New South Wales in October 1874. Appearance distinctive. Pale skin, red hair.

"But it can't be," said Forrest.

"I saw him hanged," said Macleod.

"God save us," said Boydell.

"We best be out there," said Macleod.

"Not now," said Forrest.

"But we need to go," said Macleod.

"You are in no shape to travel. We will go first thing in the morning. God knows we don't want to be on those roads at night."

Macleod realized there was no use arguing. Forrest and Boydell had made up their minds, and he was not sure whether he had been cut-out of the investigation altogether or they really feared to tread the roads at night. Either way, he resolved to return to Reynella.

"Your horse is waiting," said Boydell. "You will need to see Collinson tomorrow to have that dressed."

He made his way to the stockyard where Collinson was holding his horse. He walked the horse down the stock track as the sun dipped low on the horizon. Ravens gathered in the trees above him, wailing as if to signal his demise, as he made a solitary procession back toward Reynella.

15

Macleod's horse whinnied as it approached Reynella. The sun was setting, a chill accompanying the mist that was settling over the landscape. The bullocks were lowing in the paddocks as they grazed freely, the drivers having settled in for the evening, with heavy clouds overhead threatening a storm. The mist and clouds added to the dimness, making it seem later than it was, and an all-pervading feeling of doom swept over Macleod as he tethered his horse and undid the saddle and bridle. He laid them over the undercover rail and winced as his shoulder wound pulled.

The spectre of McCoy haunted him and he was pondering the story the Gringai had related when Nell Bird approached him.

"Will you be having dinner Mr. Macleod?"

"I will, thank you, Nell," he said.

"You look pale," she said. "Are you feeling well? Can I get you something?"

"I'm all right, thanks Nell," he said. "Just some trouble with a wound but it is passing now."

In the background the noise within the wine bar was ramping up, the drovers fuelled by alcohol playing the fiddle and stamping their feet as they sang.

"It will be a boisterous night," said Nell, smiling.

"I am sure you will keep them under control," replied Macleod, smiling back at her.

She led him inside the smoke-filled room and found him a table in the corner. Bringing him a glass of fortified wine, she left the bottle with him. He lit his pipe and was deep in thought. The noise in the room was becoming raucous, the drovers grateful for a dry place to stay for the night and releasing their tension into the room in boisterous song. Patrick Bird was moving quickly between the tables serving drinks and Bridget O'Donnell approached him as he took a puff from his pipe.

"Welcome back Mr. Macleod," she said. She placed a bowl in front of him, the steam rising as the piping hot stew beckoned him. "You'll like that. Spiced mutton stew."

He took a mouthful to please her and nodded his appreciation, complimenting her on the dish.

"Would you like me to get McDermott to join you, and those other nice gentlemen who are visiting?"

Macleod stopped.

"Other gentlemen?" he asked.

"The men from Sydney. They said they knew you well. They arrived late this afternoon and have been talking to McDermott in your room. I can go and get them now to join you for dinner if you like."

Macleod pushed the bowl away from him. "I think not," he said. He could see that she sensed that something was wrong, but she resisted the urge to ask. "I'll go and see them in the room. We'll join you for dinner later. Would you mind putting this aside for me?"

"I can Mr. Macleod." She took the bowl, looking at him quizzically and gathered the bottle of wine with her free hand. "I'll keep the table for you."

"Thank you," said Macleod.

He didn't need details of who they were. He hurried out of the noisy room and turned around to the front. The outer area was empty, and he moved quietly down the corridor to the room he and McDermott shared. He placed his ear to the door. Inside he could hear low voices and he calculated they were at the far end of the small room. He reached into his coat to ensure that his knife was handy, took a deep breath and turned the lock. The door opened with a creak and the room was dimly lit with candles. His heart sank. McDermott was sitting bound with twine to one of the chairs in the room. There was blood on his shirt streaming from his left ear, where the earlobe had been removed. There were two men, one standing to his side and the other sitting on the bed. Macleod scanned the room quickly to make sure there were no others. He eyed them carefully. One was a large beefy man with ruddy skin, a gaudy neck chief tied around his neck. The second was smaller and wiry, like a whippet, grinning sardonically at Macleod as he entered the room and shut the door. The beefy one spoke first.

"Ah, Inspector Macleod, it's so nice of you to join us. We have been entertaining your constable, as you can see, haven't we Patrick?"

"That we have," said Patrick, holding up a small filleting knife in his right hand and in the left he held a small piece of an earlobe he had removed from McDermott. "He has been most amicable," said the whippet man, his grin turning into a laugh.

"You with me McDermott?" asked Macleod.

McDermott nodded.

"Oh, he's all right," said the beefy man. "Don't you worry. We've been keeping him company waiting for you. It seems you have been having trouble solving the murders up here Macleod. Maybe they need a real policeman up here, not some ring-in who spends most of his time on the grog."

Macleod let the insult pass.

"What's your business here?"

"You know our business," said whippet man. "Our chief is not happy with you and McDermott here. You see, his son was the one you murdered."

"He fell to his death while we were pursuing him," said Macleod.

"That's right. You murdered him," said the beefy man. "Now, our chief doesn't like people getting away with things like that and he is very angry that it was his son. You see, it was his eldest son, one of his favourites."

"His eldest son was a killer," said Macleod.

"So you say!" said the whippet.

Outside the rain fell harder, and the noise in the adjoining bar became louder, with the stamping of feet and singing reaching fever pitch.

"And what do you want from us then?" asked Macleod.

"Oh, you will surrender," said the beefy man. "You will kneel on the floor here in front of me and I'll bind your hands and then we will see what happens."

"I'll not yield to you," said Macleod.

"Is that right?" said the whippet.

Macleod sensed a nervousness about them and in that instant recognized the beefy man in front of him was the one he encountered in Reynolds lane in Sydney. As his eyes adjusted to the darkness, he could see the teeth missing. He sensed the unease in the man.

"Oh, you see me now," said the beefy man. "Well, I'll not be taking a beating again from you Macleod. So you will be kneeling and my friend here will be binding your hands and then we will see what happens."

Macleod took a step forward and the beefy man stepped back. The whippet took his filet knife forward and placed it near McDermott's face.

"Oh, I wouldn't do that," he said. "You don't want your little friend here hurt any more do you?"

Macleod weighed the situation. He knew that if he yielded McDermott and he were finished. The methods of the push were never moderate. If he knelt and was bound he was signing their death warrants.

Deciding to take them on, he took two rapid steps forward but halted as the whippet took the fillet knife and plunged it into McDermott's right eye. McDermott groaned as the vitreous drained out, the right eye closing as blood seeped down his cheek.

"Now you don't want your boy blind, as well as no ears, do you?" asked the whippet. "He may just get out of this alive but *you need* to yield."

There was no other way out. Macleod nodded acquiescence and put his hands up.

"No more," he said to the whippet who held the knife. "No more."

Dutifully the whippet man put the knife down by his side, indicating that Macleod should kneel. McDermott's head was down on his chest and Macleod was not sure if he had passed out.

He dropped to his right knee and then his left knee and put his arms forward.

"No, no..." said the beefy man, "behind your back."

He had a piece of twine in his hands and Macleod put his hands behind his back and the beefy man carefully walked toward him, clumsily fumbling the twine in his hands as he moved around behind Macleod.

"Now, nice and easy, hands together," he said.

Macleod seized the moment. He lurched forward before his hands were bound and rolling onto his left side came up fast, right fist poised striking the whippet man blunt on the nose. He yowled in pain as his nose splintered and Macleod brought his knee up, breaking his jaw in one movement. The beefy man was moving behind him, and he turned, grasping the whippet man's hand with the knife in it plunging it up beneath the beefy man's ribs. He sagged, the knife going deep, staggering backward and falling heavily onto the floor. Outside the rain pelted down and the maelstrom of sound from man and nature, coupled with the noise of music from the bar, became deafening.

The beefy man was down and jerked on the floor. Macleod made to move toward him, to make sure he was finished but at that moment he felt a tightness around his throat as the whippet man closed a piece of twine around his neck. He was a wiry small man but strong for his size and his breath smelled of whisky and rotting gums as he breathed into Macleod's ear. His voice was garbled, drops of blood spitting onto Macleod's face from his broken jaw and streaming nose.

"When I'm finished with you, I'll make sure I kill the boy slow, piece by piece," he hissed.

The rope tightened. In front of him, Macleod saw the beefy man twitch his last, death claiming him. The world was swimming in front of him, the whippet pulling tighter as Macleod put his hands up, scrabbling at the rope, attempting to loosen it. Instead of straining forward he pushed backs that there was a second where the twine was loosened and he had a moment to turn and grasp, bringing his elbow around and striking the whippet in the right temple. His assailant stunned momentarily, Macleod released himself, as the whippet pulled another knife from his jacket pocket, his bloodstained shirt testament to the beating he'd already received from Macleod.

He advanced toward Macleod and Macleod took his own knife from his pocket and they stood transfixed for a moment, knife hands outstretched, weighing each other. In the candlelight Macleod glanced to look at McDermott who was conscious and watching the action, his right eye closed. The whippet and Macleod were frozen in time, the bar next door reaching its thudding crescendo as the rain drummed outside rhythmically.

The whippet stepped forward first and Macleod stepped aside, parrying the thrust with his arm and punching the whippet three times in quick succession in the face. He staggered back, but he was wiry and tough and shaking his head, filled with rage, he lunged forward at Macleod. Macleod grasped his knife arm and pulled him forward, smashing the hand over his knee so that the man's knife clattered to the floor. In the blink of an eye, the whippet had turned and had kneed Macleod in the stomach, doubling him over. Macleod fell to the floor, catching his breath, his knife hand on the floor. When he looked up, the whippet had recovered and had regained his knife and was advancing towards him at speed. He launched at Macleod, toppling him over and straddling him, and in the melee Macleod's knife clattered off to the side. He was pinned on the ground as the whippet pressed down on him, bringing the knife closer to his face. Drops of blood from the man's mouth and bleeding nose splattered onto his face as the whippet's gruesome visage was silhouetted above him in the candlelight, pushing closer and closer as the knife tip reached Macleod's neck. Macleod wrested his right hand free and brought it up into the whippet's stomach, doubling him over and, grabbing the knife, he turned him over and in one quick movement plunged the knife into his neck. Blood squirted onto the ground, great arterial spurts as the whippet put his hand to his neck to stop the bleeding. Surprised and horrified, he lay flat on his back, looking up at Macleod, pleading.

Macleod stood up, realizing that nothing could be done to prevent him dying and watched as his life slowly ebbed away, the blood pumping out of him. After a moment he was still and the rhythmic thudding of feet next door and rain stopped as if nature and man had sensed the dreadful thing that had happened. Then it began again, on cue, the rain and drumming of the feet and the fiddle next door drowning out the murder.

Macleod went over to McDermott. "Are you with me, boy?" McDermott nodded. "You're tough. I'll give you that," said Macleod.

"I'm sorry," said McDermott. "They were in the room when I came here. They got me before I could do anything."

"It's all right," said Macleod. "You did your best. Let me untie you."

The knots binding McDermott's hands were a mess. He searched around on the floor for a knife and found his that had clattered away and slit the bonds, placing the knife back in his pocket.

"Let me look at you," said Macleod. The earlobe had stopped bleeding and dried blood was spattered over his neck on the right side. The eye was closed.

"We'll need to get something to bind those up, then we'll have to deal with these bodies."

Macleod looked at his jacket. There was blood on him and he took the jacket off so as not to arouse suspicion. Underneath his shirt was clean, the jacket having taken the sprays of blood.

"Wait here," he said to McDermott. He walked into the corridor and Nell was there.

"Is everything all right Mr. Macleod?" she asked.

"Yes Nell, but I will need some linen strips for bandages. McDermott has cut himself using a knife to slice food."

"I'll bring something and some water. Can I help?"

Macleod put his hand out. "No, we don't need any help but thank you."

He went back into the room, leaving Nell to fetch the items. The blood from the whippet had pooled.

"We need to move," Macleod said. "We can use the jute bags and wrap them."

"Where will we take them?" asked McDermott. "We can't cover this up."

Macleod nodded, understanding he would need to explain the nature of things to McDermott.

"Reporting this at this point would give us no advantage. Our best course is to bury these bodies and forget that they were here. By the time the morning comes this place will be cleaned and the two gentlemen that were here would have returned to Sydney, their business finished."

"But Mr. Macleod that's...."

"That's the way of things," interrupted Macleod. "It's how it has to be."

McDermott nodded. There was a knock at the door. Macleod went out, closing the door behind him and took the items of warm water and bandages from Nell.

"Thank you, Nell."

"Will you be requiring dinner later?" she asked.

"No thank you," he said. "We've had something to eat together in the room here. We are exhausted. Our guests will stay with us, on the floor."

"Can I get them anything? Food or...."

"No, they won't be requiring anything. Thank you very much. They must leave very early in the morning but I'll be sure to look after them."

Nell paused, not understanding what Macleod had said and wondering why he was refusing her hospitality, but she knew better to ask anything further. She bowed her head and walked back to the din at the bar.

The music and stamping continued as Macleod cleaned McDermott, wiping the blood away. He bandaged the eye and ear and McDermott took a clean shirt.

"We need to bury this shirt with them," he said. "Your jacket?" asked McDermott.

"I'll wash it. I don't have another and I need it with the weather here. There is plenty of water around at the moment," Macleod said, nodding to the rain outside.

They took the jute bags from their bed and, laying them open, lifted the beefy man in first, moving his knife and placing it on his stomach. He was heavy and his head lolled around as they lifted him into the jute bag and bundled him up.

"Use the twine McDermott, we'll tie him up."

His feet stuck out at the bottom but they managed to cover his head. The whippet was easier, lighter and much easier to manage. They wrapped him likewise, his feet sticking out the bottom and the knife from his neck placed on his chest and wrapped in the jute shroud. They moved him over next to the other man, their bodies side-by-side.

Macleod got on his hands and knees and used the rags that Nell had supplied to clean the blood from the floor. It took him some time and by the time he had finished the rags were blood-soaked but all signs of the struggle had been erased from the room.

Macleod opened the jute bags and threw the bloody rags into them, bundling the crime clean-up in with the crime.

The noise in the bar continued.

"We will need to get rid of this water," said Macleod. "Bring my jacket."

Macleod looked out into the corridor and seeing no one he hurried along with the dish, moving out to where the rain was pouring down and tipped it out on to the earth. The pouring rain soaked it in immediately, dispersing the blood and the evidence. Macleod dipped it in the horse trough, cleaning away any remaining blood. Standing in the rain, he washed his jacket in the horse trough, rivulets of blood flowing from it and onto the ground. Satisfied that he and McDermott were clean and the crime scene was secure, he returned to the room.

The noise in the bar continued but he could hear Patrick calling Nell to calm the men and he knew that soon all would soon retire to bed. The hour was getting late, and the rain continued to fall.

Merciful cover.

Not a word passed between them over the next two hours as they waited in silence. The bodies of the men that had been slain lay mute on the floor. At length, the noises in the bar and scuffling of feet settled as the time approached eleven. Macleod stole out of the door into the main inn, checking that all had been cleaned and put away. Bridget O'Donnell, Nell, and Patrick were nowhere to be seen.

He went out to the front of the building, calming the horses and taking them around to the side before saddling and putting the bridles on them. The rain continued to fall, less heavy now, but still steady as the droplets dripped from his hat. He crept back inside and he and McDermott took the whippet first. Macleod carried the head end and McDermott the feet, carrying the body to the horses and laying it over the saddle so it was balanced evenly.

"With me," said Macleod.

They left the body; the horse taking the weight without complaint. The beefy man was heavy, and they struggled, his body swinging backward and forwards as they grappled with him up the hallway and out onto Macleod's horse. The horse protested the weight but then acquiesced.

"Wait here," said Macleod, nodding to McDermott.

As Macleod moved back inside he checked the inn, noting no witnesses, and then stole back to their room to check that all was clean. The bowl was unsoiled, and they had removed all traces of blood from the dirt floor. He was satisfied, and he shut the door, content that if any in the house wandered into the room, they would find nothing amiss. To be sure, he locked the door. He walked out the front, as the rain eased, now becoming a fine mist. Taking the reins, they led the horses south along the road and back into the darkened bush.

The rain softened and then stopped, with clouds parting and the moon shining brightly. Nature was removing its concealment after the deed that had taken place and shining strong moonlight on the aftermath.

 They trudged on for an hour, following a bush track by the soft light of the moon, before arriving at a suitable place within a valley, surrounded by trees.

"This will do," said Macleod. They tied the horses up to the trees and Macleod, taking the spade he had lifted from Reynella, dug into the soft moist earth.

"We've got 'til dawn, "said Macleod. "Best we get to work,"

McDermott was looking up at the moon. McDermott did not answer, his left eye fixed on the orb in the sky.

"McDermott!" hissed Macleod.

McDermott looked at him blankly and nodded, holding his hand out to take the spade. Macleod handed it to him and McDermott dug, taking his shift. They took it in shifts over the next hours toward the dawn, digging graves deep enough that animals could not disturb the bodies. Once the side-by-side holes were completed, they heaved the bodies in, the soft earth yielding easily to the spade as they took turns in piling the dirt back on. The morning birds twittered, signalling that dawn would soon arrive.

Macleod stood watching as McDermott piled the last of the dirt. As he was watching, he heard a movement in the bush. Suspecting an animal, he looked up and beyond a great ghost gum in the distance, he saw a shadow moving. There was a low growling. McDermott sensed it as well and stopped his work, looking to Macleod, questioning. They both stood silent for a moment as the growling intensified and then stopped. It was replaced by a low hiss then a shape darted, so rapid they could barely discern the blur. But both Macleod and McDermott saw it. A streak of red, a pale body, racing through the undergrowth, hissing as it went crashing through the bush and then disappearing.

McDermott looked at Macleod and Macleod nodded.

"Must have followed us," said McDermott. "And you say you don't believe in ghosts Inspector."

He smiled, almost a sneer, after he spoke, and then laughed. Macleod eyed him carefully, weighing his state of mind. McDermott's shoulders twitched as his laugh came to a halt, and his voice became vacant, as he stared at the lightening sky.

The words hung heavily in the air as they rolled stones and boulders over the graves and scattered leaves and bark to cover the crime. As they completed the task the light of dawn was beginning. They led the horses back down over the rough ground with the kookaburra signalling the rise of the sun and a whip bird calling in the distance. As they took their horses on to the track, the darkness dispelled just before the sun touched the horizon. Ravens gathered in the trees above and called to Macleod and McDermott as they travelled along the dusty bullock track, their shoulders sagging, heavy with the crime they had committed.

16

Macleod awoke to the smell of bacon cooking, and he could feel the rustling of feet in the adjacent dining room as drovers dragged themselves from their alcohol induced slumber to satisfy their hunger. The wound on his neck tugged at him as he tried to sit up on the bed, dragging himself forward and upright. Dizzy for a moment he sat still with his head lowered and then, as it passed, he opened his eyes to look across at McDermott. The boy lay flat on his back on the bed, staring upward. His right eye was bandaged, the blood-soaked material dark and murky, his left eye open as he gazed at the ceiling.

Macleod stood, his right thigh grabbing him, the muscles sore as he took a step over to observe McDermott. The boy did not acknowledge him, continuing to stare at the ceiling, as if transfixed by something that was there. His mouth moved as if he was speaking but no sound came. Macleod reached down and touched him on the shoulder.

"McDermott?" he asked.

The boy shuddered and started, drawing back from Macleod as if he were a demon, and then finally recognizing him and settling back on the bed.

"Are you with me boy?" asked Macleod.

"I am," said McDermott.

"We must get that eye cleaned up. You'll need to see Collinson."

McDermott nodded and Macleod sensed that the boy was broken, his will to resist or fight bent and misshapen after his ordeal. He helped McDermott to sit, surveying the damage. The boy's earlobe where it had been severed showed proud flesh with dried caked blood. His left eye was half closed, the right covered in the murky bandage. It was the blood-stained material of a battle wound.

"Come, boy," said Macleod, "I need to get you up and get you something to eat. Then up to Boydell's so you can see the bush doctor."

A knock at the door interrupted them. Macleod quickly scanned the floor, making sure that all was in place and there were no signs of the events from the night before. Satisfied, he moved quickly toward the door and opened it a crack. Nell Bird was there, her face worried and concern etched upon her brow.

"Is everything in order Mr. Macleod?" she asked. "We are expecting you at breakfast."

"Nell, thank you. Could you be so kind and help me before we come to breakfast? I need water and more bandages for the boy. The injury was worse than I first thought and I must bandage it again this morning."

"Yes," said Nell. "But, Mr. Macleod, I must tell you that something terrible has happened overnight."

Macleod took a breath, not wanting to hear what she was about to say, fearing that someone had discovered them. He opened the door to let Nell move closer to him, uncertain what he would do if she had been a witness to the destruction of the night before.

"It's our pigs," she said. "Killed in the night in the most dreadful way. Bridget is beside herself. She says the devil is here. Patrick is inconsolable."

"What do you mean?" asked Macleod, exhaling and relieved that she did not speak of the matters from the night before.

"Someone slaughtered all of our pigs during the night."

"And you heard nothing?" he asked.

"Nothing at all," said Nell "There was no sound from the yard during the night. They slipped in silently and did it, but with such malice," she said, shaking her head. "Mr. Forest has asked for you to go up to the Boydell's this morning and report to him on the pigs and other matters," she said, nodding her head.

"We will, thank you for informing me," said Macleod, feeling increasingly relieved that Nell had no knowledge of what had transpired in that room during the previous evening storm.

"Fetch me the things I've asked for and I'll clean up McDermott. Then I'll investigate what has happened with your animals. We'll need to make haste to Boydell's afterward Nell. Could you arrange for us to take our breakfast with us?"

"Yes I can," said Nell, "I'll have something appropriate made for you that you can eat on horseback.

She bowed and left the room, not turning her back on Macleod until he had disappeared from her view, and then scuttled from the hallway and back toward the main house.

Macleod moved back to his bed and shook his jacket, damp from the night before, and turned it around him quickly. He helped McDermott with his boots, lacing them up and then keeping him upright as he put his jacket about him. He then helped him to his feet.

"Pigs..." McDermott muttered.

"Yes, we'll investigate and then I'll take you to see the bush doctor," said McDermott.

"Poor pigs..." said McDermott. "Poor little pigs."

Macleod had seen it before, in Lucknow, a young man so full of life, his mind battered by what he had seen, the madness slowly creeping in. There was no time to lament or ponder. He shuffled McDermott towards the chair, ensuring that he was sitting safely, and then turned toward the room tidying, ensuring that all was in order. He checked the floor to ensure the blood stains were erased, making the scene clean. Satisfied, he took a debreath and picked up his knife, examining the blade and ensuring it was clean, before placing it inside his clothes.

There was another knock at the door. Macleod opened the door wide, now content to let Nell into the room. She came in with a bowl of warm water, towels and bandages. As she placed the water down beside McDermott, she took a step back and put her hand over her mouth.

"He'll recover Nell," said Macleod. "He's had an accident is all."

"Will he be...?" She stopped short of asking, almost not wanting to know the answer.

"He'll mend," said Macleod. "I'll tend to him. You go now and gather Bridget and Patrick. I'll need them to come with me to see what has happened to your animals."

Nell scuttled from the room, Macleod sensing she did not want to be around the blood and madness.

He gently unwound the bandages from McDermott's face. Underneath the eyelid was closed and using his thumb he pried the lid open. The globe was flat, and the vitreous deflated.

"Can you see?" asked Macleod.

McDermott shook his head, pointing to his left eye. "Only from this one."

He carefully cleaned the damaged right eye, wiping away the blood from the boy's face and making sure he was clean. Then he applied the fresh bandage, ensuring all the blood was out of the boy's hair and he was presentable. As he bandaged, McDermott stared at the floor, not wishing or daring to speak. His bottom lip moved rhythmically as he seemed to mouth, talking to someone who wasn't there, but no sound emanated from his lips. His mouth moved constantly as he repeated a phrase, almost an incantation. Macleod completed his work and was satisfied. He tidied the bowl and helped McDermott to his feet.

As they opened the door Nell was waiting outside. "All ready," she said, "out there, near the elm tree."

"Will you come with us?" asked Macleod.

"With respect sir, I don't wish to go over there again. I've seen enough." Macleod nodded in understanding.

"Shall I keep the young man in the dining room with me?" asked Nell

Macleod thought for a moment. "No, it's best he come with me. But thank you, Nell, I appreciate your kindness."

Macleod linked his arm through McDermott's and walked him along, as the young man stared blankly ahead, and made their way along the corridor and out to the elm tree where Bridget and Patrick were waiting. Ned was absent and Macleod assumed he was down at the yard where the animals had been slaughtered. Bridget was fumbling with her rosary beads and making the sign of the cross. Something haunted Patrick, and he started as Macleod walked out.

"'Tis the devil Mr. Macleod," said Bridget. "The devil is here."

"Now Bridget, let me examine things," said Macleod.

"No, you listen to me," she said. "Nothing human would do this. Nothing that lives on this earth and created by God would do what has been done. It is the devil's work."

As she spoke she kissed the cross on her rosary beads and made the sign of the cross twice over. Patrick did the same, mirroring her gesture and fell in behind as she walked briskly, military style, toward the pig yards. Macleod gripped McDermott as his pace slowed, urging him to walk faster.

"Are you with me boy?" he asked.

"I am," said McDermott, his voice vacant and his eyes searching the bushland around for something. "It knows what we did," he whispered. Macleod knew it was no use refuting him. His mind was slipping gradually and Macleod knew of no way to stop it.

The bullock trains were being brought up by their drivers and Bridget weaved a haughty path through them, urging them to get out of the way. The drivers were craning their necks to see what the fuss was about, as Bridget and Patrick led Macleod and McDermott down the side of the house, out the back where the pig pen was. Bridget stood back, unwilling to approach the pen and Patrick stood behind her.

"There," she said, "nothing of God would do such a thing."

Macleod took McDermott to the side of the pen, placing McDermott's arms up on the rail. "Stay there," he said. McDermott nodded.

Within the pen the six pigs had been slaughtered, each of them had had their throats deeply cut and there was pig's blood spattered all over the pen, wiped in handprints on the walls. Pig's blood covered every inch of the structure, the shed, the fence, and the open gate. The intestines of the pigs had been removed and scattered about the yard, helter-skelter, thrown in anger or fury. Flies buzzed, and the stench was awful. The mutilated carcasses lay thrown about the yard; they had been hefted and hurled during the assault. As Macleod looked closer, he saw ten eyes in a line on the feeding trough. The dilated black pupils, sitting atop the white glow of the bloody flesh.

Macleod put his hand over his mouth as the stench wafted toward him. Swarms of flies were moving in now and Macleod closed his eyes. When he opened them, there were bodies of men all around him, groaning and pleading for help. They stretched their hands towards him as they lay on the stretchers within the field hospital, their uniforms ripped and torn, their bodies mutilated by musket shot and sabre, bayonet injuries baring open flesh. He staggered back as the ghostly figures attempted to rise from their beds toward him, reaching to him for help. He closed his eyes again, as Bridget's voice reached him.

"Mr. Macleod," she yelled. "Mr. Macleod."

He broke from it and when he opened his eyes, the pigs were there again. As he looked along the row of eyes, seeing them watch him in silence, he understood the message was for him.

McDermott was beginning to jibber in the background and Macleod strode over to him, grabbing him by the jaw. "Quiet now boy," he said.

McDermott whispered. "He saw us. He knows. He knows what we did. They eyes saw us. The eyes see us now." His face contorted in a grin.

"Stop it now. Stay with me boy!" said Macleod. He grabbed him by the chin and squeezed it tight. McDermott pulled back from him and shook his head, then became quiet once again.

"Macleod!" Bridget's voice was insistent.

"Do you have any enemies Mrs. O'Donnell? Anyone who would do such a thing? Patrick?"

"No-one in this district would do such a thing. No person would do such a thing. This is not the work of any animal. This is the devil himself, brought to this place by something or someone. Mr. Macleod, I can only see these things have visited upon us since you have been here and I must insist you find somewhere else to stay. That's all. You must find other lodgings."

Macleod nodded. There was no point arguing, her face was set. She blessed herself again and walked away. Patrick followed her.

Macleod took a last look at the pigpen and then stepped out to take McDermott, ushering him back.

Edward Bird was there, having saddled Macleod and McDermott's horses. He looked at Macleod suspiciously.

"Best you be off Mr. Macleod. We'll give you one more night."

"I understand," said Macleod.

As Ned handed the reins to him, Macleod took McDermott's horse as well and Ned moved quickly away from them as if to be in their vicinity would bring evil upon him. Calming his horse, Macleod helped McDermott onto his, lifting him into the saddle and ensuring his feet were in the stirrups. As he was preparing to mount Nell ran quickly from the building, carrying a small basket with her, covered by a cloth.

"I prepared this for you. I'm so sorry Mr. Macleod, but Bridget's mind is set. I tried to tell her it is not you that has brought this. This was here before you came but she won't listen."

"I understand," said Macleod.

"I'm so sorry," she said, glancing at McDermott. As if to distract herself from her thoughts, she looked to her basket. "There are scones and beef in there, and water as well. There's fortified wine if you need it. Take it with you. I've wrapped it so it will fit in the saddlebags. Please make sure Mr. McDermott eats."

"I will," he said. "Thank you." He took the items from her and put them in his saddlebag, passing a piece of the damper to McDermott. He took it from him and chewed it noisily, staring ahead as he did. Macleod took a swig of the fortified wine and then placed it in his saddlebag with the other items, taking a piece of dried beef for himself for the ride to Boydell's. As he mounted his horse, he could hear Bridget's shrill voice.

"Nell! Nell!" she was screaming.

"I best be gone," said Nell. "Don't tell Bridget about the food."

"It's our secret," said Macleod, smiling at her.

She pulled her skirts up and rushed back into the house as Bridget's shrill voice had reached screaming pitch. "Nell, where in God's name are you?" Macleod turned, taking the reins from McDermott's horse and beginning the short journey to Boydell's. As they rode away, he could feel the eyes of the drovers' on him, wary and untrusting, their suspicion heavy upon him.

17

As Macleod turned into the Boydell property, St Mary-on-Allyn loomed in the distance. The cloudless sky and sunshine failed to lift the gloom from the little church. A stableboy took the horses as Macleod helped McDermott to the ground, linking his arm in his as he pulled the boy on, taking him into the homestead. Boydell was waiting in the parlour, sitting forward in his armchair, hands clasped upon his lap. Forrest was opposite, and they spoke in low tones as Macleod and McDermott entered. They stopped talking as soon as they saw Macleod entering the room and Forrest stood.

"What happened to the boy?" he asked.

"An accident," said Macleod.

"And I don't suppose you will tell us any more about it, will you?" asked Forrest.

"There is nothing more to tell, a simple accident, that was all."

Forrest eyed him carefully and nodded his head. Macleod could feel Boydell's gaze heavily upon him.

"Do you know anything about what happened to those pigs?" asked Forrest.

"Nothing," said Macleod. "But the way they were killed....."

"I agree," said Forrest. "And your visitors had nothing to do with it?"

"They left early. They had to get back to Sydney," answered Macleod.

"And their business here?" asked Forrest.

Boydell was now standing, intently interested in the conversation. Macleod knew that he had to be careful.

"They were sent from Sydney police, on orders of the superintendent, Fosbery," lied Macleod.

"Enquiring about the progress in the investigation?" asked Forrest. "Such a long way to come when the information could be conveyed by telegram."

"Fosbery has requested that we not use the telegram to keep the gossip to a minimum. He wants the news kept silent."

Forrest nodded, weighing Macleod's story.

"And so they visited...and?"

"We passed on the information regarding the investigation and they have conveyed it back to headquarters in Sydney."

"And they left on horseback?" asked Forrest.

"On foot," said Macleod. "They were to pick up with one of the bullock drays on the way back to Paterson."

Forrest nodded again, staring intently at Macleod. There was a heavy silence in the room as Boydell and Forrest regarded each other, an imminent decision hanging in the air, but unable to proceed, they both relented, accepting Macleod's story, or at least knowing that pursuing an alternate version was not possible. Macleod changed the subject quickly.

"The boy has been injured. A branch went through his eye while he was riding last night. I've bandaged it best I can but he will need to see Collinson."

"I'll have him sent for," said Boydell. "And your wound Macleod?"

"Much better thankyou."

"Well, he can look at that too while you are here."

"The pigs?" asked Forrest. "Our murderer?"

"Most likely," said Macleod. "The scene is mayhem. Pieces of the animals ripped to shreds, eyes removed."

Boydell put his hand to his head. "My God! What have we done to have this visited upon us?"

"There's something else," said Forrest. "At the O'Malley farm last night... Eamon O'Malley." Forrest stopped and looked at Boydell. Boydell nodded, indicating for him to go on. "The family found his body this morning."

"And?" asked Macleod.

"Murdered," said Forrest.

"And the details?" asked Macleod.

"Bite marks, fresh. They found the body on the O'Malley property this morning and sent a rider, their son, to bring the news."

Macleod's shoulders stooped, and he looked at the floor, the notion he had failed miserably, unable to halt the tide of murder despite his expertise, weighed heavily upon him.

"I've sent word to Sydney via telegraph," said Boydell.

"But..." said Macleod

"No details of the case," said Boydell. "I've requested Fosbery to allow me to hand this over to the Paterson police. The magistrate and police will be on their way."

"But you don't have jurisdiction," protested Macleod.

"The jurisdiction I require is your failure to make any impact upon this case. Murder after murder and you are no closer to finding the killer Macleod. I have no other option but to bring my people in to solve this and to stop it."

Macleod had no answer. Boydell's intervention was understandable. The town was in a panic.

"But if I can only get out to the Shea's I am sure..."

"You'll do no such thing," said Boydell. "You will go with Forrest, investigate and report your findings back on the O'Malley property and this afternoon the Paterson police will take this over and you will return to Sydney."

"But they don't know what they are dealing with," said Macleod.

"Neither do you," said Boydell. "You said you know this thing, and you saw it hanged. So how can it be here again? How is a thing that is dead, that you saw dead, here? How could such evil visit again from beyond the grave?"

"When we spoke yesterday a telegram indicated that an individual was transferred to the Shea property," said Macleod.

"Yes," Boydell answered impatiently.

"If only I can go out and question the Shea's..."

Boydell put his hand up and cut Macleod off. "You are finished, Macleod. Your time is up here. Do as I ask you. Collison will look after McDermott and see to your wound and then you and Forrest will travel to the O'Malley property and prepare a report, give ascent for burial of their son and be back here to return to Sydney. Are my instructions clear?"

"They are clear sir," said Macleod.

Boydell turned and left the room. Collinson readily appeared, flustered and breathless, having made his way as quickly as he could. "I will see to you now Mr. Macleod, and Mr. McDermott," said Collinson, trying to hide the shock on his face at McDermott's' appearance.

"Mid-morning is approaching," said Forrest, "and I would like to be on the road in an hour."

"You shall be sir," he said.

Forrest eyed Macleod carefully and then turned and walked from the room. Collinson gestured for Macleod and McDermott to join him in the study that was off the main area. Macleod sat heavily on the chair in the corner as Collinson helped McDermott to the table, placing a roll under his head and gently removing the bandages.

"I will tend to you in a moment Mr. Macleod," he said, "but I think Mr. McDermott needs my help more urgently. What is the nature of the injury?"

"A branch into the eye when we were riding," said Macleod. "It pierced the eyeball."

Collinson unwound the bandages as McDermott stared blankly at the ceiling, expressionless and mute.

"Be still son," said Collinson. McDermott nodded but did not speak, his limp body pressed against the table and his head loose upon the support. Collinson pried open the right eyelid with his fingers. "My God, the eye is lost. He is at risk of infection. I'll have to get it out. If I leave the globe in the wound will turn putrid and he could die. I will have to eviscerate the eye contents."

"Can you manage it?" asked Macleod.

"I'll have to manage it," said Collison. "McKinlay showed me. I've seen it done at least twice."

"But you've never done it?" said Macleod.

"By the time we get him over to McKinlay in Dungog it will be putrid. There is no chance he would survive."

"Then do it," said Macleod.

"You will need to hold him," said Collison. Macleod stood from his chair and came over and placed as much weight as he could on the boy's shoulders and arms. McDermott did not move, submitting completely to the mutilation of his eye and the trauma that would follow. Collinson removed a surgical implement from a canvas roll. He took a bottle of spirits from a side-table and poured it on McDermott's eye. McDermott hissed and tried to move his head but Collinson held firm. Collinson looked at Macleod. "Hold him, hold him tight."

Macleod pressed his weight heavily onto McDermott. The boy struggled as Collinson pried open the eye and plunged the sharp instrument in, twisting and turning it. McDermott screamed and Macleod held him as firmly as he could, his body writhing as the sharp implement removed the contents of his eye. Collinson moved quickly and in moments vitreous, iris and the globe were removed with the extra-ocular muscles left and the eye socket clean.

"Hold him," he said urgently to Macleod, pouring alcohol once again into the wound. McDermott hissed and screamed but then lost consciousness, falling limp on the table.

"Are you finished?" asked Macleod.

"It's done," said Collison. "It's less likely now to turn putrid. It's been cleaned with alcohol but we need to keep it bound up and he needs to stay here with me. He can't travel. Quickly, I'll bind him up while he is unconscious.

Taking fresh dressing, Collinson cleaned and bound the young man as he lay unconscious, his head flopping back and forth as the bandage went around his head. Having finished, Collinson dressed his ear. He asked no questions of Macleod regarding the injury but cleaned it with alcohol, ensuring that it would not become gangrenous. Having finished, he placed the boy's hands over his chest so, corpse-like, he lay quietly on the table.

"Take off your shirt," said Collinson. "I need to see that wound."

Macleod dutifully removed his shirt and sat with his arms on the table.

"There is still some redness there. I need to open it again to get the muck out and clean it."

"Do what you have to," said Macleod.

Macleod winced as Collinson cut once again across the wound and he felt a sudden release as the collection of pus and muck squirted out onto his back. "This will hurt," said Collison, digging down into the wound and Macleod felt he was piercing him down through his chest. He then doused the area liberally with spirits before binding Macleod. "It's cleaner. There's still muck there, but it will not turn putrid. I'll need to dress it again tomorrow."

Macleod nodded, grateful for the attention of the bush doctor.

"Will you look after the boy?" asked Macleod.

"I'll care for him physically but I'm no expert in matters of the mind." said Collinson.

Macleod nodded, taking his meaning, but did not respond. McDermott's mental state weighed heavily upon him and he doubted that he could keep his promise of returning the boy physically and mentally well to his mother.

"Mr. Forrest is waiting outside," said Collinson. "You best be off."

Macleod took the spirits from the cabinet and drank a deep draught, and then handed it to Collinson. Collinson placed the bottled into a saddlebag. "Take it with you," he said.

Macleod said no more, gratefully taking the bottle and turned to walk outside where Forrest was waiting. The stableboy handed him the reins of his horse and Forrest did not speak, turning his horse as Macleod mounted, showing that he should follow. The sun was high in the sky as they moved down the track toward the scene of the crime at the O'Malley's farm.

18

The afternoon sun blinded Macleod as their horses turned into the O'Malley property. The barn and homestead were quiet. There was no wind and the crops in the fields were motionless, a sense of mourning gripping the place.

In silence, Forrest and Macleod wound their horses up the dirt track, tethering them next to the barn and dismounting, carefully approaching the homestead. Patrick O'Malley stepped out with a musket and pointed it at them. His eyes were wild, and he glanced anxiously around and across the fields. Satisfied, he lowered the musket and beckoned the policemen to approach. Macleod could hear weeping from the adjacent room.

"I told you," said, Patrick. "And when I bury my boy, I'm going over to the Shea's to settle."

"You'll do no such thing," said Forrest. "I'll be keeping the law in this town and if I hear any whiff you've gone over to the Shea's I'll lock you up Patrick."

Patrick gritted his teeth, sneering at Forrest, but Macleod sensed that the man knew better than to break the law.

"Well then, you should be over there," said Patrick.

"And I will do my duty, and you will leave that to me," said Forrest. "Put the musket away and take us to see your son."

At the mention of his son Patrick O'Malley's shoulders sagged, he dropped the musket to the ground and wept. Grief enveloped him. Macleod and Forrest waited, allowing him time, and as he recovered he shrugged as if nothing had happened, and led them to the kitchen where the boy's body was laid out on the table. He had been cleaned and dressed in his best. His arms were folded upon his chest. His only pair of shoes were on his feet. Forrest stepped forward. Macleod could see the ragged tracks on the face and arms. Forrest opened the boy's shirt and nodded. Macleod did not need to ask.

"Who found him?" asked Forrest.

"I did," said Patrick.

"Where?"

"Over near the barn this morning," he said.

"And when did you last see him?" asked Forrest.

"Last night. He went to bed early. He'd had a big day in the field. We spoke briefly after supper and there he was safe and sound."

"And nothing happened during the night?" asked Forrest.

"No," said Patrick, his left hand gently brushing his son's arm. "Nothing at all."

"And then you found him?" asked Forrest, leading O'Malley on.

"I went out early to the barn to check on the animals and found him inside. He was..." O'Malley choked and could not speak anymore. Forrest allowed him a moment but continued on.

"You saw no one?"

"Nothing," he said.

"No one about the property you didn't know?"

"Don't be stupid!" O'Malley spat. "I'd know if someone was here. I would have seen them. There was no one. We need to bury him Mr. Forrest so that he can be resurrected in heaven. Will you give us permission?"

"I'll notify the priest," said Forrest. "You can bury him as soon as you are able."

With nothing left to say Forrest and Macleod exited the room. Patrick stayed behind for some time and as they waited, they could hear the howling of Eamon's mother.

Macleod felt her grief heavy upon him, as if he was responsible. He turned away to escape the sound. O'Malley reappeared soon after, and Forrest and he spoke in low tones as Macleod contemplated the farm outside. The two men spoke for some time before Forrest retreated from the conversation, joining Macleod and urging him to the veranda outside.

"We will talk by the horses," he said. "He's convinced it is someone out at the Shea's, but I've warned him not to go out there."

"It's a good thing. We don't want vigilantes muddying the waters," said Macleod.

"Not that they could be any muddier," said Forrest, looking at Macleod. "Now we take our findings back to Boydell and tomorrow you return to Sydney."

Macleod nodded.

"You're finished here, Macleod."

Forrest turned to mount his horse and as he did Macleod moved swiftly, striding across, removing his knife from his clothing and striking Forrest at the base of the neck with the butt. Forrest became limp almost immediately and Macleod struck him again, his body falling down behind the horse, one foot still in the stirrup. The horse whinnied and Macleod steadied it as he unhooked Forrest's boot and then dragged him into the barn. He checked that the man was still breathing and, sure he was alive, he brought the horse inside as well and hid it beside Forrest's unconscious form. He knelt down beside him.

"I'm sorry Forrest," he said.

Moving out he mounted his horse, surveying the property. Seeing no signs of any witnesses he turned his horse down the O'Malley track and onto the main. He urged the horse along the bullock track, down toward Eccleston.

As the sun was low on the horizon he passed the chapel and spurred the horse along until they reached the entrance to the Shea property. Turning along the track, the horse cantered up towards the property, and Kitty Shea was waiting outside the slab hut. Her plump form a shadow silhouetted by the setting sun, her brown hair pulled back tight, and hands folded in front of her. It was as if she knew that Macleod was coming for her.

19

Macleod dismounted from his horse as Kitty Shea stood unmoving, her gaze fixed upon him. They squared off at the front of the slab hut, she an immovable object, protecting her flock. She waited for him to speak.

"I fear that you have not been as truthful as you could have been Mrs. Shea," said Macleod.

"In what way would that be inspector?" she said.

"There is someone who has been staying here," said Macleod.

"I don't know what you mean," said Kitty Shea, lifting her chin, so she looked down her nose at Macleod.

"Well, perhaps I'll speak to your husband," said Macleod.

"You'll do no such thing," said Mrs. Shea. "My husband is busy and has no time to speak with you. You'll speak with me or no one," she said pursing her lips.

He noticed that she was wringing her hands and her lower lip was trembling, anxiety and fear betrayed by her gestures.

"Boydell had a telegraph," said Macleod slowly. "It says an individual was delivered to Eccleston, to the Shea family. An individual with flaming red hair and pale skin."

Kitty Shea's face became white and then ashen. "I know of no such thing," she said. "The telegram was wrong."

"I'll tell you my theory," said Macleod. He saw that she was breathing rapidly, and he pressed his advantage home. "I would say you had a sister who lived in London. I would guess that she died from consumption some years back."

Kitty Shea's face contorted with abject horror as Macleod continued.

"And I would guess that she was married to a man who hanged for murder and that when she died, the sons disappeared and her daughter went to an orphanage. Through the goodwill of people in England, they found you even though you had come all the way here to New South Wales to escape from the stigma, to escape the prejudice of those who knew what your sister had married. For your family's sake, you moved all the way here, all the way to the end of the world. And here you could escape the prejudice, the knowing looks and the low voices talking about you. But no matter how much you tried to hide they found you and they sent the child here, to you." Kitty Shea was rocking backward and forwards now. The weight of the truth was upon her. Macleod said no more but waited.

"She came here," said Kitty. "I've tried to keep her from trouble. She would not stay in the house and she looked so much like him, I could barely..." she stopped. "I could barely look at her because she reminded me so much of *him*. When she came here, she was in a dress with her monstrous face, those eyes, the pale skin. She was like his ghost, haunting me. I tried to keep her in the house but she was better in the lean-to. She was like an animal. She killed the chickens and tortured the animals, so we kept her here outside."

"Where?" said Macleod.

Kitty Shea looked at the ground.

"Answer me," he said.

Kitty Shea pointed to the lean-to that Macleod had inspected previously where the bones had laid. "In there, during the day. At night she roamed. I know not what she did."

Macleod could barely comprehend the complicity and willingness to cover up. He shook his head at her and pivoted, striding towards the lean-to. The sun was setting and darkness was enveloping the slab hut and barn. Macleod pushed inside, using the fading light to guide him. There were bones there as before, and two jute sacks used as bedding. He searched quickly with his hand along the roof and along the ground but there was nothing, no clue that would help him. He stood quietly regarding the place, feeling it. Then he noted in the corner that ants were crawling in unusual numbers, crawling moving and writhing. Stooping, he took his knife from his pocket and dug into the earth. The earth gave way easily, a sod of grass covering the area loosely and he pulled it aside. Underneath ants swarmed over a wooden box, a box that would have held goods at some point, but now held something altogether more sinister. He brushed aside the ants with his knife as they swarmed over the box. He swallowed. In his mind, he knew what was inside but did not want to see it. His memory was full of horrors and he did not wish to add to them but to complete his task he knew that he must go ahead. He pried the lid with his knife and turned it exposing the contents. Inside ants swarmed. Human parts, strips of flesh, were roughly strewn inside the box, jumbled together as the ants feasted on the human remains. Macleod closed his eyes, shaking, he took the lid and placed it on the box before lifting it gently out of the ground, so as not to disturb the hideous contents. Ants swarmed along his hands and arms as he lifted it and carried it outside of the lean-to and toward the house. He strode along, the ants now crawling to his elbows and up to his arms, as they swarmed around flesh and blood.

Kitty Shea was waiting, her mouth open in horror. Macleod put the box on the ground and flipped the lid off, pointing. Kitty Shea fell back, stumbling backward along the veranda of the slab hut until her back hit the timber and she sank down until she was sitting, her right hand to her mouth and eyes wide.

Macleod took a cloth from his saddlebag and wrapped the box tightly. Once it was secure, he placed it in his saddlebag, securing the evidence.

"Now tell me where she is," he said.

Kitty Shea was mute, her hand still over her mouth as if she wanted to scream but could not.

"Stand up woman!" he said, dragging her to her feet. "Tell me where she is! She has the blood fever and if I don't stop her, she will murder again tonight."

"I don't know where she is. By night she disappears," said Kitty Shea, her voice returning. "I don't know where she goes."

"I know." A voice came from the left and Kitty's husband, Richard, stepped out of the slab hut. "I'll show you," he said.

Kitty looked at him and shook her head.

"No Kitty," he said. "It's time to end this now. We need to walk inspector. The horses won't go there."

The shadows of the night were encroaching as Macleod followed Richard Shea down past the barn and down the bank toward the river. They walked in silence, Macleod not wishing to question the man but understanding his complicity. As they approached the river, Richard turned to the left, following the line of trees along the riverbank. The shadows deepened as they reached a crossing and Richard guided Macleod across the river boulders until they reached the other side. They walked on to the long grass as the sun set and evening began; the moon beginning to show itself and stars appearing in the sky. Readily they approached a small clearing surrounded by trees. Within there was a lean-to and Macleod could see bones of animal strewn here and there. There were remnants of a fire but the place was deserted.

"This is where she stays during the night," he said. "She must be abroad somewhere."

"Where?" asked Macleod, turning to Richard and grasping his shirt. "Where is she?"

"I don't know her whereabouts during the night Inspector. I only know that she comes back here when she has prey, an animal that she has killed. She dismembers it here. If you wait long enough, she'll be back."

"Then we wait," said Macleod. "Are you armed?" he asked.

"I have a knife."

"Good enough. You at that side of the clearing and me on this side. We wait until she returns. We'll take her alive if we can," said Macleod.

"Mr. Macleod," said Richard, "I must warn you she is violent. She will not be easy to take."

"Take your side of the clearing and be on the ready," said Macleod.

As the darkness fell Macleod settled between two fallen trees at the side of the clearing out of sight. As he waited, two ravens landed on the tree above him and croaked, as if to signal and warn of his presence. Taking a nearby stone he threw it at them and dispersed them, and then settled down to wait as the night sounds of the forest surrounded him.

20

The stench from the ragged shelter confronted Macleod as he stepped in through the tent flap, peering into the gloom of the makeshift hospital. As his eyes adjusted, he saw the mess of stretchers strewn about the room. Bodies scattered here and there, half on the stretchers and half off. He saw colleagues and friends, those who were succumbing to their injuries slowly, as the tide of blood ebbed from them, their lives slipping away. He recognized a young corporal, his lower limb torn away by cannon shot, the ragged flesh seeping blood. He reached out to Macleod, pleading for help. Elsewhere, the corpses of those that had died from cholera, their pinched faces and hollow sockets telling the tale of their terrible dehydration, witness to their suffering, while others were still to succumb. Their muffled groans filled the room, some lying on the floor where no stretchers were available, left to die in their own filth as the death claimed them.

Macleod wound his way through the stretchers as hands grasped at his uniform, pulling him this way and that, as he forced his way toward the corner. He did not know what he was searching for but something was drawing him to the far corner. Something was pulling him there. He walked halfway across the room and looked down to see a captain trying to whisper to him, his bloody throat and smashed jaw preventing intelligible speech. He reached to Macleod and then, giving up, laid back and died, succumbing to his wounds.

The stench of stool and blood, fear and sweat became overwhelming as he pushed his way through the stretchers, making his way to whatever horror was in the far corner of the tent. There was something standing there in the shadows, beckoning him, dragging him to it. It swayed malevolently in the shadows, close to the bodies strewn on the floor near it, all around it was dead. The faces of the once living young men, eyes open, mouths slack with dehydration or musket ball wounds laid as mute testimony to his inaction, his inability to save anyone.

Macleod took another step and then saw what it was. It was smiling, its sharp yellow teeth gleaming from the shadow and pink eyes regarding him with contempt. The red hair was there, ethereal, floating about its head and then its fingers extended toward him, pointed yellow nails. In its hand it held the flesh of its victims, holding them towards him as if he was complicit in his failure to stop the murders and was part of them. It beckoned him to join it and when he resisted it pulled back and came forward towards him with unnatural speed, its arms held out toward him to embrace him, mouth open with drool spilling from the bottom lip. It embraced him, enfolding him as if he and it were one.

Macleod took a sharp breath, held it for a moment, uncertain of his surroundings or of his own mind. He lay deathly still, staring. He felt the pressure of the twin trees either side of him, the brush at his back. There was a cloudless sky above with twinkling stars and the full moon was bright, a blue hue saturating the eucalypt bushland. He could not guess at the time or how long he had been asleep. He listened intently for any sound before deciding whether he should move. He took shallow breaths, not daring to make any noise. The bush was silent and the floor of the eucalypts provided hiding places from the evil in the forest.

There was a low hiss. At first, he thought a snake, but it was more than that, a low hiss and growl, soft footfalls across the clearing. It was coming towards him slowly, stealthily and measured. He swallowed and held his breath. He moved his right hand and realized his knife was out of reach and to move would give his position away. He closed his eyes and kept his breathing shallow as to make no noise, and listened as the footfalls drifted towards him. The slow measured crack, the deliberateness of the footfalls continued and the low hiss became a constant growl. The footsteps stopped, and the growling ceased. Macleod stopped breathing, breath held in hope, a talisman against discovery.

For an eternity he held, daring not to breathe as the silence of the eucalypts surrounded him. And then the footfalls retreated slowly. There was a low hiss as the creature moved away. As he listened, the footfalls further retreated and then were gone.

An age passed before he moved. He laid stock still, staring at the eternal sky and the twinkling lights of the everlasting stars, waiting for the moon to shift, to be certain danger had passed. Then slowly he moved, his right arm first and then the left, feeling the tightness over his back where the wound was still seeping. His right leg resisted him as he tried to move, but he forced it, breathing through the pain, turning to his right side and peering over the tree that had hidden him. The clearing was empty, save for a formless shape lying toward the outer side. Slowly, stealthily, he pushed himself to his knees and then stood, the dizziness from being supine so long making him wait, and then allowing him to step out of his hiding place and softly into the clearing.

He scanned the bush and listened carefully, on high alert, adrenaline flowing and senses sharp. He stepped carefully across the clearing, measuring his footfalls to make the least sound, his knife drawn in defence. The shape at the other side of the clearing became clearer as he walked toward it. Richard Shea was lying on his back, his legs and arms spread-eagled with his throat cut viciously, at least three slashes, a frenzy. He had been bitten savagely on the face and chest.

MacLeod searched the man's body and took his knife. As he stood he scanned the bush once again, but there was no sound or sign of movement. He contemplated his position carefully. There was no chance that he could make it back in the darkness and he realized that he would have to make the best of it for the night, keeping himself safe.

As he contemplated a low hissing began. He twisted, searching behind him and to the left and right, but could not make out the direction of the sound. Then a low growling began, deep and guttural, becoming louder and louder as Macleod frantically searched the landscape around him for the direction of the sound.

When he finally realized that it was coming from above him, it was too late. It landed on him, arms clawing around his neck and legs sticking to his body like a spider taking its prey. He felt the piercing pain as sharp teeth bit his neck; the head of the creature moved backward and forwards savagely tearing flesh as its hands went to his eyes and clawed at them. Macleod cried out and lurched forward, throwing himself to the ground and then over on to his back so he squashed it beneath him. It let out a scream, a banshee-like yell as its arms and legs released. Taking a chunk of flesh, its head snapped back. Macleod felt the blood from his shoulders seep through his torn shirt. He leaped up from the ground, its hand grasped at his right leg, nails digging into the flesh. Macleod drew out his knife, plunging the knife into the creature's forearm, the nearest vulnerable point. It screamed as blood spurted and pulled away; the knife slicing once again at flesh; the gaping wound sending gouts of blood onto the floor of the forest as the creature rolled away and scuttled off into the brush.

Stunned, Macleod put his hand to his neck. The wound was deep and bleeding fast. He applied pressure and then, removing his shirt, he tied it around to staunch the flow. Dizzy, he stood for a moment to regain his footing and saw the trail of blood, black in the moonlight, leading off into the bush. He staggered off in the direction, following it to the edge of the clearing and then into the bush where a torrent of blood covered rock and leaves, leading him deep into the forest. He stumbled on, staggering between trees until he lost the trail, blood petering out. He stood on the leaf-strewn floor of the bush, between two enormous eucalypts, listening to the sounds of the night.

It hit him from the side, careening into him with its shoulder pressing into his ribs and taking away his breath so he hit the ground with a thump. He tried to roll over and get to his knees but it was on him again. Flailing at him, arms moving pinwheel. He was able to squeeze back and brought up his knee to kick it off so it flew across to slam into a tree. It sat at the base stunned for a moment and then crouched like an animal weighing its prey. Macleod and the creature stood opposite each other, neither moving as Macleod brought his knife forward.

She was fifteen or sixteen. Her skin was white and her eyes light, the pink reflected in the moonlight. Her dress was ragged and feet blackened, bloody. Blood from the forearm had seeped into the dress and continued to flow. But it was the long red hair that struck him. It was constantly moving, tangled, an unruly, unholy mess. It moved around her head as if powered by its own energy as she swayed. She hissed and growled and then bared her yellow pointed, serrated teeth. She was the image of her father. Macleod stood opposite her and realized that all of his sins from that day to this had brought him to this moment, facing his demon.

Without warning, she leaped toward him at an unnatural speed, leaping across the space between them in one step. Her hands went immediately to his face and eyes, sharp nails digging into the sockets. She screamed as her legs clamped around him and he flailed with the knife, slashing this way and that, making contact here and there but no blow slowed her. She dug in deeper, pushing hard into the eyeballs. Macleod felt himself fall, the ground coming to meet him as his skull smashed against the ground. The jolt released her grasp just for a moment and he brought the knife up, slashing against her side. He felt the knife plunge home, into her thigh, and she screamed as her fists pounded him in his face and nose so he was bloodied.

Now her right hand grabbed his ear, twisting and trying to tear it off. He brought the knife around, slashing at her again, this time catching her other forearm so that blood squirted on to him, soaking him, as he rolled away from her. She was flying towards him again, as if suspended by an unnatural force, flying to meet him, her red hair surrounding the pale face. He slashed at it, making contact and then slashed again, the second contact deeper, meeting more resistance. She stopped and when he opened his eyes and looked, she was standing next to a tree with her hands to her throat as blood poured out. She took her hands away for a moment and looked at them, unbelievingly, and then glared at Macleod. Blood spurted from the arterial sever, splashing across the clearing, soaking the dirt and leaves and grass of the forest floor. She fell back against the tree, still standing, and then slunk slowly down, legs splayed, hands to her throat trying to staunch the loss. She growled and hissed at Macleod as he moved toward her. He stopped, keeping his space, as he watched the life ebb from her. Her hands dropped to her side and her head bobbed, blood soaking her dress, soaking into the ground and then pooling around her body, spreading out, free at last, free to move and ebb and flow. As Macleod watched, her head bowed and body slumped, and the blood flow slowed, the supply exhausted, all the blood from her seeping on the forest floor.

As the silence of the forest surrounded him he looked at her body, head slouched and throat slashed, blood surrounding her. The night closed in on him; the sky becoming earth; the trees bending toward him, silent witness to the horror that had .

21

Macleod guided the horse gently up the slope. The early morning mist was still rising from the ground as the horse slowly made its way along the road toward Caergwrle. Occasionally the horse snorted, protesting the extra weight, and Macleod had to sooth and pat it, cajoling it to continue its journey. His neck was tight, the bite continuing to ooze and his slashed arms, the open wounds oozing blood and serum, continued to stain his ruined shirt. His hands were slick on the reins, blood slippery, making grasping the leather difficult. He felt the exhaustion, his eyes closing as he drifted in and out of consciousness as the horse slowly wound its way towards the destination. In front of him, the jute wrapped body of the girl was slung over the front of the saddle, hanging limply and swaying gently with the motion of the horse. As they came to a bend they turned right and Macleod, with a slight twitch of his knees on either side, gently coaxed the horse up the hill.

The sun was beginning to peak through the fog, the early morning chill had become part of him and had seeped into him. He had never felt so heavy. As they approached the rise he could smell wood smoke and cooking meat, perhaps it was bacon. In the distance he could just make out St Mary-on-Allyn, shrouded in the fog as the rise levelled out and the horse slowly made its way across the open stretch of ground toward the waiting men.

Forrest was there with two constables that he did not recognize, both grim faced wearing uniforms. They were large men, one beefy and ruddy, and the other taller and wiry. Their eyes were fixed upon him as the horse gently moved towards them. Macleod took his hands off the reins and raised his hands above his head in a gesture of surrender. The taller one stepped forward, walking cautiously toward the horse and taking the reins, bringing the horse alongside. Forrest took some time to speak, spending considerable time examining the horse, the body and the blood covering Macleod.

"You stay where you are Macleod," he said. "Constable, we will need to get that off."

He pointed to the body on the front of the horse and the beefy constable, his burly form moving awkwardly across the ground, walked to the front of the horse, took the body and put it over his shoulder, moving back slowly, always facing Macleod.

"Take her to St Mary-on-Allyn. There is a table set up there. Place the body on it," said Forrest.

"There is more to take in the saddle bag," said Macleod.

"Easy," said Forrest. "We'll get it."

Forrest moved cautiously along the horse and opened the saddle bag, removing the gruesome tokens. Macleod dared not move - the wiry constable holding the horse had brandished his rifle upwards and was pointing it directly at Macleod. A move in the wrong direction would mean a bullet. He heard a sharp intake of breath behind him.

"What in God's name...?" said Forrest.

"That's evidence," said Macleod. "I found that on the Shea property."

"Enough," said Forrest. "We will hear from you soon enough."

"But I need to tell you Forrest, I need to tell..."

"You don't need to tell us anything," said Forrest, moving back toward the front of the horse, wrapping the ghastly treasures back in the canvas that surrounded the box. "The Shea boy has been here this morning. We know what happened."

"But he won't have told you..."

"Quiet!" said Forrest. "There is no need to hear any more from you. I need you to get down from that horse easy."

Forrest took the reins and motioned to the wiry constable to take a step back so that he could keep a close aim on Macleod. Macleod put his arms down slowly, and as he did, gravity lent its weight, blood oozing down his arms and dripping off his hands. He took his foot out of the stirrup and put his weight on the right side, slowly dismounting, and upon reaching the dusty ground he put his hands up. The constable pointed the rifle directly at his face, motioning for Macleod to put his hands back in the air. He could see the hatred in the man's eyes and rather than looking directly at him, he chose to look at the ground so as to not challenge him.

A stable boy scurried out and Forrest gave him the reins of Macleod's horse. He led the horse away and Macleod lowered his hands slightly, the weight of holding them making him feel more heavy. The action the rifle wielding constable - startled he stepped forward and turned the butt of the gun striking Macleod on the forehead - as he was falling he struck him again on the back. Macleod felt a piercing pain and saw the ground close to him, the out of focus stones and gravel swimming before he lapsed into unconsciousness.

A searing pain woke Macleod. There was a stinging and a then a deep aching sensation in his neck. The room swam about him. Macleod's arms were splayed to the side, crucifixion pose, his arms tied so that he could not move but to expose his wounds so that Collinson could work.

"I'm sorry," said Collinson. "This will hurt. I thought I could get most of it done while you were asleep."

Macleod nodded, acquiescing and indicating to Collinson that he should continue.

"I am going to have to cut this a bit, there's something in it," he said. "I'll tend to your arms then. If I don't get this thing out it will fester and become purulent."

Macleod nodded that he understood and after pouring more alcohol into the wound on his neck Collinson dug in deep. The searing pain shot through Macleod from the base of his skull to his tailbone, he shuddered in pain, but he did not cry out. He closed his eyes as Collinson dug and toiled, turning the implement this way and that. "I'm sorry. It's deep. Perhaps we should wait."

"No, get it out," said Macleod.

"But Mr Macleod, Dr McKinlay is on his way. We have sent a telegram and called for him."

"No, I'd prefer you to get it out now, whatever it is," said Macleod.

Collinson took a deep breath and dug deeper and using a pair of forceps he pushed down so deep that Macleod could feel the pain through to his chest. "Got it!" he said and pulled it out.

Macleod heard the sound of a solid object on metal. He glanced behind him, looking over his splayed right arm and saw a whitish object in the metal dish. Its sharp form was obscured by blood but Macleod knew what it was. Collinson poured more alcohol and the burn increased, taking Macleod to screaming pitch. Then mercifully it was over and Collinson dressed the wound.

"I will still get McKinlay to look at this when he gets here later this evening from Dungog."

Macleod nodded.

"I need to do your arms as well. This won't be pleasant," he said.

Macleod looked across his left arm and saw the slashes, five or six across his left in a haphazard pattern. His palms were cut, the open flesh oozing blood. Collinson took a clean piece of cloth and poured alcohol over his left arm and hand. Macleod stiffened with the pain, the burn traveling up but then he felt the sensation in his arms dulling, as if the pain had reached a level that his body could no longer bear. The room began to swim again and he resisted falling into unconsciousness. Time slowed until it was finished and the bandages were on. He sat bare-chested as Collinson cleaned the remaining blood from him and Macleod put his head back. The beefy constable sneered at him, having witnessed and ensured that Macleod had not escaped his bonds during the procedure. He walked over and tightened them before turning to leave the room. Macleod tried to move his feet but they were tied fast, his arms splayed.

"I am sorry," said Collinson. "There is nothing I can do. It is clearly not a humane way to care for someone but these coppers from Paterson are brutal."

"I don't imagine Forrest is too pleased with me either," said Macleod.

"I won't speak for him," said Collinson.

There was silence in the room as Collinson cleaned the mess of blood and tissue from the floor and table. Macleod recognized the room. It was off the Boydell main parlour, the room where Collinson had attended to him before.

"I'm not permitted to speak to you about the case Mr Macleod."

"I understand," said Macleod, respecting Collinson's honesty.

"Boydell and Forrest have a lot of questions and I wish you well in answering them," he said, bundling up his instruments and turning to leave.

"Wait," said Macleod. "McDermott? How is he?"

Collinson stopped, keeping his back to Macleod, his form silhouetted by a candle in the room.

"Physically he is in good health. He is eating when we feed him, his eye is healing and there is no suppuration."

Macleod nodded, waiting for a further response. Collinson began shuffling toward the door.

"And the rest?" asked Macleod.

Collinson turned to him. "His mind is....his mind is not with him. He barely recognizes anyone.   He shuffles up and down the room by day and night. Mrs Boydell has helped look after him and has taken him in as one of her own but even with all of her care we can't bring his mind back."

With nothing left to say Collinson turned to leave the room and Macleod let him go. He bowed his head, his blood stained trousers framed against the dusty floor as he waited for his interrogation.

Macleod took a sharp intake of breath as the water hit him. The stocky constable was leering at him as his thinner comrade held Macleod by the hair. He threw the water in his face again. "Wake up you scumbag!" he said. "There's some questions need to be asked of you."

They roughly began untying his hands as Collinson entered the room.

"Easy gentlemen," he said. "You'll disrupt those wounds."

They ignored him and roughly untied the bonds, pulling Macleod's arms sharply behind his back, binding his hands tightly so he could feel his palms oozing as the increased pressure caused them to bleed once again. His feet were untied, and he was dragged upright to his feet, his jelly legs refusing to stand. Then half dragged and half walking he was marched out of the room into the parlour where Forrest and Boydell were sitting behind the large table. He was roughly shoved into a wooden chair and his feet tied again. His arms were tied to the back of the chair so that he could not move. He bowed his head and was slapped.

"Look up at the magistrate. Show some respect."

The ruddy constable slapped Macleod again across the face before Forrest put his hand up.

"Enough thank you constable," he said.

"Yes sir." The constable stepped back, leaving Macleod in the centre of the room as Collinson retreated.

Boydell was sitting at the table with his right elbow on the edge, palm on forehead, resting and looking down and as the mid-morning sun dispelled the fog and the rays threatened to disperse the gloom in the room, Boydell eventually spoke.

"She was a young girl Macleod. She's cut up brutally."

There was silence. Boydell put his hand to his head and looked down again, rubbing his forehead as if to dispel the images of the body from his mind. Forrest took up the conversation.

"We will need to hear your version of the events Macleod. The Shea boy, William, has told us some, but we'll need your side of the story."

Macleod related the events of the previous day, the finding of the gruesome evidence, the clearing and the fight that ensued.

"But she is only a whip of a girl," said Forrest. "Surely you could have captured her and brought her in."

"My wounds are testament to her ferocity," said Macleod. His voice was soft, almost a whisper. He almost did not want to defend himself against what he had done, for what he had become, but he knew the truth had to be told.

"She was ferocious and strong, stronger than any man I have ever fought. I thought I was going to die in that clearing, in fact I was sure of it, and I can admit to you that the slaying of her was more luck than anything else. I struck out against her as she slashed at me and caught her throat."

"And you found the body of Mr Shea?"

"Yes," said Macleod. "He had the bite marks. She must have got to him while we were waiting."

Boydell broke in. "It is against nature," he said, looking at Macleod. "How could you bring yourself to kill someone like this? She is a girl," he said, accusing Macleod. "You're a grown man and you killed a girl, slashed her throat. Whatever she did, she did not deserve death. I've heard your story Macleod but I'm not convinced of your part in this, nor am I convinced of your story."

He looked at Forrest. "When McKinlay arrives we'll have him examine the body and then inspect Macleod. We will see if he can work out from a medical perspective what the truth is."

Boydell got up to leave and Macleod took a chance. "May I see McDermott sir?" he asked.

Boydell glared at him. "Whatever you have done to that boy, you don't deserve to see him. He is ruined," he said, almost spitting at Macleod as he turned and left the room.

"Mr Forrest," said Macleod.

Forrest shook his head. "No-one is going to let you near that boy Macleod." He turned to the Paterson constables.

"Take him away."

They closed in, undid his feet and dragged him from the chair, pushing him roughly against the door jamb as he went through. He felt the pain shooting through his shoulders. They dragged him back into the ante-room, tying his feet and leaving his arms tied tight behind his back so that the engorged veins continued to ooze blood. He sat in the darkened room, the candles put out. The door slammed shut, leaving him in darkness, alone with his demons.

22

Macleod shivered, the cold seeping into his bones. He woke with a start, for a moment not being able to discern where he was, but soon adjusting to his surroundings of the cold room and darkness. He feared the darkness more than anything else and waited for the shapes to appear. Hearing noises outside, he realised his waking had been precipitated by shuffling outside the door. The door opened abruptly and the beefy constable stepped in.

"Good, you're awake," he said. "They want you back in the room for more of the hearing."

Macleod remained silent and looked at the ground. The constable hustled towards him and grabbed him roughly, shoving him forward so that the stumbled onto his knees.

"Get up! What's wrong with ya?" said the constable. He grabbed him by the arms and pulled him up straight. "Stand up!! Get up!"

Macleod could feel his hands and arms oozing again and the bite on the back of his neck seeping heavily into the cloth as blood dripped down his chest. He raised one foot and stood carefully, waiting for the blow but it didn't come. Using the butt of his rifle, the constable pushed Macleod forward, into the chair. The room was empty, the table strewn with paper. The wiry constable appeared and they stood at either side of Macleod, anticipating the other attendees.

The door opened quietly and Boydell entered, steadfastly refusing to meet Macleod's gaze. Forrest nodded at Macleod as he entered and sat at the other end of the table with Boydell in the middle. Then there was McKinlay. The gentle Dungog doctor ambled into the room, his wispy white hair making him seem ethereal in the afternoon light. Impeccably dressed, his waistcoat and suit buttoned, he folded down his cuffs as he entered the room and nodded to Macleod. Macleod could see the sympathy on his face and he nodded quickly back, before looking again to the ground.

"I'll hear further evidence from Dr. McKinlay," said Boydell, "and then further evidence from the constables from Paterson and Constable Forrest and then I'll make my decision." He glanced at Macleod. "Put a shirt on that man for proceedings."

The constable left the room and returned with one of the servant's linen shirts. He put it over Macleod's head and pulled it roughly down his back without untying his arms.

"There, now you're decent."

The blood immediately seeped into the collar of the shirt, mopping up the bodily fluids. Boydell was satisfied that Macleod was clothed enough to face the courtroom, and he began the proceedings.

"Let the record state we are hearing evidence in the case of Inspector Cormag Macleod. The charge is striking a police officer in the person of Thomas Forrest and the second charge of murder of a minor."

Macleod took a sharp intake of breath.

Murder. How could they possibly think he had acted in anything other than self-defence?

Aghast, he sat anxiously listening as the proceedings developed.

"Let the record state we have heard the evidence from the witness and this has been documented. Dr. McKinlay, you are requested to report your findings regarding the body and your assessment of Mr. Macleod's wounds. Please confine yourself to your medical assessment."

McKinlay coughed and then nodded. He stood to address the makeshift court. Moving away from his chair and around so he stood equal distance between Boydell and Macleod.

"The findings of the body: the girl was malnourished. I have documented the physical features, hair and so forth and you know the background of her lodgings with the Shea family. I will not detail these further," said McKinlay.

"Granted," said Boydell.

"The body was malnourished and unkempt. There were signs of scurvy with the gums bleeding and ecchymosis over the body. There was flesh and blood under the nails. The cause of death was transection of the carotid artery on the right with subsequent haemorrhage and exsanguination. Examination of the internal contents revealed nothing untoward. The contents of the stomach were unremarkable, containing putrid meat and horse manure."

"God save us," whispered Boydell.

"The teeth were ragged with two front teeth missing and one of the incisors recently removed."

Boydell considered for a moment. "Anything further to add?" he asked.

"She was an albino. She had an unusual appearance with pale skin, the hair red and the irises were pink. She was an unusual specimen, very rare."

Forrest stared intently at Macleod and Macleod returned his gaze. Macleod hoped that he was remembering their discussion of the events in London and that might weigh into their decision. Abruptly, Forrest tore his gaze away to look at McKinlay to continue his evidence.

"And your opinion of the wounds on Macleod?" asked Boydell.

"I have not examined the wounds myself yet, but I have spoken to Mr. Collinson. The wounds suggest a defensive pattern and are consistent with Macleod's account. The slashing pattern on the forearms suggests a knife. By Collinson's account, the bite mark on Macleod's neck matches the one he viewed previously when he dressed it."

"Subjective," said Boydell. "It is difficult to decide based on this medical evidence alone?"

"There is something else," said McKinlay. He took from his pocket a piece of cloth and unwrapped it to reveal a small item. It was an incisor.

"This was taken from Macleod's wound. It matches the incisor missing from the girl's mouth."

"She bit him," said Boydell, unbelievingly. "But those bites, the ones Collinson described, they were from an animal. Surely they are not human? Dr. McKinlay, could a human inflict such a bite? Really?"

"It's possible," said McKinlay. "But what I can say objectively is that tooth is from her mouth. No-one else could have inflicted that bite."

"When you examined the O'Dell girl, the governess...in your opinion?"

"The bite marks are similar," said McKinlay. He paused for a moment, glancing at Macleod before continuing. "These things are difficult. The biting was undertaken in such a frenzy, it is difficult to be absolutely certain that the bite marks from the previous victim match those on Macleod."

"And the body of Richard Shea?"

"The bite marks on Macleod seem to match those on the body of Mr. Shea but I cannot say for certain. Circumstantially I..."

"I don't need circumstantial evidence here," said Boydell. "I need your medical opinion."

"Then I will tell you the bite marks on Mr. Shea's body are like those on Macleod and these in turn are similar to those that were found on the first victim."

"The tissue retrieved by MacLeod. Your opinion."

McKinlay paused.

"I can't determine the exact nature. It's rotten, putrid, unidentifiable."

"Anything else?" Boydell asked McKinlay.

"Nothing else rom a medical point of view," he said.

"Then thank you," said Boydell.

McKinley nodded and returned to his seat.

"Anything further to add Mr. Forrest?"

"The report that Macleod gave me, that I have related to you, fits the description of a man he saw hanged in London." .

Boydell sighed. "Anything of fact Constable Forrest?"

"No sir," he said looking chastened.

"All right then," Boydell sighed and looked down for a moment, spreading his hands on the table. His waistcoat puckered slightly as he took a deep breath. The call of a whip bird punctuated the silence in the room.

"In my opinion, I cannot be certain Mr. Macleod of your intentions and therefore I am remanding you to the custody of these two police officers from Paterson. You will return there to face the magistrate."

McKinlay interrupted. "But Mr. Boydell, the evidence we have given you...."

"Do not argue with me," said Boydell, his face reddened. "We are all too close to this, can't you see it?" We all wish to see this finished, myself and Forrest because this has happened in our community so close to us. Everyone in this room, excepting the policemen from Paterson, are so entwined with these events that we cannot make an objective decision. That is why I am referring this to a magistrate in Paterson who can calmly sift through the facts and make a decision. I do not wish to remand Mr MacLeod to custody but I am compelled to do. That is my decision." Boydell brought his hand down heavily on the table, showing that he was finished and stood and left the room. Forrest stood and addressed the Patterson constables .

"Take the prisoner away. Make sure Mr. Collinson takes him some food and water."

They hoisted Macleod and marched him across the room, shoving him heavily back into the chair in the anteroom, his arms remaining fastened under the shirt and his feet bound.

"I'll tend to him now," said Collinson.

Knowing better than to antagonise Collinson, the constables retreated, smirking as they closed the door behind them. Collinson went around the room, lighting all the candles that he could, and pulled the shutter on the windows so that the late afternoon light streamed into the room. Macleod welcomed the light to dispel the darkness. After ensuring there was plenty of illumination, Collinson approached Macleod. In his hand, he held a wooden cup with water and a plate of maize meal with small pieces of meat.

"You must be thirsty and hungry," said Collinson as he offered it to Macleod. Macleod acquiesced and nodded, relenting so that Collinson could hold the cup to his lips and he drank his fill, slaking his thirst. Collinson sat beside him with a spoon and tended to him, feeding him, as Macleod gratefully gulped the maize and mutton.

"Thank you," he said when he had finished. Collinson nodded.

"I wish it were different," he said to Macleod, "and I'm sorry." Macleod nodded, acknowledging his distress.

There was a knock at the door and Collinson stood as Dr. McKinlay entered. He held a bottle of whisky in one hand and two glasses.

"I've got permission to untie him," said McKinlay. "Bring him to the bedroom, the third on the left, and I'll be waiting for you."

Collinson nodded and promptly undid the bond that surrounded Macleod's hands first and then his feet. "God, they've made a right mess," said Collinson. "I'll have to clean this up before Dr. McKinlay sees you or he'll think I'm a hack."

Collision briefly left the room and returned with his implements, a bowl of water, and spirits. He busily undid the cloth and Macleod endured as he wiped the dried blood and serum from his arms before rebinding them. He tended to both wounds on his neck, the former bite mark now healing and much less painful but the latter acutely tender and continuing to ooze.

"McKinlay may want to do something different with that, but I'll dress it up for now so that he can look at it. I've left the bandages loose so he can examine you. Come with me."

Macleod went to stand and his legs buckled but Collinson held him up, slipping the shirt over his head and putting it over his arms. "I'll get you a clean shirt. That one is covered in blood."

He helped him through the empty parlour and Macleod could hear the loud raucous laugh of the Paterson constables as they became more boisterous, grog hitting them as they indulged themselves. Collision helped him down the corridor, into the bedroom where McKinlay was waiting, sitting on the chair next to a single bed in a dimly lit room. The room faced the fields at the back and in the west, the sun was swinging low on the horizon, lighting the golden fields of corn and maize with the last rays of the day.

McKinlay nodded, indicating that Collinson was to remain. "Here, you best drink this," he said to Macleod. "I'll need to examine these closely." Collinson undid the loose bandages and took the cloth off Macleod's neck as he sat hunched on the bed, gratefully accepting the whisky from McKinlay and downing the full glass in one gulp. He felt the heat press through him, surging to every limb, and the tremor left him, the heaviness that had plagued him lifted. His muscles felt loose. McKinlay poured him another glass, and he drank it without hesitation, the second glass dulling the burning, searing pain in his arms and back as McKinlay began his work.

McKinlay murmured to Collinson using the language of medicine. Macleod could not understand them as they examined his wounds together and discussed the best poultice for here and type of dressing for there. "Eucalypt and sage I think," said McKinlay. "If you make it up now, we can put it on."

Collinson disappeared from the room and returned quickly with a mortar and pestle filled with leaves. Oil was poured in and he macerated the leaves before pounding them into a pulp. McKinlay put it as a salve on the wounds, a large amount used to fill the gaping hole in Macleod's neck. "Now we bind them in a clean cloth and leave them in place for at least two days. This should stop the festering."

McKinlay and Collinson wound the linen together, clean bandages applied, and together they helped Macleod into the oversized shirt before helping him to lay back on the bed. Collinson bid them goodnight before quietly leaving the room and taking the medical paraphernalia with him. McKinlay sat opposite Macleod and took a glass of whiskey and poured another for Macleod and, helping the injured man, lifted his head so he could drink it in one draught. Then he sat opposite him on a mahogany chair.

"I'm sorry," he said. "Boydell's mind is set. He is a man with compassion, but for him, this is too close."

"He can't think I murdered her," said Macleod. "For God's sake!"

"I don't think he believes that," said McKinlay, "none of us do, but he fears making the decision here in the town. If he sets you free the people of the town will riot. Like it or not, misery and murder have followed you whilst you have been here and many in the town who are superstitious fear you have brought something here with you. By moving it to Paterson for judgment he is absolving himself. He is doing what he can to ensure that he can govern this village."

Macleod nodded. The two gentlemen let the silence fall in the room as the sun hovered above the horizon and the last rays of the day shone into the room, desperately holding against the ensuing darkness.

"I've examined the boy," said McKinlay. "Physically he is well. Collinson has done a grand job. But I am afraid his mind is gone, Macleod."

"Can anything be done? I promised his mother."

"It's beyond my capabilities," said McKinlay. "I promise you I will take him with me to Dungog when we are finished and I'll do everything I can to restore him to health."

"Thank you," said Macleod. "I can't send him back to his mother the way he is."

McKinlay took a draught of whisky and nodded. "I hope he can recover with time and care," said McKinlay.

Macleod was drifting, the room swimming, alcohol, fatigue and blood loss claiming him.

"You are weary," said McKinlay. "I'll leave you now."

"You are staying overnight?" murmured Macleod.

"Yes," said McKinlay. "I'll see you in the morning before you go to Paterson."

"Will they let me see McDermott?" asked Macleod.

"I'll entreat Boydell, but I can't promise," McKinlay said. He stopped at the door, nodded at Macleod before looking at the ground and taking his leave, shutting the door quietly.

As Macleod swam on the edge of unconsciousness, the shapes appeared in the corner as the darkness filled the room. The soldiers were there, their limbs missing, and their uniforms torn and bloody. But the pale white face of the murderer was now everywhere, red flaming hair wraithlike in the darkness. They swam on the edge of his vision, floating, and he struggled away from them into the darkness..

23

Macleod awoke at first light. The blue-hued landscape was picking up the rays from the east as a low mist surrounded the trees and crops. He tried to sit but his body resisted, stiff and sore; severed skin and muscle had tightened overnight. He groaned and taking a deep breath he swung his bare feet over the bed and to the floor. The room swam for a moment but he held, adjusting to the room. The door opened slowly and Collinson was there.

"Good morning Mr. Macleod. You will need to eat," he said. He pulled the chair over in front of Macleod and placed a tray on it containing two eggs, bacon with maize meal, water and hot tea. "Would you like me to stay with you?" asked Collinson.

"No. But thank you," said Macleod.

Collinson exited from the room but left the door ajar and Macleod could hear shuffling in the room outside. Boydell and Forrest were speaking in low voices as the light increased and the shadows in the room retreated. Hungrily he attacked the bacon and eggs, the aroma making him realize how ravenous he was. He slurped the water and carefully drank the tea. Sweetened with sugar it chased the weariness away. Outside he could hear the groans of the two Paterson coppers. Forrest admonishing them, chasing them out of their beds.

They appeared, dishevelled and stinking of grog. They bustled into the room; the stocky constable's face pale and sallow from a night on whisky, his breath stinking of rotten meat and alcohol. He pulled Macleod's hands roughly behind him and tied them tightly. The constable stood back, looking like he would empty his stomach at any moment, his face grey, bags under his eyes. His beefy lips were pale as the hangover wreaked its havoc on his body.

"Stand back," said Forrest as he entered the room. He brought with him a pair of boots, Macleod's boots that had been cleaned, and he placed them on Macleod's feet.

"You all right then?" he asked.

Macleod nodded.

"We'll leave soon. We won't be able to release your hands but you will be safe enough on horseback. They have fed and watered your horse and she is in good nick. She'll take you all the way to Paterson."

Macleod nodded, accepting all that was happening, letting go of any resistance, yielding to those around him.

"Bring the horses," yelled Forrest.

Macleod heard the stable boy, or some other servant, scuttle off.

"I'll take him with me," said Forrest. "You get your horses."

The wiry constable gave Forrest a look of distaste but Forrest did not acknowledge it.

"As quickly as you can," he said.

The two Paterson coppers ambled out of the room as Forrest addressed Macleod.

"It's a clear road to Paterson."

"McDermott?" asked Macleod.

"He's going with McKinlay to Dungog. They'll look after him there. Boydell wants every trace of you and McDermott banished from this village. You've made your mark Inspector Macleod."

He turned and indicated that Macleod should follow and he did so, walking through the door and into the parlour. The fire was being stoked by a servant who looked quickly at Macleod and averted her gaze, looking down, as if she met his eyes then some awful evil would befall her. As Macleod shuffled past there was a call from outside.

"Mr. Forrest! Mr. Forrest!"

Out the window, Macleod could see the beefy constable wobbling toward the building.

"Mr. Forrest!"

Forrest met him outside and he pointed to the distance. Macleod could see Kitty Shea and her children on horseback making their way toward Caergwrle. Her face was pale and as the morning mist surrounded her and her family, it was as if they were ghosts appearing from the forest. Macleod heard Forrest yell to the stable boy.

"Get Mr. Boydell! Mrs. Shea is here!"

Macleod sat on his bed. He had been ushered roughly back inside by the hung over constable, his feet bound in his boots. In the hour since Kitty Shea had arrived he had been kept in the room with the door locked but he listened carefully as voices came and went in the parlour outside.

He did not allow his mind to wonder what she would say. He expected the worst, she was there to incriminate him further. He could not allow himself to think such dark thoughts.

By mid-morning Collinson appeared with a sweetened cup of tea but would say nothing to Macleod, his face fearful. Then the door was opened and Forrest was there, striding into the room to undo the bonds at Macleod's feet.

"Walk with me," he said. "I need to leave your hands bound for now."

Macleod followed Forrest into the parlour. Sitting at the table Boydell was engaged in a low murmured discussion with the wiry constable from Paterson. Kitty Shea sat next to the fire with a vacant stare, as the flames engulfed the wood hungrily.

Boydell finished his conversation and looked up, acknowledging Macleod. "Sit Mr. Macleod. Mrs. Shea wishes to provide us with information."

Macleod sat, watching carefully as Boydell beckoned for Kitty Shea to join him at the table. She stumbled over, sitting heavily on the seat next to Boydell. McKinlay joined them, sitting opposite with Forrest completing the witnesses. The hungover constable was nowhere to be seen, but the thin constable stood fast at the door, barring anyone else entering.

"Begin when you wish," said Boydell.

Kitty Shea took a deep breath and put her hands on the table. She spoke slowly, her eyes fixed on the centre of the table at all times, refusing to acknowledge anyone else in the room.

"She came to us from Paterson. I knew she was my sister's daughter as soon as they gave me the description. After her father hanged in London, the two sons took jobs in the north, eager to escape the city. The girl stayed with her mother; they barely left the house such was the anger toward them. People spat at them in the street, and so they retreated. And slowly she died of consumption while her daughter watched. We took them food but there was naught the doctors could do.

God rest her soul. He was a monster. My sister lived a life of abuse and violence and it was God's mercy that she died. After he was gone, she had to live with that thing, she looked so much like him, a constant reminder. She was so strange, so *vicious*, that when my sister died we paid them to take her. She wasn't one of us, and I had my own family to care for. The orphanage took her, and kept her locked up.

But even then it didn't stop. They turned on us. Us! What had we done? We became the focus for their superstition and anger, our children beaten and bullied, Richard shunned and unable to find work. Degrading and vile and we had done nothing!"

She slammed her fists on the table and wept, the memory of her family's persecution raw. After a time she composed herself, placing her hands flat on the table, her head down, refusing to look at them as she spoke.

"When the chance came to flee to the colony we took it. We took it to make a new life as far away from London as we could be, far from our tormentors. Land was cheap here and we could afford it. We settled, we began to build a life anew."

Her face twisted as she prepared to speak again, the anguish on display as she clenched her fists repeatedly. She spoke through gritted teeth.

"When the money ran out, the orphanage wouldn't keep her anymore and they transferred most of the troubled children here to the new colony. So she ended up in Paterson, and they tried to make her work but they didn't know what they were dealing with, did they? No amount of punishment would tame her, the lash made her more violent. And then they found us. I don't know how but they found us, and once they knew where we were, they gave me no choice."

She stopped for a moment, raising her face to look at those in the room, before slumping lower in the chair before continuing.

"They gave me money, but that wasn't the point. They said if I didn't take her they would make sure that everyone knew who we were. And I couldn't have that. We had made a new life for ourselves, and I would not let my family suffer again. So I agreed to take her, but I was determined that she would not live long enough to cause me trouble again."

Boydell shifted in his seat, the creaking of the chair punctuating the silence in the room. He spoke slowly , choosing his words carefully.

"Am I to believe that you planned to murder her?"

Kitty Shea clenched her fists.

"Yes, I was going to kill her, to rid the world of that abomination. You see I had to do it, to keep my family safe. But I'm not uncivilised gentlemen, I couldn't kill her outright with my own hands. And so I deprived her, tainted her food, kept her out of sight. Let nature do its work."

She looked up for a moment at all of them around the table and then her eyes went back to the centre, avoiding their accusing stares.

"I kept her hidden from the governess and the people of the district. It wasn't hard; she slept all day to avoid the light and roamed during the night. I kept her concealed from the other children so that they would not be troubled by her ever again. But she was strange, unreachable, violent. She had something for the O'Malley boy no doubt; in some twisted way she felt something for him but could not express it. Then he courted the governess, and the violence increased. It was animals first, she strangled them or cut them, biting them after they were dead."

She bowed her head low, breathing hard. After a deep breath she raised her head and closed her eyes.

"Then she killed the girl. Richard and I knew it was her; we knew she had done it. She had done things like that to animals before here. But we couldn't tell anyone. She would have hanged but we would have hanged with her. I could not have my family subjected to that, that dishonour. We'd had it once, and I would not have it again. So, I locked her up. I kept her under lock and key in the barn so she couldn't get out and I starved her, so that she would die. But she was wily.

You see, once she killed once she got a taste for it. And I couldn't keep her captive, she was too strong. I lost control and she fled into the bush, made a camp away from us. We eventually found it but we could not trap her, we could not *stop* her. On occasion, she'd haunt the lean to around the back of the property, but she never let us get close enough to capture her. She became a wild thing, roaming the bush."

She opened her eyes and spread her palms in supplication, looking for forgiveness but expecting none.

"Please understand, I had to lie; I had to lie to protect my family. When she killed those other people, the boy from on the Kenny property, and then she went after the O'Malley boy himself, I suspect in her mind she was punishing him for what he had done. And then my Richard... she killed the man who had taken her in. You *must* see", she said, tears in her eyes, "what I did was only what any mother would do. We escaped to this place and made a new life, and I would not let that happen again. I would not let my children have the stigma they'd had, the bullying, the name calling... I only did what *any* mother would have done. I protected my family."

Kitty O'Shea looked at Boydell, and seeing pity but no mercy, she laid her head on the table and spread her arms wide, as if to sleep. She shuddered, sobbing slowly and then remained in that position, as if to hide from those in the room, from the confession she had made.

24

Macleod let the horse amble slowly down the dusty cattle track, the grooves from the oxen deep and furrowed, the dust rising as the four horses ambled along. He looked back to check on McDermott, the young man slumped in his saddle, the reins of his horse held by McKinlay. Ahead Forrest led the way, his grey horse slowly meandering back toward Reynella. As the afternoon sun shone in the blue cloudless sky whip birds called around them and starlings darted across their path. The familiar site of the oxen trains grazing brought them back to Reynella, where he was pleased to see the familiar site of Nell Bird waiting at the front with a smile upon her face. The smile was forced, but he appreciated she was doing her best. News had travelled fast and no-one would smile under such circumstances. But for their sake, she was putting a smile on and he was grateful for it. Patrick appeared as the horses approached and nodded to Forrest, taking his horse as he dismounted and rounding McKinlay's as he too landed his feet on the ground. Thanking him, he turned and helped McDermott from his mount, the boy murmuring to them as he got down, clean bandages around his head creating almost a turban as his brown hair stuck out at the top, unkempt and unruly. He staggered and was steadied by McKinlay. Macleod was down and helped Patrick with the horses. As they were tying them up and removing their saddles Patrick whispered to him. "Bridget does not want you here Macleod. My father has been drinking heavily." Patrick made the sign of the cross. "She says there is evil about you. You will probably not see her while you are here. I will serve your dinner in your room tonight, they've moved you inside, less noise in there."
He was doing his best to be hospitable but Macleod could see he was struggling, his superstition and fear overtaking him, as he fought not to meet Macleod's eyes. Nell broke the trance as she walked towards him.

"Mr. Macleod, if you could come with me," she said. "I have your room set up inside."

Macleod murmured his thanks and, leaving his horse behind, followed Nell into Reynella, away from the main area which was just filling up. As he walked past the bar, there was an immediate silence that descended over the place as men watched him. As he passed, the usual din returned, first a low murmur and then the clinking of glasses as men returned to their drinking.

"I have you in here with Mr. McDermott," she said, as she led him into a twin bed bedroom. Macleod appreciated the comforts, the wooden floor and the meticulously clean room with a waiting bowl of warm water.

"Dr. McKinlay and Mr. Forrest are just next door," she said. "I'll bring dinner to your room Mr. Macleod to save you any trouble. Mutton and maize tonight," she said, smiling and dusting down her house dress. "Is there anything else I can get you?" she asked, searching his eyes. He could see the compassion in her, the empathy. She did not judge him, nor wanted anything from him. She wanted to help him as much as she could, to ease his suffering.

"All is in order. Thank you, Nell," he said.

She backed out of the room brushing at her house dress and scuttled away as Bridget called her from the bar.

"Nell!" The stern Irish woman's call echoed throughout the building and Macleod was grateful that he would not have to see her during his stay. He took the flannel from the side and wiped his face and his hands. Nell startled him as she returned to the door.

"I hope you don't mind Mr. Macleod, but I have run you a bath. I hope it is not presumptuous."

"Thanks," said Macleod, "but I'll not be needing it. One of the other travellers can have it."

"I'll offer it to someone else." She backed again from the room, scuttling away.

Macleod moved over to McDermott who was sitting on the bed, looking into the corner of the room. He mouthed words, but no sound emanated from him. Macleod sat on the bed opposite watching him. Finally, failing to speak, McDermott stopped and put his head down staring at the floor. Macleod took the flannel and dipped it in the water and wiped the young boy's face, and his neck, and taking each hand he wiped them so he was clean and ready for dinner.

McDermott made a sound, unintelligible.

Macleod bent to look at McDermott and saw he was speaking to no-one in particular and his response was the learned response of the mindless. McDermott looked up again into the corner of the room and mouthed, trying to form words but could not pull a sentence together. He gave up again and looked at the floor.

As Macleod sat opposite McDermott the afternoon wore on. He felt a great sense of heaviness cloaking him. His memories of being a father, soldier, policeman or a decent man were gone now. He was none of that anymore. He did not recognize anymore who that man was, or who he had been. He shuddered as a chill passed through his body and he settled back against the wall, resting in weariness.

Macleod was startled awake as Nell shook him. "Dinner Mr. Macleod."

McKinlay and Forrest were there and Nell led the stupefied Macleod, shaking off his slumber, out into a common area to the side, a veranda of sorts. There a table had been set away from the crowd and Macleod was glad. As the din of the inn reached its peak, he was relieved to be separated from the noise; the prying eyes and accusing glances of the other patrons. There were three chairs and Macleod took his place opposite McKinlay and Forrest. Nell answered quickly the question forming in his mind.

"I'll feed Mr. McDermott in his room. You leave that. You gentlemen have your dinner here."

Presently she placed a plate in front with a yellow maize meal, littered with pieces of mutton. She offered them fortified wine and Macleod gratefully accepted. The three ate in silence, none wishing to speak of the events that had occurred. As Macleod took the third draught of fortified wine Forrest broke the silence.

"I received this today from Sydney, for you."

He reached into his coat pocket and handed a telegram to Macleod. Forrest had already read the correspondence but Macleod made no protest. As he opened it he saw the insignia of the chief of police, Fosberry.

Do not return to Sydney. Take McDermott to Dungog. Await further orders.

Folding the telegram, he slipped it into his coat pocket and sighed.

"Well, I have my orders," said Macleod.

"You can stay with me," said McKinlay. "I'll look after the boy and you'll be safe in Dungog."

"You become more of a mystery each day Inspector Macleod," said Forrest, eyeing him carefully. "I don't wish to know what the danger is in Sydney but I wish to know that it will not visit us here in Allynbrook."

"Well, with me gone that won't happen, Mr. Forrest. Dungog is big enough to hide."

"I will not ask who you are hiding from or what you are hiding from. I don't want to know anymore. I'll accompany you to Dungog tomorrow to make sure you get there safely."

Macleod knew that Forrest was not so much worried about his safety but more concerned to make sure that Macleod reached his destination. He took another drink of wine, his muscles relaxed.

"Well gentlemen," said Forrest, "we leave at first light. With your permission, I will take my leave."

"Sleep peacefully," said McKinlay, "thank you."

Forrest stood and almost bowed to both gentlemen before turning and hurrying away. Nell once again appeared, always seeming to choose the right time to be present.

"Can I offer you anything else?" addressing McKinlay and then turning to Macleod. "I am afraid I don't have any quince pies. Hanson stopped us using the quinces from over the fence. I have rhubarb pie if you wish for it."

McKinlay waved his hand as if to say no and Macleod did the same.

"Thank you very much but our bellies are full. Perhaps a whisky if you have it available."

She nodded and disappeared, returning promptly with a bottle.

"Mr McDermott is tucked into bed and is asleep so you take your time and enjoy the rest of the evening."

As she turned to leave them Macleod could hear a song beginning in the distance from the bar. They had brought a fiddle out and people were stomping to the rhythm. McKinlay poured two full glasses of whiskey and handed one to Macleod. They clinked their glasses and drank at the same time.

McKinley finished his drink and poured another, offering Macleod the same as he spoke.

"I've lived a long life Macleod and seen many strange things, both at home and here but I wish not to see the things that I have seen in these past few weeks ever again."

"Aye," said Macleod.

"Slainte"

Macleod smiled. "Slainte agad-sa," he said and lifted his glass.

McKinlay lifted his glass as well and they drank deeply as the noise from the bar reached its crescendo.

25

Macleod took the reins from Patrick Bird as the young man put his head down and stood back, not wanting to touch or see the man in front of him. Behind him, Bridget stood in the doorway with her rosary beads in her left hand, repeatedly making the sign of the cross with her right. As soon as Macleod noticed her, she stepped back into the doorway to avoid his gaze. McDermott settled into the saddle, McKinlay and Nell had applied fresh bandages and had him looking smart, a waistcoat and jacket and borrowed hat atop his head. As Macleod was mounting his horse McKinlay and Forrest turned their horses to leave, McKinlay leading McDermott on. Nell Bird was there with Macleod, standing aside the elm tree, the smile upon her face yielding as she bid them goodbye with a tear in her eye.

He stopped for a moment and she ran over to the horse. She put her hand on his boot and said: "Go safely and look after Mr. McDermott." He could see the tears in her eyes and wanted to acknowledge them, to comfort her, but he did not have it in him. None of that man was left, only the shell, the bare bones of the man he was.

"Yes," he said. "I'll look after him. Thank you."

He urged his horse on as her hand fell away.

As the horse moved along the dirt track and out into the oxen grooved pathway, he turned back to see Nell waving at him. He waved back and then turned to the road.

They rode in silence, the sound of the whip birds and magpies filling the morning as they reached the end of the road and turned into the bush to ascend the mountain on the overland track to Dungog. A great heaviness came over Macleod and his shoulders stooped as his steed weaved its way slowly through the bush. They rode deeper, and the sound of the magpies retreated.

As the horse troop plodded on, a large black raven landed in the trees above them. Its white eyes regarded them, as it cocked its head this way and that. Macleod saw it and then heard its call, a long and mournful wail, like an animal trapped or cornered, meeting its demise. Another joined it and then another. They sat atop the high tree, calling to the company as it ambled past. Macleod watched as McDermott looked up, his mouth open. As the ravens wailed and cawed, McDermott's mouth moved and he mimicked the sound. The birds responded, calling louder and louder as McDermott joined them. Macleod watched the ravens and forgot about McKinlay and Forrest, riding up next to McDermott. He listened as McDermott copied the sound of the raven exactly, the cacophony of human and raven filling the surrounding bush.

For a moment he was inclined to join McDermott, to surrender to the ravens' call. But he clung to what was left of him, and riding next to McDermott he placed his hand on the boy's shoulder and whispered to him.

"Stay with me boy, for God's sake stay with me."

McDermott stopped calling and was silent. He looked at Macleod and for a moment Macleod thought he saw a flash of recognition, but then it was gone and McDermott stared blankly at the sky above.

Macleod turned to the wailing ravens as they gathered in the trees above.

"Be gone with you" he yelled, " be gone with you and go to hell!"

As one they flapped and took flight, their calls fading as they disappeared.

Macleod glanced at McKinlay and then turned, facing the path ahead.

As the sun rose, the shadows lightened, the darkness retreating.

Author's note

This is a work of fiction. The main character Cormag MacLeod, is a fictional character, but has been constructed to inhabit historical events, occurring just prior to, or during the time when this story is set. The murders and the event s surrounding are also fictional, the perpetrator a work of imagination.

The history of the region, however, is genuine. The townships of Dungog, Gresford, Allynbrook and the settlement of Eccleston exist today and I have attempted to accurately represent life as it was in 1875 in this region using the abundant historical sources available. Many of the characters in the novel are drawn from real life figures from 1875 in the Allyn River Valley.

The traditional owners of the land in this region, the Gringai people, are represented in this novel by one of their elders. I have based my description on European descriptions of the Gringai, flawed as they may be. I mean no offence to the indigenous persons of the region, and trust my representation is accurate.

Dr McKinlay was a larger than life figure in Dungog, with ample historical evidence to guide me in formulating his character. William Boydell, Thomas Collinson, George Hancock and Thomas Forrest are well recorded in historical documents and while I have taken some liberty in recording conversations between the characters. I hope that I have not caused any offence to surviving family members in representing these individuals.

Likewise, the Doohan family and the Bird family are my ancestors, and the inn at Reynella stands today, now a private residence. The characters were recorded in history, but I have had the advantage of interviewing family members as part of the background research for this novel. They provided a rich and vibrant history of the region and the characters herein.

The Shea, O'Dell and O'Malley families are fictional, but have been crafted using historical documents and drawings, the ensure that these characters are authentic.

I have taken some liberties in the timeline (Nell Bird for example went to Reynella several years after 1875) but any alterations of this kind have been kept to a minimum, and I trust are acceptable to the reader within the context of the story.

SK Falconer June 2019
Sydney

Acknowledgements

My Great grandmother, Nell Bird, ran the wine bar at Allynbrook and her grandson and my father, Noel Bird, continues to document our family history within the context of the Allyn River Valley.

The Dungog Historical Society, and the Gresford Historical society provided invaluable material for the research aspects of this novel and I am indebted to George Sales and Allan Hancock for their willingness to provide a wealth of information regarding the region. In particular Alan Hancock was kind enough to cheerfully give several hours on a Saturday afternoon at the Beatty Hotel in August 2018, patiently answering all of my questions and providing a rich history of the characters and events in 19th century Allynbrook.

Denise Jordan lived with Nell at Reynella for many years, and her knowledge of the personaility and kindness of Nell as well as the workings of Reynella was invaluable.

A special thanks to my elder brother, Christopher. His passion for the history of the region and for this novel have been a welcome encouragement. He has worked as creative consultant, copy editor, marketing manager, history expert and media liaison. His contribution has been invaluable.

My brother Andrew has been a wonderful supporter of this novel, accompanying me on tours of the Allyn River Valley, as well as acting as history consultant and genealogy resource.

SK Falconer

https://www.skfalconer.org/

Made in the USA
Monee, IL
18 December 2021

86351348R00177